...In the Beginning

Squatting in the darkened cell in Sharafim Glasshouse, toward the end of their sentences, Walker asked, "What are your plans Johnny when you get out?"

Offer said very distinctly, "I'm not going up the Blue, my friend, I'll break out."

"They'll bloody pick you up in no time Johnny, and back you'll be here for another dose of the Wall."

"Don't you think I'm a lot cleverer than a mob of M.P.s and screws with no more brains than would fill a teaspoon? ..."

He hadn't started this war, and he was for getting out of it. The war against Rommel could wait; John Offer had a war of his own to fight, a war against the brutal sadistic jailers who staffed the Glasshouse, the callous officers in charge, and the Higher Authority which tacitly encouraged the destruction of men's minds and bodies. John Offer would never forget what they had done to him, and to so many others, inside those walls, and he would get his revenge ...

THE GLASSHOUSE GANG

Gordon Landsborough

HAWK EDITIONS

A MANOR BOOK

MANOR BOOKS

Manor Books, Inc.
432 Park Avenue South
New York, New York 10016

Copyright, ©, 1967, by Gordon Landsborough.
All rights reserved.
Published by arrangement with Tandem Publishing Ltd.
Printed in the United States of America.

ISBN CODE 0-532-15255-7

THEY came to him in the punishment cell shortly after Himmler had handed over the morning parade to the Killer. He heard them coming down the passage outside, heavy boots stamping, and even his nerves ran riot and set him trembling, and the muscles of his stomach gripped into knots that were as solid as the fists soon to cripple them.

Outside was the maniacal screaming from staff-sergeants drilling squads or sending them on to the Walking Wall; within the Punishment Block silence, save for those ominous advancing footfalls, while every unhappy man there listened and hoped that the boots would not halt at his cell.

Outside the door of the man who had had two names, they halted. He stood with his back to the whitewashed wall of his windowless cell, lit only by a naked bulb set into the concrete roof, and his eyes watched the tiny peep-hole set in the solid wooden door. An eye appeared; Private John Offer caught the gleam of reflecting light on the eyeball. It regarded him for a full two minutes, while outside there was silence. The eye was intended to instil the utmost fear in the solitary occupant of the cell. It succeeded.

Then the massive lock was turned and the door went hurtling back against the wall with the maximum of noise and violence. Two screws walked in. Two, though only one was needed for an undersized runt like Offer. Only one would take him on, if the pattern was normal, the other watching, expressionless, but quietly thrilling to

5

every bone-crunching smash of the fist, every rake of the steel-plated boots on unguarded shins. But don't show it, that was the rule. Never show emotion except hatred and ferocity.

Private Offer watched them guardedly, waiting for the first blow. They all looked alike, these staff-sergeants of His Majesty's Field Detention Prison, he thought. They were all narrow-gutted, ex-Regulars, lean hard men, fined off to muscle and bone by this life of constant physical exertion – this life they chose; for no man was conscripted into being a screw. They all wore cheese-cutters, peaks well down over the nose, like guardsmen, and their faces were thin and brown and seemingly fleshless, their eyes recessed and set close together aside the hard beak of bone that was their nasal organ. Most noses were twisted, as if they had been broken at some time or other on His Majesty's service. And they contrived to emit an aura of latent violence, a projection of suppressed fury within – a feeling that it only needed two words to have them lashing out.

They were men who wanted to hurt – that was why they had been accepted into the service – and in every subtle way they conveyed it to their hapless victims.

But Staff-sergeant Andrew Milkin did not immediately pitch into the smallish man waiting for the beating. Oh, no, that would have been assault and irregular, according to their book. There had to be an excuse, a reason for a tearing away of the bonds that held back sadism.

The other screw – Staff-sergeant Anacard, 'Knackered' to all men including his fellow screws – rammed the door shut, then stood with his back to it. Milkin advanced to within a yard of the smaller man. His eyes were nasty under the peak of his hat, frightening to a man who was alone and felt his utter helplessness.

'You was shouting just now,' Milkin said ominously. 'What was you shouting about?'

6

Offer, thin little man, spoke quickly. 'No. Staff, it wasn't me. I can assure you, I did no shouting.'

It was a good voice, incongruous from that wasted form in sweat-stained shirt and KD shorts. It was what is sometimes called 'cultured', which meant it had had money spent on its education through prep schools and public schools and perhaps even university. Offer, though, had got no further than public school, and that wasn't of much account, but it had left its stamp on his voice. That voice was upsetting to the staff-sergeant. He called it la-di-dah in the mess, and thought he was being talked down to, and it filled him with resentment and anger.

'You calling me a liar, Private?' His tone was frosty.

'No. Staff, just mistaken.' Offer knew it was no good. Staff was going to pick a quarrel. Staff had to pick a quarrel to satisfy everyone that what happened was justified.

Staff said, 'You was shouting your head off. Think we can't recognise your pansy voice, Offer? Eh, Sar'nt Anacard?' His head turned to bring his colleague into the argument.

'It was him.' Anacard was contemptuous. 'Shouting.' Both sergeants embraced the same lie, and having done so were now convinced it was Offer who was lying.

' 'Ear that? Staff Anacard heard you. You was calling for something. Now tell us what you was calling for.'

He had his cane up and was punctuating his words now with a steady thrust into Offer's body. The first hard poke was between the private's breasts. The next was a little lower. The third lower still. They hurt a bit, a bruising feeling, but Offer knew what the pain would be like when Milkin began to use his stick on his privates. Once down there the bastard would concentrate, going for them until no man could stand the anguish.

He hadn't called out. No one had called out in the punishment cells. No fool drew attention to himself in

7

that block by shouting. The two sergeants had come in looking for trouble. They'd probably worked it out over their greasy English breakfast in the sergeants' mess.

'That new pansy bastard – what's his name?, Offal?'

Roars of laughter, very encouraging to the wit.

'Reckon he wants taking down a peg.' The others nodding emphatically, always in agreement when someone decided someone ought to be taken down a peg. 'Doesn't seem to understand he's here to get discipline.' With a matchstick, Staff-sergeant Milkin dug pasty white bread from between smoke-browned teeth, parading the old lies. 'Do 'im good to know who's boss here.' The others nodded grim agreement.

Milkin rose. 'Come on, Knackered, let's knock the shits an' offal out of 'im.' Another roar of laughter at the crude humour, but work shit into a sentence and you were halfway there to merriment always.

And here they were, intent on trouble, though he'd done nothing out of step. But they were going to push him out of step, Private Offer knew, and for a good-humoured, easy-going man – his prime fault – he had plenty of guts.

'I'm in for a hiding,' he told himself, and was depressed at the thought of the pain to come. But it would come – nothing would stop it – and he wasn't going to crawl to these bastards or plead with them and beg for mercy. That wouldn't hold back the pain. So he planned exactly what he would do.

'You've as good as called me a liar.' The stick went hard into his stomach, hurting him and making him gasp, but this wasn't the time yet. Propriety said he had to take a lot more pain before he responded. 'Staff, you remember that. Prisoner was creating a nuisance. Upon going to enquire the reason for the noise, prisoner denied he had been shouting and accused me of lying. He did, didn't he, Staff?'

'I 'eard 'im,' said Anacard loyally.

You don't have a chance against these lying bastards, everyone said. They made up charges and Higher Authority believed them against the word of prisoners, though Higher Authority knew who was lying, having come up through the ranks themselves.

Milkin began to work himself into a suitable fury. 'I don't like being called a liar, not by a shanker-mouthed git of a poxed-up whore's son. You hear that, you prick-headed bastard of a trouble-maker?' He was goading Offer – that was the accepted routine – but every foul word designed to hurt the Private was fuel for his own mounting fury. Soon there would be an explosion within, and Staff would go berserk, and would kick and strike and go as near to killing his victim as he dared. In fact two men had already nearly died under his hand in the interests of discipline in this Glasshouse.

The stick was stabbing in the lower groin, and by God that did hurt. But not yet. It had to go lower. A man was supposed to stand any amount of hammer up top, but it was when his manhood was assaulted that he had excuse for reckless retaliation. Excuse? Not in this place.

Milkin was beginning to shout and to sweat now, knowing he was within inches of violence. It would begin within seconds, next time he lowered his stick. These were the moments he wanted, the things to go over and over in his mind for months and even years afterwards, remembering the breaking of bone and the squirt of blood and the terror – oh, that was what made it, the blubbering, awful terror of the bloodied thing under his fist and boot.

Staff-sergeant Milkin never needed to go out of the Mess for entertainment. Give him a dozen pints of wallop – never touched whisky himself, rotted the constitution – and he could go off in a daze where all the brutality of his life floated in Glorious Technicolor pictures before him.

Offer, who knew life better than most men, read the signs correctly and stared into that lean brown face shouting obscenities to drive him into retaliation – 'Sir, Private Offer assaulted me when I walked into his cell to enquire why he had been shouting. Staff Anacard will tell you that it was unprovoked ...'

He knew the moment that Milkin really intended to hurt. He could see it somehow in the eyes, perhaps slightly widening, in the saliva that came with the shouting. Offer knew the stick had lowered those three inches. The next time it would drive mercilessly into his testicles and the pain would be unbearable, and yet it would come again and again. Nothing could stop it, and what's more, nothing could make it worse. He was up for a working over and he knew what that meant.

The stick moved. Offer pivoted instantly and the stick went hard into his left groin. Even that pain was a shock to him, so that he knew what it would have been like if it had connected with his privates.

Milkin caught the movement, and began to shout, 'You sod –' as if the victim wasn't playing fair, not standing to be hurt. Then he got it himself.

Private Offer grabbed for the stick in both hands and rammed back hard. Staff Milkin went sick as his cane rammed into his own testicles. Then Offer was at him, a man who had had a soft round body until coming here, but never a soft little mind. He knew he had only seconds in which to hurt, and he wasted neither time nor effort to attain the maximum of satisfaction before they gave him the hammer.

He kneed and got Milkin's bruised members again. Kneed again as Milkin staggered. Kneed again, inflaming the pain to unbearable proportions. Kneed yet again, keeping up with the staggering Staff. Rammed down hard with his ammo boot heel on top of Milkin's instep. Slashed twice with the bony side of his hand across

Staff's already broken nose – '*Hit the nose hard with the side of the hand, thumb fully extended to create the hardest cutting edge possible. Hit with a downwards motion, and at the same time draw the side of the hand across the nose. These two movements are calculated to detach the cartilaginous material from the bone of the nose, leaving it broken.*' Instructions to Commandos in training, H.M. Instruction Manual 33/GT/8883387/42.

Staff Anacard said afterwards, 'Like a fucking cat, he was, so fucking quick. Gave ol' Milky the one-two before he knew what was fucking hittin' 'im.' There was something of respect in his voice for the quick-moving Private Offer, skinny little man. Not even young. Thirty-four?

Anacard came leaping in, shouting, 'Stop that, you bastard!' and started to swing at the Private, but Milkin halted him.

That sudden eruption of ferocious in-fighting by Offer would have put most men out for days. Not Milkin. Milkin wouldn't even miss a parade as a consequence, but pride would help him there.

Staff Milkin had been in many a brawl just as bad as this, and had taken many a hammering, but he was an iron man and always came back. Now he came back within seconds. Fury little different from insanity engulfed him, anaesthetising pain.

He shoved Anacard away. 'My man!' he snarled, and came in.

Staff Milkin was a specialist in three things. First was the toe-end to the groin, swift as light and unstoppable. The second was the rake down the shin with the side of his steel-plated, steel-studded boot while the victim was still standing, shocked. Third was a double-handed chop to the neck as his man went down writhing. After that the boot went in ... and in ... and in. Ribs and soft part of the anatomy. Leave the face, it put the M.O. to a problem. Faces showed and bodies were clothed.

11

Offer got the heavy ammo boot in the groin. The pain enveloped him, tearing him to pieces. He began to scream, as most men scream when the boot goes into their crotch. The boot raked down his right shin. The skin, near to the bone, flailed off so that for weeks he would have the sores and bruises to remind him of this working over. His scream became a sob of unbearable agony . . .

In the punishment cells alongside his fellow prisoners would hear the cry of torment and would be glad. Glad it wasn't they who were copping it. Though some already had.

Then the cries ended suddenly as Offer fell and took the two-handed rabbit punch. The boot went in. Offer showed remarkable toughness, for he tried to roll away though he was gagging with vomit from the pain of his lower region. Milkin accidentally kicked him in the face and was sorry about it. Never faces, he'd always said to rookie staff-sergeants. But this was an accident which would have to be explained. The heavy boot smashed Offer's nose and there was blood and snot all over his face and he was choking for breath.

Anacard hauled back on Milkin's shoulder, Staff still wanting to go in with his steel-toed boots. 'Hold it, Andy. You've given the bastard enough.'

He dropped on his knees to examine the face. He even gave medical advice to the patient. 'Keep your fucking mouth open, you stupid git, or you'll fuckin' choke.'

Milkin's fury was running out, but his eyes smouldered as he became aware of the pain down below – the other damage didn't affect him; nothing did beside the raging pain in his loins.

Anacard said, 'He'll be all right. We'll get the M.O. to see him. Pity you had to hit him so hard to stop him kicking you, Andy.' He was already fabricating the fiction that would have to go on the report sheet.

'It was him or me,' said Milkin, and he wanted to hold

his tortured privates but wouldn't do it in front of his fellow staff-sergeant and the bastard prisoner. In the Glass-house, Staffs were recruited for their hardness, and iron men never show pain.

Milkin drove his boot a last time into the moaning, gagging form on the concrete floor, then they went out into the sunshine and into the Mess for cold beer, and in time they went to talk to the M.O. who, Hippocratic Oath or not, was on their side, anyway.

And Private Offer lay in his blood and sick and ached so terribly that he wanted to die. He had been worked over, and he knew it. Not in any interests of discipline, justice or reform, but because he had a voice that was different, a posh voice.

He had also been an officer, and that was unforgivable in the Glasshouse.

Outside in the torrid Egyptian summer sunshine, the poor sods also went through it. From the moment he passed through those awful blank doors set in that high wall of concrete, topped with barbed wire, a prisoner did everything at the double. Never go sanely about anything, but always as if your life depended on it. And never speak unless you were spoken to; never even talk to your mates in the cells when it was over, or the eye at the door would spot you and have you in the punishment block in no time. Everything at the double, in that awful heat, and with a bare minimum of food to keep one alive – thin porridge, weak soup, and margarined bread. And abused, abused all the time, sworn at obscenely, goaded into acts of indiscipline by raucous voices that never let up the whole day long.

Lying half-conscious in his cell, Private Offer could hear the bellowing outside, and perhaps in his agony he wished he was with his mates on the square. They were suffering, but not like this.

They were drilling, three squads, thirty to a squad, each in the charge of a staff-sergeant. Everything at the double, though they wore full marching order even to a filled water-bottle (but no bayonet in their frog; if they'd had one they'd have used it, carving the drill-sergeants).

'About turn! Lef' ri' lef' ri' lef' ri'. Up, up, up! Up with them flamin' legs, you shambling shower of shit! Up, up, up! About ... turn! Lef' ri' lef' ri' ...'

Hour after hour. Five minutes rest, but only standing at ease under that hot sun, each hour, that was all. At the double, their packs weighted with small bags of sand, feeling a ton as the hours passed, bruising the skin and tearing it away as the packs swung to their frantic movements.

Up, up, up. Get your feet high or you'll be in dead trouble. The pain in the leg muscles through this doubling and lifting the legs high. The searing agony of each movement, but it had to go on. Dropping out brought greater punishment. Do it now or you did twice as much later. At the double. Up and down the sandy parade ground. About turn, about turn, about turn. The sweat running until there was no sweat left to run. Mouths open and gasping for air and the throats so dry the moans hardly came through them. Wanting to drop. Can't go on, despair in their minds, can't move another step. Anything's better than this. But going on. Finding the energy to keep moving, to keep running with those weights on the back and at the side. Because no man dared stop.

And all the time the stream of obscenities. The drill-sergeants, very natty in dhobi-pressed KD shorts and immaculate shirt, swagger sticks in hand, thin brown faces shadowed by the cheese-cutters down their thin brown noses, snarling and bellowing and showing their contempt. Trying to hurt with words, and too often succeeding, and so the punishment cells had occupants.

Most staff-sergeants were unoriginal, using the same limited words and phrases that had been handed down to them by previous staffs. Staff Anacard in particular never said an original thing, relying mainly upon one word to show he was coarse and by implication, tough. But Sergeant Milkin was different. He carefully thought out original expressions of abuse before taking to the parade ground, and he knew he was admired and respected for it in the Mess. Even the R.S.M. complimented him on his originality – 'Don't know where you get all them words, Andy. You crease me, you do.' All the other sergeants said Staff Milkin's obscenities creased them, too. In another way they creased the luckless prisoners who had to receive the abuse.

Not that Staff Milkin was particularly original. Sex and bowels, associated with a man's wife or mother, almost completed his restricted circuit of imagination. Yet he was content, particularly if his vicious tirade got a man into retaliating.

Today Staff Milkin's voice was not to be heard drilling the prisoners, but three other staff-sergeants did their best without him. They drove the men and gave them hell, and if the prisoners hadn't been young and fit they would never have stood it and would have collapsed under the strain.

They kept going at their drill, yet each knew that worse was still to come. When they had done their two hours of drill at the double, they'd have two hours on the Wall, and that really was punishing.

Men hated the Wall and went in horror of it. The mere thought of a two-hour stint on it filled them with unholy dread. It was worse – many, many times worse – than square-bashing, even at the double, and no one could get out of it.

Every Field Detention Prison has its Wall, or something equivalent to it. The worst punishment that can be given a man is to drive him hard to create something, then drive him hard to destroy what he has created. That knocks the guts out of a prisoner. So each Glasshouse uses its ingenuity to provide the painfully futile, and in Sharafim Glasshouse, along Egypt's Sweet Water Canal, the first commandant had devised the Walking Wall. He was restricted for materials, just a lot of sand about, but triumphed magnificently over shortages, and so came the Wall that Walked.

It was a huge sandbagged wall, ten feet high, sixty feet long, and six sandbags wide, and in daylight hours it was always on the move, crawling slowly round the edge of the parade ground. It contained 3,600 sandbags, and each weighed about sixty pounds. A hundred tons of sand. Each squad had to make that Wall walk fifteen yards in their two hours (less one five-minute break), which meant that each prisoner had to transport over a ton of sand from one end of the Wall to the other in that time.

When men saw what they had to do, even the stoutest heart quailed. Under that sun? In full marching order, all webbing worn, a pack on the back, a side pack, both stuffed with sand, and a full water-bottle? The staff-sergeants loved that Wall. It broke every heart. It killed every spirit. It was murder.

The Wall itself was a neat thing, properly laid with headers and stretchers and never out of line or bulging and threatening to collapse. Any man who simply dropped his sandbag or laid it badly caught the full ferocity of the staff-sergeant and never did it a second time. A neat Wall, but at either end it was ramped, so that men could climb to the top, run along the Wall and descend at the far end.

That was all there was to it, as month after month, staffs told new squaddies with mirthless humour. All they had to do was pick up a sandbag from the rear of the Wall, climb to the top, proceed to the front, descend and lay their sandbag properly there. That was all. But it had to be done at the double, with staff screaming at them all the time, sixty awkward pounds of sandbag held in arms that soon seemed empty of strength, with sixty pounds of kit on their backs to start with, and that sun sapping them, and they having to climb up treacherous sandbags that could grab a man's ankle and sprain it, then run along the top – no easy thing, to run on sandbags – then down and then stooping, with the heart threatening to burst and the blood pressing up behind the aching eye-balls and making them giddy, but the bag had to be laid exactly right. Then at the double round the base of the Wall, and another bag and another climb, and your only hope was that someone would fall off the Wall and break something and for a few minutes while staff ran up to see he wasn't shamming you could halt and grab a few mouthfuls of air.

The Wall had walked many times round the edge of the parade ground since its sadistic inspiration. It had mangled arms, legs, and ribs, had sprained too many ankles to count, and had broken every heart that had kept a hundred tons of sand moving at a rate of 0·175 m.p.h. It was a curious way to help the war effort, but Higher Authority, military and civil, presumably felt that it made its own contribution.

On the Wall that afternoon, while Private Offer lay in his blood and vomit and envied them, his cell mates laboured. Eddie Walker was one of them. Pomegranate Face another. Straw-haired Bert Holder, a depressive, was with them, and so were Cruiser and Busker, the fair-ground bully-boys.

Eddie Walker, big, strong artillery-man, was in for enjoying himself. He had turned a twenty-four hour pass into Ismaelia into a seven-day one in Cairo. He hadn't intended to, he told everyone – told it engagingly, for he was an easy-going man and able, even inside the Glass-house, to communicate the good-humour inside him. There were these chaps, he kept explaining. Bofors men, on the jag and each with a seven-day pass. They'd all got to drinking in the Y.M.C.A. canteen in Ismaelia, and before long it had seemed quite reasonable for Walker to get into the truck with them and keep them company while they spent seven hard drinking days in Cairo. On the eighth day he had been heading back to camp along the Canal when the M.P.s picked him up. The trouble was, his mob had moved while he was living it up with the Bofors crew, and at the court-martial he was declared to have deserted rather than go up the Blue to fight the enemy. Very serious. Sixty days in the Glasshouse.

Pomegranate Face, noisy little two-faced bastard, was in for pinching rations from the cookhouse and flogging them to the Wogs. It was not the first time he had done so.

Bert Holder, nineteen and looking fifteen, was in for being simple. He was slow and he was afraid of the world. Physically he was only a boy, but his age had got him conscripted into a man's army which terrified him. He was confused by non-coms who shouted at him, and therefore made a hash of everything he did. Because he was weak, he became the butt of sadistic N.C.O.s, so that life was one long round of misery for him. He began to slip under the wire to go home to his mother, who didn't want him because she had trouble enough with a husband and too many children. He kept being hauled back to camp and punished, then was finally sent overseas, where he couldn't stand it and ran away again. The Redcaps picked him up, but instead of being sent to some kind medical officer, he was slapped into the Glasshouse for the offence. Now he only wanted to die. There were many Bert Holders in His Majesty's Armed Forces at that time.

Cruiser and Busker were in for rape. Quite a number of Glasshouse inmates were there for rape; for not only were the weak and unfortunate inside those high walls, but a lot of nasty villains, too. They'd spotted a little Wren – 'on her Todd', explained Busker, as if it mitigated the offence. It was dark and they had simply lifted her into a doorway in the Ezbekiah area, where the Forces' clubs were and each in turn raped her so that she was off men for many years afterwards. In the process, for fun, they had stripped off intervening clothing, and afterwards walked away with a fragile garment. Unfortunately for Cruiser and Busker, that night the Wren was not wearing Service issue bloomers but her own dainty silk ones, for she was going out and issue bloomers didn't make a girl feel smart. Damn' fools, as everybody said; some M.P.s had spotted them flaunting the silkies in the Forces Club not much later, and now here they were, sweating it out for a few thrusting motions in a shadowy doorway.

Villains, the ex-fairground boys. Massive, rubber-limbed men who moved lightly on their feet like the pugs they were, men with huge hands that had broken many a jaw and enjoyed doing it. They had loyalty to no one, ever on the make and taking what they wanted by bullying force. Loyalty to no one, that is, except to themselves, and neither would ever betray the other.

The Wall was killing, and even Cruiser – that had been his fighting weight for a long time; now he was well into the heavyweight area – and Busker wilted under the dual strain of sun and field-punishment. Walker, taller than the fairground boys though not as heavy, one-time bouncer at a Mecca dancehall in London until he was bounced into hospital by some rougher lads, found the going murderous. For the smaller men, including Holder and Pom, it was an agony not to be repeated under any circumstances. But it had to go on.

When finally the day was over, they returned to their cells and dropped as if lifeless to the cold concrete ground that was their beds, shagged, in their own terms, but unable to break their kit just yet and get a blanket beneath them. A moaning filled the cell block, as unhappy men counted the cost of their ordeal of the day, and staff-sergeants went from door to door, eyes at the peep-holes to try to detect those who made unpermitted noise, ready to take them once more over the Wall 'to teach them a lesson'.

No one was allowed to talk, yet within a few hours the whole block knew of the terrible beating John Offer had taken, alone in his cell. The trusties, those long-service prisoners broken beyond further punishment, the sweepers and fatigue men who picked up everything, saw to that. They even knew that Staff Milkin had had to see the M.O. because of a badly bruised central area, and described luridly the colour and awesome size of Staff's most intimate parts.

When they heard of it men growled their hatred of the tormentors, fear bringing on a ferocity of emotion; for all knew it could happen to them. The staffs on cell duty went from door to door, banging with their sticks and shouting, 'Stop that bloody row, d'you hear? I'll 'ave you all out on the Wall for another two hours if you don't shut up, you bastards.'

It shut up. The Wall, or the threat of it, always shut them up.

In Offer's cell they reacted typically. Lying facing away from each other, heads towards the walls so that the eye at the door couldn't see their lips, they talked it over. The big fellows, Cruiser and Busker, said, 'The flamin' bastard! Someday I'll break his fuckin' neck.' That was Cruiser. Busker's contribution was that he'd geld the soddin' bastard when he got out.

Pomegranate Face – he had a wide mouth full of small teeth that looked like pomegranate seeds, some even edged with green because he never cleaned them – yapped on and on, the same old sexual nastiness, and all the time he was saying that someone ought to top the bastard, and tried to work up a hatred among his companions so that one of them some day would go for Milkin. A cunning little swine, Pom, always stirring, always trying to get someone else to do the dirty work. As treacherous as they came, and they all knew it, but he was one of them, a comrade of the Glasshouse, so he was accepted.

Gunner Eddie Walker also said that Milkin was a bastard. They had limited use of words, and however else they decorated their sentences, in the end they relied heavily on illegitimacy for insult. But Walker's whispers were more corrosive. He had taken to Offer, his own amiable spirit amused by the small ex-officer's impudent personality. 'Christ, let me get my hands round that murdering bastard's neck and I'd break it. I tell you, I'd break it and laugh when I did it.' He meant it, too, and he lay there and worried a bit about poor old Offer alone and battered in his punishment cell.

Only Private Bert Holder said nothing. He had nothing to say. He felt dead and wanted to die and with that part of his brain which could still function above his misery he tried to plan his own death.

Offer was an ex-officer, yet was completely accepted by his Glasshouse mates. And that was unusual. Once a man had carried the taint of the King's commission he was somehow set apart by the other inmates of the prison; he'd been the enemy, and there was still mistrust of them, even when they had fallen.

But no one held his former rank against this man now busted down to private. Offer was engagingly easy-going, with no suspicion of holding rank, as some officer-inmates, incapable of shedding habits, managed to do. Much more important, he was accepted because the prisoners instinctively knew him for one of their kind, a man derisive of authority and rank and all that went with it, even though he had enjoyed being a lieutenant. Above all they took to him because they knew him to be a rogue.

John Offer had been an actor in Civvy Street. 'Only rep,' he would tell them with disarming candour. 'Three quid a week if I was working,' which wasn't all that often. But he had loved the life, with its vagabondage and Bohemianism, and used his wits to supplement his meagre income.

Part of that process was to join the 'week-end soldiers', His Majesty's Territorial Army. It brought him a few extra pounds each year, and provided him with two weeks' quite pleasant holiday in camp in summer. Being a man clever with his head he worked his way into the Q stores and in time reached the exalted rank of quartermaster-sergeant. It provided him with an opportunity for a glorious fiddle.

In the months after call up, in 1939, when Britain went to war with Germany, Q-sergeant John Offer lived, by his standards, richly and in great style. The number of blankets he got out of the stores and flogged to a pal down the East End was astonishing. There were other things, too, in demand by the world outside the army, and where they were in store, John Offer provided them, doing a service to the public and nicely filling his own pocket in the process.

He was a generous soul, too, never forgetting his hard-up companions of the theatre, and on leaves would look them up and take their starving bellies for the best meal Soho could provide. John became a most popular man with London's poorer acting fraternity. Unfortunately, the good luck didn't last for ever.

Some officer with a suspicious nose got going on Offer's stores, and in no time was asking awkward questions of Q Offer. The actor in him survived the first round, but Offer knew it was curtains for him if he had to have another go with that knowing bastard, so he took off one night and disappeared.

Having great cunning Offer hid in the safest place for a man on the run. He volunteered into the army. This time, though, he joined up using his stage name, Robin Raeburn, and as Robin Raeburn he rose through the ranks, and was finally sent on O.C.T.U. and eventually commissioned. In time he embarked for overseas service and found himself in Palestine, where he wangled himself the lovely job of Entertainments Officer for Jerusalem.

Offer, now First-Lieutenant Raeburn, did an excellent job and was highly popular in Palestine, until one day in an hotel someone said loudly, 'Q Offer! What are you doing here?' Unfortunately, before Offer had time to shut him up, a major who knew him as Robin Raeburn heard the remark and asked questions. It ended with the inevitable court-martial, Offer being stripped of rank and sent down to Egypt to serve a sentence in the Glasshouse on the Canal. That was thoughtfulness on the court's part. Never jail an officer locally where he is known and might have made enemies, is the ruling. Not that Offer had any in Palestine. So he came across the Sinai with two escorting N.C.O.s, was delivered to the Glasshouse, and became acquainted with the Wall.

He met with no trouble with the prisoners, but from the start the Staffs had a go at him because he had once been a cut above their kind. Offer took everything with a resilience surprising for a small man, his innate good-humour helping to control his temper. In the end they got him, of course.

Staff Milkin was sweating them out on the Wall. 'C'mon, double up, you shower of crap!' he kept exhorting, and he had them going over the Wall, staggering under their burdens until they were dropping.

Offer did finally drop his sandbag, his muscles trembling uncontrollably with fatigue, towards the end of their two hours on the Wall. Unhappily he dropped it right in front of Staff Milkin, who promptly worked himself into the usual fury. Milkin stood over the sandbag, fallen off the top of the Wall, and had Offer come round at the double to pick it up, all the time cursing the luckless man with obscenities that held no originality for the moment, but did nothing to maintain a man's dignity.

Just as Offer was stooping to take the sandbag in his tired arms again, Milkin really touched the ex-actor on a nerve. 'You're not poncing around Civvy Street now, Private Offer, or in the Officer's Mess. Get that bag up on the Wall! What were you in Civvy Street? A puff? An actor?' He was going to dwell on it, to develop a theme which connected homosexuality with acting.

But Offer for one bad moment lost control of his tongue and said, 'A bloody sight better than being a commission-aire!'

Milkin got him into the punishment block for that. 'Prisoner persisted in talkin' on parade, sir,' he glibly told the Prison Commandant, a nasty Scotsman, Major Tul-loch. Prisoners never had a chance against staffs' lies and distortions. 'Talked back at me, sir, he did. Wouldn't stop when I gave him a warning.'

'Ten days,' said Major Tulloch, usually known as Himmler to staff and inmates, and little different from the S.S. leader in outlook, only less successful in climbing the promotion ladder.

The sentence disappointed Staff Milkin, for he wanted something infinitely more savage. He was sensitive about his civilian career, and tried to hide the fact that until he took to prison service the last job he had held in Civvy Street was a very humble one. He wasn't even commission-aire outside some big West End hotel or St James's club. Proud, authoritative Andrew Milkin had stood outside a provincial cinema in the Midlands, marshalling folk into orderly queues for the sixpennies, ninepennies, and one-and-threes. It was a flea-pit of a place, and he wasn't even supplied with full uniform – just a braided coat too long for him, and a peaked hat that had to be stuffed with paper to hold it above his ears. In between commission-airing he tipped up cinema seats at the end of the day and swept out the fag ends and choc-bar wrappings. He wasn't proud of his career before the army, and Offer was a marked man for his incautious observation.

In due time, Offer came back to join his mates in their cell. The day he returned Bert Holder, poor bewildered boy of nineteen, tried to end his sufferings. They heard him sobbing as he struggled over the Wall beneath the weight of kit and sandbag, and Milkin gave him hell with his tongue.

Then Bert dropped his sandbag, unable to go on. They saw him standing there, high above the ground, crying in despair. Then he jumped, going over in a deliberate dive to land on his head, to kill himself.

He didn't die. He broke his neck and both collar bones, but it got him off the Wall and into an army hospital and no one seemed to know what happened to the boy after that.

It was that day of the attempted suicide that ex-Lieutenant Robin Raeburn's sentence ended and he was released from the punishment block by Staff Knottley, cell officer for the day. His cell door was hurled open with much noise, and Knottley did the usual bellowing of 'Lef-ri, lef-ri – halt!' and Private Offer was marched back 'home'. Knottley, of course, glared maniacally at the five cell occupants, and in his most intimidating manner warned them that they must not speak to the prisoner or indeed to each other. Satisfied that he had put the fear of God into them, he stamped out, all boots and bone-brain, and paid for no higher virtues.

Everyone started talking immediately, of course, though

they stopped the moment a threatening eye showed at the peep-hole.

Eddie Walker, head averted from the door, asked, 'The bastard did you up? Milkin?'

Offer nodded, sighing with relief as he settled against tne cold cell wall. It was good to be back with his mates, good to be with someone, even villains like these. The awful part of punishment was the knowledge that one was alone. 'Milkin,' he agreed.

'The bastard,' said Walker. 'We heard. Nose bust, they said.'

Offer's nose was an awful shape and the colour still hung darkly around his eyes. 'It wasn't this shape when I went in. Did it with his boot.' His voice was drawling again, sounding good-humoured in spite of what he had gone through.

His words worked up the fury in his audience. Walker, more moved than the others because Offer was a bit of a pal, went on for a long time about topping Milkin, and others, when he got clear of the Glasshouse. Pom yapped several times that Milkin was a bastard, and supplemented his opinion with every improper word he had learned in the army and before.

Offer listened to them tolerantly, and when they had finished he said, 'That's all talk. When you get out you'll do nothing. Nothing. That's how it always is.'

Every man from the Glasshouse always vowed to do the screws when they got out, but it took nerve to come back and do it, and in the end no one ever did. Even when the staff-sergeants transferred their hard-drinking habits to Cairo and ran into ex-Glasshouse inmates, only occasionally was leave spoiled by violence. Staffs usually went around in pairs, anyway, and could handle vengeful men better than most.

They protested. You see, they'd be back and by Christ that bastard Milkin ... Offer's good temper didn't change, but his head shook decisively. 'You won't come back.' He paused, brooding behind the bruised and swollen face that had had but perfunctory medical attention, then he said, almost lightly, 'But I will. I'll do the bastard in.' A pause, then – 'Because I know how to do it and get away with it.'

It was said with such lack of passion or heat that it was impressive, and they looked at the small man with respect. Offer was a man who would keep his word; they, they all knew, would not.

Minutes later they were called out on parade, and Bert Holder went with them and it was that day he tried to kill himself. Offer, who had a soft heart, said, 'He shouldn't have been driven to that. He was quite inoffensive, old Bert. For that I'll have all their rotten guts for garters, by God!' And for once John Offer's eyes smouldered and his face was hard. All the screws, he silently vowed, but especially Milkin, the sergeant-major, and the prison commandant. The two latter were not fit to live, and if he could he would help them off the face of the earth. But he kept quiet about those plans after his first statement of retribution for Screw Milkin . . .

There was one conversation in the cell that Eddie Walker remembered, though. It was near to the end of Offer's sentence, and Walker wouldn't be long after him, either. Squatting in their darkening cell, trying not to notice the stench from the two already well-filled latrine buckets, Walker said, 'What are your plans, Johnny, when you get out?' He knew the ex-lieutenant would never reconcile himself to the ranks after the fleshpots that went with two pips.

John Offer drawled humorously, 'I'm going to put on weight. I'm going to become my old roly-poly self again.'

'Were you fat?' Incredible to believe that this thin man might once have had more substance.

'Fat? Round as a ball, old chap. Beautifully round. And

27

I'm going to be round once more, because I'm going to eat the best food and all that I can scoff, and I'm going to drink the best brandy and I'll have it by the crate.'

Walker asked the obvious question. 'What are you goin' to do for money?' Though he used the soldier's Arabic word for cash, *feluce*.

'Money?' Offer was shocked. 'I shan't need money. I'll knock it off, pinch it!'

Walker, practical man, saw the difficulties. 'Cases of brandy? They don't leave 'em lying around up the Blue, where you're heading for, mate.'

Offer said, very distinctly, 'I'm not going up the bloody Blue, my friend. Where there's fighting and men getting hurt all the time? Oh, no, not for John Offer. I didn't start this war, and I'm opting out from it.'

'You'll scarper again?'

'I'll scarper.'

'You won't get away with it, Johnny.'

'I will, Eddie, my boy.'

'They'll bloody pick you up in no time, Johnny, and back you'll be here for another dose of the Wall.'

'They bloody won't.' Offer mimicked his companion, but it was done pleasantly, so that Walker couldn't take offence. 'Eddie, I reckon the war won't last long in Africa, maybe another year. With a bit of luck it'll all be over in a year and a half – say two years. That's not a long time to hole out, not if you're clever.'

'You think you can go on the run for two years, maybe?' Walker was incredulous.

Offer looked hurt. 'You do me injustice, Edward, my boy. Don't you think I'm a lot cleverer than a mob of M.P.s and screws with no more brains than would fill a teaspoon? Oh, my boy, you don't know me,' and he sat back and chuckled behind the broken face.

Walker was impressed. He crept a little nearer. Any moment now the light would go on and then talking would be more dangerous. 'What're you goin' to do, Johnny? Come on, tell a pal.'

Offer's whisper came back, and it carried laughter with it, as if he thought it all a good joke. 'Going to get me a commission again, Eddie boy. Only mugs stay in the ranks. Yes, a commission. Officers aren't stopped by M.P.s for questioning, not often, anyway. And I think I know how to stop them even thinking of questioning me.'

He had worked it all out in solitary, while the pain of his face and body was receding. He wasn't going to risk his life up the desert, and he wasn't going to live hard on the run in Cairo. He would end his war years in style, wine, slim women, and fat cigars, and to get the best in wartime Egypt one had to have the magic of the King's commission in evidence on one's shoulders. So, he would get a commission.

'A commission?' Walker was a loyal friend, but this he could not believe. 'Christ, man, they'll never give you a commission after being in the Glasshouse.'

At which Offer, because he trusted the big ex-bouncer, told him the truth. 'I shan't ask for one. I shall give myself a commission.' He seemed to muse. 'This time I think I'll start off as a captain.'

Walker, too limited in worldly experience to believe the smaller man, shook his head. That beating by Milkin had done for old Offer all right. Poor sod was round the bloody twist. He said so. Offer's pulped face screwed into a painful, indulgent smile. 'Don't you believe it, mate,' and something about the way he said it convinced Walker that he really meant what he said.

Offer left Gharahm, but there was the usual final interview with Major Tulloch, the commandant, with R.S.M. Fry present, before he was taken away by an escort of sergeant and corporal.

Major Tulloch gave him full warning in future to keep his nose clean, spelling out the awful punishment that would be his if they ever saw his face within the Glass-house again. Tulloch had been a prison officer in Dartmoor and other U.K. jails, had volunteered into the army Field Detention Prison service at the outset of war and had been commissioned within a year. That was because by then he had acquired the reputation of being the hardest man acting in His Majesty's interests where Service malefactors were concerned.

Now that he was a major he muted the language of his earlier years, but it was still full of threat, full of menace, calculated to intimidate any man luckless enough to be hauled before him. Tulloch never showed softness or mercy. Any sentence he gave was the maximum possible within his jurisdiction. Any brutality by his staff was not so much condoned as rewarded with praise, to encourage them to further excesses. Tulloch had the power of life and death, and under his regime men died, sometimes suicidally, sometimes by collapse under the barbarous physical torment of life under his staff-sergeants.

When men died their bodies were quietly removed from the prison and taken somewhere and buried. There was always an enquiry, of course, but in the Service men of rank are always protected by men of high rank. Such 'accidents' were expected of a brutal arm of the Services, anyway, and every Field Detention Prison has its record of men who have 'died on active service'. That was the euphemism. That was the telegram that was sent to grieving relatives. Your son, your brother, your husband has died on active service. No mention of death in the Glasshouse, though some must have guessed it, because when a man went inside his dependents could whistle for their army pay; for the army gives no pay to a man or his family while he is enduring field punishment. They too must be made to suffer.

'You do understand, Offer, that next time here your stay won't be so pleasant?' Hard Scottish accent issuing from a hard Scottish face, grim and deterring. The Scottish Himmler, he'd heard himself described, and wasn't put out by the terrible insult.

'There'll be no next time, brother, and some day I'm going to pulp your face just as you condoned the pulping of mine,' retorted the departing private, but that was in his own head, and all Himmler heard was a dutiful, 'Yes, sir.'

'You won't get any pretty parts now when you go back to the stage,' Himmler said, and the ghost of satisfaction came into that grating voice as his eyes took in the wreckage that had been a shapely nose.

'Your parts aren't going to look so pretty when I've done with them,' Offer told himself. He could listen to Major Tulloch, and could plan to avenge himself yet remain calm, no fierce swelling emotion of hatred within him, no suppressed blinding fury that would depart once he was out of the presence of this man of evil, this holder of the King's field rank. That was what made Offer dangerous. He had control of his emotions, yet he had the emotion, all the same.

'Yes, sir.'

'You've got something to remember us by,' said the Scotsman, looking again at that broken nose, and now undoubtedly he sounded satisfied.

'Yes, sir,' said Offer, and he would carry it around for the rest of his life and he was never going to forget the people responsible for it.

'Take him away, Sergeant-major.' A brusque, get-rid-of-this-thing, and R.S.M. Fry took over.

'Prisoner and escort, right turn, double march, lef-ri, lef-ri, lef-ri!'

Outside in the sun, R.S.M. Fry had to display his wickedness before the gates opened to take Offer into the great free world beyond. 'I just hope you come back. I hate nancies and I hate officers.' Offer wasn't a nancy, but Fry, like Milkin, would insist that actors must be puffs – all designed to hurt and humiliate.

'Call me Killer,' Fry used to tell his squads. He liked to use the word to frighten the men, and he was second only to Tulloch for brutality towards prisoners. No man was more dreaded, no man more hated.

'You heard me?' Fry shoved a threatening face close to Offer's, wickedness there, daring the man at the last moment to say something out of line and give him chance to have him detained a few more punishing days for 'insubordination'. Major Tulloch would back him up if he decided to hang on to Offer, both knew.

'Yes, sir.' Offer wasn't going to yield to insult, and retort in any way.

So Private Offer, that busted ex-lieutenant, was posted to a regiment in camp along the Canal, and within twenty-four hours was away across the desert, a free man again. A hunted man, true, with the Glasshouse anxious to receive him, but a sanguine Offer was pretty sure there was no one this time smart enough to catch him.

Eddie Walker was marched out, too, after the usual threats and insults – all in the interests of discipline of course – two or three weeks later. He too got no further than a camp along the Sweet Water Canal, but that was because in those weeks in jail his regiment up the desert had received such a chewing from Rommel's Panzers that it hardly existed any more. So Walker was posted to a new heavy ack-ack battery being trained in an anti-tank role.

It is the way of the army to forget transgression once it has been paid for. That is by good officers, and most officers merit that title in the British army on the whole. Walker was marched before his C.O., who told him he had been a bad lad and he mustn't do it again, and that was the end of that. He even got evening leave into Ismaelia a week or so later, and though he had been there before and thought it stank and had little to interest a squaddie, he went because hanging around a tented camp had even less interest.

He rode by truck with the other lads, and when it was parked just off Ismaelia's tatty centre, they headed straight for a canteen where they could get a plate of food and drink because their imagination rose no higher than that in foreign parts.

He was on Ismaelia's main street, waiting to cross, ignoring the excited Arab urchins who pestered the men with fly whisks, postcards, dubious highly-coloured sweets and soft drinks, and invitations to visit their sisters, all remarkably under the circumstances proclaimed clean and virgin. A utility went by, came to a quick halt beyond him, and an army officer got out.

'Gunner Walker!' A sharp, imperious call.

Walker's head turned, startled. His immediate thought was, 'Who the hell knows my name?'

The officer came no nearer but beckoned impatiently with his leather-covered swagger stick. 'C'mon, double there!' So Walker came up in a hurry. A plump officer, short, with a bristle of a moustache; a captain, he saw, counting the pips.

'Walker, you're wanted for escort duty.'

'Me?' Walker was staggered. 'Me for escort duty . . .'

He stopped, seeing that face as if for the first time. Something bloody familiar about those lines around the eyes. That voice – where'd he heard it before? And surely to God the fellow was laughing at him.

Walker said, 'Bugger me!' He couldn't believe his eyes. 'If it isn't old Offer!'

Captain Offer retorted, 'Less of the old Offer, gunner, and give me my rank in future.' And the curious thing was that from that moment Gunner Walker never thought of ex-Private Offer as anything but a captain.

He looked the captain over admiringly. He was smart

in his captain's uniform, natty bush-jacket and KD slacks beautifully ironed. He looked the part, Walker had to admit. But fatter, though, so different from the thin little man in the Glasshouse. Walker remembered how Offer had said he would eat and eat and put on weight until he was his old roly-poly self, once he got the dust of the Glasshouse off his feet. Well, he'd done it. And that bristly military moustache made a big change. If he hadn't been so close to Offer in the Glasshouse he would never have recognised him. In fact, he told Offer now, he wouldn't have recognised him if Offer hadn't accosted him – 'not in a month of Sundays!'

'That,' said Offer, 'is why I took to a moustache and filled out my figure, my dear Gunner Walker.' His stick rubbed his nose thoughtfully. It had set broken, flattened, a broad thing across his face where before had been a sharpish nose of classical straightness. 'And this adds to the disguise,' he thought. 'No one knowing the old Offer or even Lieutenant Raeburn is going to recognise me with this.'

'Walker –' Curious how from that moment he never called them by their old, familiar names, yet no one seemed to notice it. 'There's a job for you. I think it's after your own heart. Get in the truck and I'll tell you about it.'

Walker found himself turning, obediently. For the first time he looked towards the canvas-topped utility. The driver was leaning across from the wheel, grinning up at him. Walker saw steel-rimmed service-issue glasses and a big mouth of teeth that were like fruit seeds.

This time he said, 'Fuck me! Pomegranate Face!' While Pom asked him how the bleedin' hell he was. All very friendly.

'In the back,' ordered Captain Offer, impatient to be away, and Walker went round the little 5-hundred-weight and started to climb inside. Then he paused. There is never much room inside a utility truck, but in this one there was even less room to accommodate him. It was getting dark, but he could see two bulking figures squatting there. One of them reached out and gave him a hand and big Eddie Walker felt as if he were being lifted within. Then he saw their faces.

They were flat, battle-scarred maps, big faces that had taken many a hammering. Walker just sat down and said, 'Busker an' Cruiser!' His old cell-mates. 'What'n the flamin' heck ...'

The explanations came over the next hours. Offer had gone on the run. Elevating himself to the rank of captain, a protection in itself, was easy. He had simply gone to an Egyptian tailor of Service uniforms and had had himself measured for a full officer's wardrobe. He hadn't needed money, because pukka officer sahibs never paid promptly but only when they were billed. Offer had signed the chit, giving his address as H.M. Field Detention Prison, Sharafim, along the Canal. Perhaps it was absentmindedness which caused him to sign the name, 'Adam Tulloch.'

He acquired the utility by simply selecting one in good nick and driving off in it, though he had to short the leads to the ignition switch to do so. Then he had gone on the prowl, looking for men to add further to his disguise and also to implement some rather wicked plans he had in mind.

Offer needed men around him – quite a lot, in fact; the more the better, because they would act as camouflage. Even captains could come under suspicion, but a captain in charge of a squad of men never would. That was how Offer argued, and he intended to put the theory to the test, too.

The only men he could trust were his old jail-mates, so he had done a little scouting around service canteens and soon found Pom because of his loudly yapping voice. Pom had found Cruiser and Busker, who were tired of discipline already, and only too anxious to live the freer,

35

gayer life promised by Captain Offer. Quite accidentally they had spotted Walker when they were on their way to their first job.

'First job?' Walker, crouching in the back under the canvas cover too low for a man of his height, was interested. 'What's that?'

Leaning well round in the passenger seat, Captain Offer said, simply, 'We're going to do Staff Milky.'

Walker had forgotten the Glasshouse. He had even forgotten his hatred of Milky and Knottley, Palmerston, O'Dwyer, and the bastard R.S.M. and the even bigger bastard, Himmler. That was the way it was. You came out burning for vengeance, but when you were outside there was so much to occupy one that soon the fires of hatred died to nothing more than an ineffective spark. But the moment that name was mentioned, the moment Captain Offer talked of doing Staff Milkin, the blazing hatred was there again instantly.

Walker said, 'You can count me in!'

'That,' said Offer, 'was something we knew we could depend on.'

It turned out that picking Walker up was to their advantage. Pom would have to sit in the car, waiting in case of need for a quick getaway. Anyway, he was no good in a brawl. Offer himself would probably have his hands full, restraining a bint. And Milkin would be a handful for two to tackle, even though those two were the roustabouts, Cruiser and Busker.

'What's this about a bint?' Walker was pleased as hell to be with his old oppos, but he wished they'd do a bit more explaining. Offer gave the explanation when the utility halted in a quiet street outside a big old-fashioned block of apartments. It was now fully dark, but the street was well lighted and Walker, peering out, saw palm trees in a narrow garden, and balconies jutting out from a brownstone building.

'Milkin visits a bint on his time off.' Walker nodded. Everyone in the Glasshouse knew about Staff Milkin's bint. An Italian, the whisper said. For that matter, everyone inside knew just about every intimate event concerning the Glasshouse staffs. Where the news originated, no one knew, but time often proved the whispers to be astonishingly accurate.

'He's coming for his greens tonight.'

Walker wondered how Offer knew. Unless he had looked up the bird and chatted her up and got the truth out of her, he thought. Offer was smart enough for that.

So they sat in the car and waited, very quiet and very still. Less than an hour later Staff Milkin showed up. He came walking into the lamplight outside the apartment entrance, and that lean hard figure was unmistakable even though they couldn't see his face because of the shadow of his peaked hat. They became tense, watching him turn in and mount the broad stone steps. But now wasn't the right time.

Offer gave him five minutes, then said, 'Here goes.' He got out, quietly closing the door behind him. The three big men crawled out from the rear, while Pom, suddenly nervous at the thought of being left alone, lit up a Blighty Wood and started to puff vigorously. Offer, Walker noticed, had put on a denim jacket over his pips.

The captain certainly knew his way around. He led the way confidently into the apartment block. In the open hallway were the usual skull-capped and galabiaed Egyptians, squatting and talking and taking no notice of the British soldiers as they went by. Evidently they were used to seeing Britons come and go in that place.

Captain Offer took them up two flights of stairs. They stank of the polish used by all Egyptians, as did the high-ceilinged, bare corridor that stretched at the head of them. Offer walked quietly along a row of doors, finally halting at No. 28. The others closed round him there.

Silently he took a tin of black boot polish and opened it. He had a small piece of rag in his denim pocket, and this he dipped into the can, then spread the black stuff across his eyes like a mask. Not a big mask, either; just that black strip across the eyes and above the nose and no one would recognise them. And a small 'mask', anyway, was more quickly removed.

The others masked up. Then Captain Offer quite gently pressed the bell. They heard voices within, one a woman's. They expected her to call out, asking, 'Who is it?' as such women usually do when they are entertaining a gentleman friend. Instead the door began to open. Walker wondered how much Offer had paid the girl to open up to them. He also remembered the stories that Milkin was a bastard with his women, offensive when he had finished, calling them filthy cows. They took his money, but perhaps they weren't averse to seeing lover-boy getting a beating. This one, anyway.

Walker saw the door begin to open. He saw a ripe Italian beauty in silky negligée, and he could have sworn there was a hint of a smile on her face as she looked at Captain Offer, and equally was ready to swear that what happened then held some quality that told of rehearsal.

Offer grabbed the girl and hauled her outside, out of the way, for a second. In that moment Busker went crashing into the room. Cruiser was on his heels, Walker tagging close behind. Walker had a feeling of a feminine room, almost a boudoir, though no bed – that was through an open door beyond. Staff Milkin was at a sideboard, pouring a drink. His jacket was off, and his braces were dangling down his thighs in old-style army fashion. His face was startled, seeing them come running in. Then it went hard and fierce and he dropped the glass and started to pull away, but Busker was too quick with his fingers.

They stabbed, things as hard as the roots of an ancient oak and just as gnarled. They struck into Milkin's windpipe before he knew what was happening, and the pain hit him like a blinding flash and he gagged, the pipe collapsed and shockingly bruised, and he fighting for breath in an instant and unable to breathe.

That was to prevent him from shouting, Offer had explained when he briefed them.

Then Busker got his foot up in Milkin's groin, just as so many times Staff Milkin had done it on helpless men in the solitary cells. He kicked, and he kicked hard, wanting it to hurt so much that the pain would never leave the sergeant. The other two piled in in silent savagery, and Offer brought the girl into the room and shut the corridor door, and though she could have screamed, she made no attempt to do so. Offer led her to the bedroom, but she hung back, eyes greedy, watching the beating of her lover. When Offer pushed her into the room she tried to pull him in with her, but he just murmured, 'Not now ... another time, honey,' then locked the door. There he stood, watching, taking no part in the brawl.

Milkin's face was going purple, his eyes staring out of his head as he gasped for air, but he was still wickedly dangerous. He went spinning away to give him seconds in which to recover, but they were at him. Busker was trying for his groin again, Cruiser swinging with a jaw-smashing right. Walker, little less dangerous, was only a shade behind the heavier men.

Yet the reeling Milkin, fighting with the cunning and desperation of the proverbial cornered rat, got in first. His shoe – no boots when you went to bed a luscious Italian bint – came up, stabbing across Busker's shin-bone as the second kick aimed for his groin. It's an old trick, and it is crippling. Busker's swing had all his weight behind it, and suddenly it was stopped by that down-jabbing foot. Busker thought his leg was broken. He simply collapsed on the polished floor, writhing. Offer stood and let him writhe.

Milkin, still swinging away, got in another blow. It was a hard back-hander, and it caught the on-coming Cruiser smack across the broad cheekbone. It shook Cruiser, did little damage, though, but threw him off his own blow – Cruiser's right did not quite connect with that hard, recently shaved chin or Milkin would have been down. Instead it too landed on his opponent's cheekbone, and Milkin felt it and his head went jerking back.

Eddie Walker was in immediately. His hand chopped hard again for the exposed throat, that throat bruised already and a thing of aching fire. The Adam's apple took it once more, and Milkin's face began to go black. Now he struggled frantically to get away, to reach the window, to get air into his lungs.

Cruiser came leaping in, battering him with rib-breaking blows to the body. Walker leapt from behind the reeling man and put the boot in again. Then Busker hauled himself off the carpet, aching shockingly on a leg that hardly bore his weight, and pulled both of them off, then got stuck into Milkin.

The whole beating took less than two minutes. That was the thing Offer regretted. This man, Staff Milkin, had months in which to torment and mangle the men put in his charge. Nothing that could be done to him in two minutes was remotely like the hell he gave so many over a much longer time. Offer wasted no sympathy on Staff-sergeant Andrew Milkin.

Offer let them kick Milkin unconscious, then said, 'Time to go.'

Busker, still in pain from that leg, and remembering beatings from Milkin and other staffs at Sharafim, wasn't satisfied and hauled Milkin erect and in the same movement swung him. It was a demonstration of strength and terrible animal ferocity. Milkin's limp form was lifted clear into the air, to crash with bone-cracking impact against the wall. He slid down to the floor, and the blood began to run across the polished surface.

Offer held out some field-dressing pads. They smelled of eau de Cologne. 'Watch your eyes,' Offer warned. 'It'll sting.'

They cleaned their faces, a matter of seconds, Offer inspecting them afterwards. Milkin would remember masked intruders, but wouldn't have recognised them.

They went out into the silent corridor. No one appeared to have been disturbed by the ruckus, and they went down to the hallway. The chattering Egyptians, squatting there with their white galabias tucked around their knees, hardly bothered to look up at the four British tommies. They passed out into the night, into the pleasant warmth of an Egyptian evening, the palm trees tall above them, silhouettes against a starlit sky. The world was at peace here, so unlike those savage two minutes in the room above.

Offer thought, musingly, 'I'm calloused.' The violence had not affected him except to be glad it was going on. The thought did not worry him. This was a world of survival and sometimes of painful retribution. Certainly it was a world lacking in justice for the weaker brethren, and long ago Offer had decided he wasn't weak. 'Violence,' he quoted to himself, 'begets violence.' How true. Well, he, self-made Captain Offer, didn't start it.

The girl still hadn't started screaming for help. Good girl. Must look her up some time. 'Meelkeen? He is peeg,' she had declared. 'But you take his money?' The pretty mouth drooping with self-pity. 'He ees a customer. So many of my customers are peegs. A girl must smile and say eet does not matter.' She brooded for a moment, then fiercely, 'But eet does.'

Now she was keeping quiet, giving them chance to get away.

Taking his time, very casual about it, Offer removed his denim jacket and became a smart infantry captain again. 'That's the first bastard,' he said. 'We'll sort the others out when we've time to get round to it.'

They had enjoyed themselves, even the limping Busker. This was the sort of thing that kept such men happy. Pom was yapping, wanting to know the details. 'Later,' said Offer, then spoke to Walker. 'Well, that's over. Now, what about you? Going back to your mob, or throwing in with us?'

Walker hesitated only half a second. Then he said, 'Okay, I'll team up with you.' A fateful decision, made impulsively, and one which should have had considerable thought behind it. But Walker, still excited by the beating of Milkin, was in no rational mood.

They climbed into the utility and drove off. When she heard the car drive away the bint would start screaming, Offer thought, but it did not panic him and they drove through Ismaelia very sedately. Anyway, why panic? He was there for all the world and the Redcaps to see, a captain in his utility being driven by his batman on some military business or other.

Pom took the road out to Cairo, and they drove along the Sweet Water Canal for something like an hour before turning off and bumping over the sand. It was a warm, early-summer evening, and Walker in the back felt relaxed yet excited. He had been at the beating of a bastard who ought to have been topped long ago, and it did him good. He had also opted out of the army on an impulse and that was thrilling even though a voice inside him kept saying, 'My Christ, Eddie, you're a silly sod. They'll catch up with you someday, then –'

But Eddie had that touch of recklessness which reckons the future will take care of itself. He had also latterly in some curious way acquired faith in his old cell-mate, and a belief that Captain Offer *would* take care of them all – handsomely. The faith was sufficient to lull odd moments of alarm and to keep him pleasantly satisfied in the back of the lurching utility.

The lights of travelling vehicles on the busy Canal road were suddenly extinguished and Walker guessed they had put a hill of sand between them and the traffic. Almost at once, discreetly out of sight, the utility halted and Offer called, 'All out! Let's get a noggin inside us.'

Walker clambered over the back and landed on soft sand that whispered sibilantly as his boots stirred it. Cruiser got out easily, too, but Busker, his leg on fire, had to be helped down. 'That flamin' screw!' he gasped, putting his weight on the injured member. 'God, if I could get him now, I'd kill the bastard!' He was in great pain, and Cruiser and Walker had to help him walk.

Walker realised that they were in a tented area, and he was surprised. There were about a dozen tents, E.P.I.s, like miniature marquees, good accommodation for that climate because the five-foot walls could be removed to allow a cooling breeze to enter. But a dozen? And there were several trucks parked in an orderly line, 3-tonners and 30-hundredweights. Where were they, and why did his companions walk so confidently?

Pom went scurrying by. 'Canteen open in a minute, sir,' he said, and from ex-convict, ex-Private Offer, came a calm, approving, 'Good man.'

A white glow went up in one of the big tents, and they all passed inside. Pom was lighting a second glaring Tilly-lamp, and Walker saw they were in a mess tent. There were the usual orderly trestle tables and forms, and even the odour of the British soldier's invariable diet meat and two veg – hanging about the place. At the end where the lamps were was a small bar. Pom very cheerfully – it was a job he loved – had unlocked a cupboard and was placing bottles on the bar. Beer in an improvised ice-bath, though the ice seemed all to have melted now;

whisky, brandy, rum, gin, and vodka. Everything was there.

'Brandy for you, sir,' said Pom briskly, the perfect bar-tender, as if he knew what the captain wanted, and a generous four inches went into the beer glass.

'Scotch,' said Cruiser, making a satisfying sound.

'Brandy,' said Busker heavily, sitting on the end of a form and carefully stretching his leg before him.

The drinks came, a quarter of a bottle in each glass, and Walker's eyes were startled, seeing the generous measures.

'And for you, sir?' Pom showed his pomegranate teeth in a professional smile. 'Brandy, whisky, vodka, beer?'

Walker said, 'I'm skint.' Months in prison leaves a man's pocket empty. 'A beer for me, that's all I can go for.'

They all turned on the big gunner at that, shocked. Captain Offer exclaimed sharply, 'Good heavens, Walker, you don't pay for drinks in this outfit.'

'You don't?' Walker's eyes began to shine.

'No, stupid.' Pom reached for a glass and the brandy. 'Don't think we bought this stuff, do you? We knocked it off, old squire, the whole bleedin' lot of it.'

'Then give me a brandy, a big 'un!' said Walker, and he knew then he had made the right decision to leave the flaming ack-ack. When the glass was in his hand he looked round the Indian Army pattern tent and said, 'You knocked this off, too? And the trucks?'

'Every bit of it,' Offer told him. Then he raised his glass. 'Well, gentlemen, let's drink a toast. We've had our first action against the enemy, and apart from one minor casualty' – he bowed to Busker who looked indignant – 'it was highly successful. So let us drink to the future. Here's to the good life and an exciting one with the gee-gee see-you.'

Walker said, 'The gee-gee see-you?' for that was how it

sounded to him. 'What the heck's that?'

'The G.G.C.U.?' Offer delayed the toast to explain. 'That's the Glasshouse Gang Commando Unit. You've just joined a wild and desperate mob, my old china.'

Walker drank to it, bewildered, quite sure the whole thing was madness, but while it lasted it would be great.

When Private Offer, so recently purged of his sins, took off and deserted from his unit, he had three things to do in quick order. The first was to get money. The second, documentation to prove several identities. And the third was status and a screen of safety.

Getting money was no problem. He had a good-sized account with a bank in Jerusalem – Offer hadn't been entertainments officer with all that potential for rackets for nothing – though it was in the name of Lieutenant Raeburn. He had walked into the bank's Cairo branch, firmly asked to see the manager, and told him the truth. Disgraced and now a humble private. He told his story with such drawling good-humour that the manager was charmed and sympathetic and within twenty-four hours had Offer's account transferred to Cairo. Offer did forget to tell the manager, of course, that he was a service criminal once more, a man on the run, but that was none of the manager's business, so he kept quiet about it.

With a pocket full of money, Offer then went into that area of Cairo, the dangerous native quarter, which is strictly out of bounds to all ranks. Here was a one-eyed but smiling Egyptian he'd heard of while in the Glasshouse, who did a little bit of printing and quite a lot of good forging. Offer's money bought instant and charming service, with lots of *finganis* of coffee, and pleasant conversation while the work was completed. He even slept the night in the print shop – in a way the safest thing to do with the M.P.s looking for a private on the run – and felt quite safe though the area abounded with thieves and

45

cut-throats. But then Offer had a way with him which brought acceptance and friendship in any circle and with any men.

The various forms of documentation were interesting. The first to be used, and to be instantly discarded after one use, revealed Offer's good-humour. It was the usual form which said that His Majesty, King George VI, Defender of the Faith and all that mullarkey, was pleased to bestow upon his well-beloved subject a commission in the British Army. A supporting document from GHQ Cairo said that he had been granted an instant commission in H.M. Field Detention Service, and the name it was made out to in both cases was Adam Tulloch. That produced the lieutenant's uniform with no trouble, and Offer improved his rank within minutes by adding two further pips to his shoulders. And when you are an army captain you really are a person of consequence and standing.

Other documentation supported a claim to be Captain John Offer. What was curious was that he appeared to be i/c Field Salvage (Forward Area) Company. Offer was rather proud of (Forward Area) Company, but if a man's imagination could supply it, why shouldn't it exist?

And all that led up to the creation of the screen that would provide safety for him and other men until the silly war ended and they all could go back to the penury and discomforts of peace once again.

When he found Pom and then Pom found the fairground bruisers, Offer went into action. 'We've got to have establishment,' he said, though they didn't understand him immediately. And when he added, 'The bigger, the more outrageous, the better,' they were no wiser. But they soon understood.

First they nicked a couple of 3-tonners to add to the utility that Offer had 'borrowed'. Then armed with his Field Salvage (Forward Area) Company identity the quartet went foraging. As bold as brass they went down the Canal, where for twenty miles Allied troops were passing through vast tented camps, and bumped across the sand to various R.H.Q.s. Offer coolly requested to see the commanding-officers, produced his documentation whenever requested – sometimes an impressed colonel, newly out of England, didn't even ask to see his papers of identity – and made his demands.

Equipment was urgently needed up the Blue, where the Allied Forces had taken yet another mauling. He had to commandeer anything surplus to requirements – tents, blankets, tables, forms, groundsheets, cooking equipment, clothing, etc.

Captain Offer had the right manner. Very calm and assured, so that he seemed to be talking down even to officers of higher rank. There never was any bother. Whatever could be spared was loaded on to the trucks of the Field Salvage (Forward Area) Coy, fatigue parties being detailed by the local commander to do the carrying. Invariably the charming, but firm, Captain Offer was invited into the officers' mess for drinks and sometimes lunch, too, while his men fraternised amiably with their peers. Offer, who knew the ropes from his old quarter-master-sergeant days, signed for everything and left everyone happy. No one ever tumbled to the deception even in the months afterwards; but then in the chaos of war thousands of millions of pounds of taxpayers' money has to go down the drain somewhere, and who's to keep check on every item?

Loaded with the basic necessities of camp life, Offer solemnly trundled his trucks to an area he had marked out for his own. This was somewhat away from the other regiments in camp along the Canal, yet quite obvious to anyone if they bothered to look their way and if the hill wasn't between them and the road. Offer wanted seclusion, as befitted a mysterious cloak-and-dagger outfit, but did not want to arouse suspicion by appearing to be trying to hide away.

So, commandering a large patch of warm golden Egyptian sand, half a mile into the desert away from the Canal and thus beyond range of the anophelene malaria-carrying mosquito, Offer and his 'cadre' of commandos set to work to put up the tents. In all, twelve were set up, enough to accommodate seventy or eighty men, which seemed a puzzle to three sweating helpers.

'Camouflage,' said Offer soothingly. 'Size is impressive. Pinch one tent for the lot of us, and we'd have Redcaps round in no time.' But no one would think twice about a neat and orderly camp which had sprung up on a spare bit of sand.

'When we get a few more men,' Offer told them, 'we'll have a proper guard on patrol, and it will be a very efficient one. Anyone coming with questions will be told to sheer off, and if they don't sheer off, you run 'em in to me at the point of a bayonet, and I'll deal with them.' Even officers. Regardless of rank, the instruction was that they must come under close escort before Captain Offer, i/c the unit. And Offer? He would take them aside if they were officers, and speak confidentially, saying they were a special commando outfit operating behind the enemy lines. He would murmur names like Long Range Desert Group, Popski's Private Army, the Special Air Service, and the Special Boat Service – there were any amount of daring little armies operating under cloaks of secrecy, so another wouldn't create much thought except perhaps a little awe and respect for the dare-devilry of the personnel.

The absence of men around the camp would be explained away with a mythical exercise in the desert, and if visiting officers looked into the E.P.I.s they would see kits neatly laid out awaiting the return of their owners.

Offer knew he would get away with it, because the deception was too brazen to be challenged. 'Tell a big lie,' he told his men, 'and no one rumbles you. Pitch it small, and you've soon had it, chums.' And G.G.C.U. was a damned big lie, so no one was going to question it.

The activities of the Field Salvage (Forward Area) Coy temporarily came to an end when they had all the equipment they needed for camp. But to function as a pukka irregular unit, Offer needed food, water, a show of arms to impress those possible visitors, and of course cash to pay the men who joined him and keep them quiet. He went out to get what he wanted.

Before Walker joined they had made several raids in quick succession, to their satisfaction and enjoyment. The first was upon an inoffensive Naafi canteen along the Canal. It was neatly planned, and so smoothly executed that Offer knew they really had the makings of an efficient irregular unit.

They drove to the Naafi an hour after closing time, before the moon came up, so that it was dark. Sentries from a nearby camp took in the Naafi on their patrol, and had first to be dealt with. Offer, again denim-clad because officer rank was no good this night, swung down from the truck when it halted, throbbing away outside the Naafi. As he expected a sentry immediately materialised from the darkness.

The sentry wasn't expecting trouble, so his approach wasn't very formal, none of that, halt-who-goes-there stuff. He said, friendlily, 'What's up, mate? Got lost?'

'No. Got a delivery for the Naafi.' Offer dropped into the crude speech of some hoarse-voiced Cockney.

'Bit late, aren't yer?'

'We're always soddin' late in this bleedin' outfit,' said Offer, and he put bitterness into his voice. 'Never get any proper kip on this job. Talk about runnin' an army, they can't even run the bloody Naafi without making a cock of it.'

49

The sentry was quite won over by this victimisation through upper-rank inefficiency. He made equally hoarse sounds of agreement. Offer asked him where he would find the Naafi manager.

'Kips inside,' the sentry told him. 'It's Yangos, a Greek. Kick the door and waken him, though he won't like it.'

So Offer kicked the door, and when an outraged Greek manager appeared the sentry wandered off on his patrol, and it was easy thereafter. They shut off the Greek's tirade with a gag, and securely bound him. Then they started to load up, and when the sentry came wandering back they explained the movement of cases into the truck with the one word, 'Empties.' The clink of bottles appeared to confirm the statement.

The night's work provided a satisfying amount of liquor, bottled beer and the hard stuff, and a fair amount of canned food, mostly baked beans and corned beef.

Another raid, a night later, on a cookhouse at one of the camps – the sentries never worried them, and were probably playing solo in the guard tent – provided them with all the vegetables and meat they needed for some time. Bread was easy to get. Two men drove to the Field Bakery in a 30-cwt each morning and drew the amount of bread they needed. No one seemed to have to sign for anything, no questions were asked. You just shoved a chitty across with a scrawled signature and they spiked it without even looking at it.

Pom knocked off a 250 gallon tanker, so they were okay for water after that.

Altogether it was a most agreeable bout of activity, and Eddie Walker envied them the good times they had had while he had been doing guard and fatigues with the new ack-ack mob. All Captain Offer needed now was cash, but that wasn't too urgent. What he did need immediately was more men, so that at least on the surface they would appear to be a proper fighting unit, even though irregulars.

Nothing untoward happened for nearly two weeks after Walker joined the G.G.C.U., nothing, that is, to upset the happy existence at their camp along the Canal road. They raided an Army Pay Corps office, and beat up another Glasshouse screw, but all that was pleasurable and seemed in no way to endanger their existence. And all the time they looked out for likely lads to join them.

Offer was recruiting fast. Each evening he and his men would go into Cairo, John Offer to regale himself in those many pleasure areas reserved for officers only, his men to enjoy themselves in cruder surroundings and at the same time try to recruit new personnel.

They knew who they were looking for, and they knew that the bait they could dangle was almost irresistible. They went for men who had been inside, men they had personally known within the Glasshouse. For men who had the marks of the screws on their bodies were men bitter against authority, and leapt eagerly, fiercely, at any chance to escape the routine discipline of an army which they felt was their implacable foe. The Germans, the Italians? They were remote. They didn't feel like an enemy. But *their* army, with the forbidding array of officers looking after themselves, N.C.O.s trying for more stripes, and Redcaps and screws down the road, here was the real enemy. That, at any rate, was the way Glasshouse men looked at the world when they came out.

They were men ready to listen to any plan to get them away from drills, parades, guard duties, and fatigues, and when Pom, Walker, and the bully-boys talked of the easy life without army bullshit, and with all the liquor they could drink without paying for it, they were won over without much talking. Offer's followers picked their men carefully, though, opening up only to the hard cases and bitter rebels who were likely to take the big gamble of deserting their regiments.

Each night the trucks came bumping back to the desert camp with new recruits. So another gunner, Jimmy Milborn, a bit of a comedian, joined them, and Charlie Crookshank who had done some boxing in his time and showed it, and Arthur (always Art) Weybright and Angus O'Keefe became patrons of the only free bar in the Canal Zone. Before the balloon went up – and it went up with startling suddenness – Captain John Offer had a handy little force of fourteen men in his camp, and a tougher bunch of thugs no one could have recruited.

Angus O'Keefe, for instance – Offer thought it a marvellous combination of names – turned out to be an ex-L.R.D.G. sergeant, and men had to be very, very tough to have held that grade in the Long Range Desert Group. But O'Keefe was a man with a pathological hatred of Military Police, and usually when he came out of the desert and took leave he got himself into trouble with the Redcaps.

The last time had been too serious to be ignored. O'Keefe had resisted arrest after drunkenly challenging two Redcaps to do their worst with him. When they took him up on it, both ended in hospital, and the Military Police do not like their men to have their bones broken. Even the L.R.D.G., who moved heaven and earth to protect a comrade, wasn't able to keep O'Keefe from the Glasshouse.

The former sergeant was a tough man, with periods of manic activity followed by long depressions. Offer was always careful in his dealings with the man, yet liked him and in a way felt sorry for him.

Art Weybright was a signaller from the Royal Corps of Signals, quite a dab hand with radios, who went off on his own and knocked off some excellent radio sets (and a transmitter for himself; he liked playing around with the 'wireless', as he still called it), so that the Glasshouse Gang's camp was soon a place of lively music, every tent with its own set.

The one minor worry for a time was lack of cash. Offer saw no sense in paying his followers out of his own bank account, though for the first weeks he did, but he'd see that he got it back later. He knew where money was, but for the moment couldn't lay his hands on it. He explained the difficulty to his men when the recruits started to roll in.

'There's a lot of pay due to us,' he told them, and they, deserters from the army, managed to look indignant. 'It's just down the road in the Army Pay Corps office. The trouble is, they're a suspicious lot of so-and-sos, and they don't exactly leave it lying around.'

That was the trouble. At night, when it was most convenient for the Glasshouse Gang to collect their money, the Pay Corps put all their cash into a nasty great safe.

Offer said, hopefully, 'Any of you men know how to blow a safe?'

It wasn't altogether a wild hope. Offer was seeking among the bad boys for recruits, and several had most interesting backgrounds. Perhaps he would find a locksmith or safe-blower among this lot ...

Gunner Jimmy Wilborn sucked a tooth in the silence that followed Offer's question, then casually flicked away half a cigarette – no one bothered to smoke fags more than halfway when they were free.

'A Pay Corps safe?'

Captain Offer looked at him with sudden interest. 'Yes.'

Jimmy sucked that tooth again. 'Piece of cake,' he assured them. 'A doddle. All I need's a bit of jelly.' He knew where he could lay hands on some gelignite, too. Everyone was very courteous. No one asked Jimmy where he had served his apprenticeship in safe-cracking. They were content to know they had found the man they needed.

They raided the Pay Corps office, and it proved a knock-over. The guards who watched over the long wooden building, stuck out in the desert a fair distance off the road, concentrated their vigil on an adjacent cookhouse, where tea was on brew most of the night through.

Offer and his commandos, faces blackened, came stealing through the night on foot and broke into the building with ease and no disturbing noise. Jimmy Wilborn blew the safe most neatly, piling so many sandbags around it that the guard, knocking back the old char only fifty yards away, never heard a sound. They got away with less than £2,000, but if they had been there earlier that day they could have lifted over thirty thousand.

For the moment £2,000 was satisfying. Captain Offer didn't immediately share out the loot with his men, and the men didn't ask him to do so. By now they had so entered into their role that they appeared to believe in it; and when Offer said there would be a pay day each week, all accepted the situation. They lined up and received a satisfying amount of pay, including back pay for the time when they had been inside the Glasshouse and the army had stopped their payments.

That was the mistake Offer made then – he put too much money into the hands of some extremely wayward characters, and he should have expected trouble as a consequence.

The beating up of another screw – it turned out to be Staff-sergeant Anacard – came just before this trouble, however. Flushed with triumph at their success in raiding the Pay Office, pockets full of Egyptian ackers and minds already beerily contemplating a riotous next visit to Cairo, they had a celebration drink in their tented canteen after they got the commando blacking off their faces. In fact they all, except Offer, had a lot of celebration drinks.

And as they drank they grew noisy and truculent, and a demand began to shape that they embark on another commando raid, though this time it had to embrace their old tormentors, the Glasshouse screws.

There was nothing positive, no plan about it, just drunken memories surfacing of past indignities and terrible sufferings out there in His Majesty's Field Detention Prison, and a fierce rage swelling, mutually bolstered by talk rapidly becoming incoherent. Just hatred; no plan. Except in Captain Offer's mind.

He listened, and what he heard satisfied him. So in time he called them to silence, and when he called — voice good-humoured and almost gentle — they quietened instantly for a smallish, roundish, softish impostor of an army captain who yet held the gift of command. He told them what was in his mind. Swiftly he sketched out a plan of vengeance that set them back on their bench seats at the audacity of it, and then got them on their feet, roaring approval, hard, sweat-running faces inflamed in that oil light, savage men committing themselves to a deed of outrageous daring.

The plan no less was to assault Sharafim Glasshouse and cheekily beat up a screw right bang on his own pad.

John Offer was a rational man, singularly down-to-earth. He had a flexible intelligence, and a perennial humour that put restraints on excesses. Yet in one direction now he was not quite balanced, and that was in his fierce desire to hit and hurt all those men who had marked him while a prisoner in the desert Field Prison.

In some way it wasn't quite satisfying to lie in wait and pick up the odd staff sergeant and beat the bones to marrow as they had done with Staff Milkin. What Offer wanted, somewhere deep in the recesses of his sub-conscious, was to make his gesture of revenge against the place itself, the pit of torment. He wanted to batter against the grim walls that encircled the dreaded Walking Wall, an instinct that was futile because battering wouldn't bring them down or do anyone any good. But if they could assault the prison and beat up a screw right there on his own doorstep – ah, that would be satisfying!

Part of the satisfaction, of course, would come from the startled shock to military authority, particularly within the Glasshouse, at their effrontery. No one in their right senses ever thought men would return to attack the place that had done its best to knock the guts out of them. So they would do it. And Offer thought, 'If it comes off, we'll do it again.' And perhaps again. The pity was he couldn't leave his calling card, so that they would know who had done the deed. His hatred of Sharafim would never reduce, much less leave him, because every time he looked into his mirror he had reason for sustaining it.

They made the assault the very next night. There was no need to wait longer; one night was as good as another, and they knew all they needed to know about the Glasshouse, particularly about its routine.

Just on dusk three trucks lumbered off the desert and then bowled along the Sweet Water Canal road towards Sharafim. Offer's plan called for three trucks but only a few personnel. Few men were needed for the operation in mind, and anyway all had to be accommodated in the small utility for the return journey.

So Pom drove off alone in the utility – a bit jittery, the tricky, gutless Pomegranate Face, because he did not relish the lone role he would have to play later that evening. Behind the canvas-topped 5-cwt lumbered two 30-tonners, a Dodge and a Chev, both expendable.

In the Dodge Offer sat next to the driver, Gunner Walker. Offer had adopted sergeant's stripes for the night, though his own tunic was in the utility with Pom. Behind was the L.R.D.G. man, O'Keefe, ex-sergeant made up to sergeant again for the night's performance. He squatted on the cold metal floor, silent all the way because all he could think about was going in with fists and boots into the face and body of a screw.

With him squatted the flat-faced bulk of Cruiser, the 'prisoner' being returned to the Glasshouse for another stretch of torment.

The Chev, grinding in the rear, was driven by Busker. Six men on commando, a sufficient final load for a small utility.

It was completely dark long before they reached the desert jail. Offer was sufficiently relaxed and rational at that moment to enjoy the ride. Out on the desert the world seemed clean and boundless, the horizon low and the great sweep of sky brilliant with stars and dazzling quarter moon. And warm, pleasantly warm after the oppressive heat of the day. Even the native villages like Tahag and el Kebir, stinking, unlovely abominations, but alive with noisy humanity, could be tolerated, and anyway were soon passed through.

Though Pom did not pass through the last smelly village, a few miles short of Sharafim. According to plan he pulled up, his hand reluctant on the handbrake, just on the edge of the sprawling Canal hamlet. Here was open space, a hard-trodden area before the cultivation began, a place used by the entire village as a communal toilet, of which they were well aware the moment they halted.

Offer leaned out of his cab. 'Turn her round – no time to waste when we return.'

'Yes, sir.' Offer caught the unhappy glint of Pom's steel-rimmed army-issue glasses. The little bastard was already wetting himself at the idea of being left alone. Still, it wasn't altogether the best place to be, Offer thought, looking at the dark, silent hovels and mean alley entrances to the village. A lot of flaming cut-throats in these Gyppo villages, he'd heard his men telling Pom, just to cheer him, at the start of their journey.

57

'We'll be back in half-an-hour.' If they weren't, something had gone wrong with the plan. 'You'll be all right till then.'

'Yes, sir,' said Pom dolefully, and Offer nodded to Walker and they picked up speed and went briskly on their way. Seeing that huddled little figure behind the wheel of their all-important escape car, however, Offer felt a stab of unease. After all, their entire operation depended on this one frail utility driver, and Offer had no illusions about Pom's courage or sense of loyalty. A weak link in his chain, but Pom looked the part of batman-driver and that was why he was so necessary this night.

Until that moment Captain Offer had been in his usual good-humour, but perhaps those uneasy thoughts on leaving Pom came to dissipate it. There was a sudden spiralling down of confidence, a kind of flat feeling that was the wrong mood at the start of a hazardous enterprise. By the time they had turned off the Canal road, heading across the desert towards Sharafim, the good-humour had entirely departed. Instead, Offer's mind went blank. It was dangerous, this operation, and if it went wrong they might all spend the next years of their lives in this awful prison. Only when they were finally committed did he and his men really appreciate the enormity of the risk they were taking.

Then Offer saw the isolated series of buildings behind the high wall, bathed in a pool of yellow electric light, coming towards them over the bumpy road. At once he threw off his momentary attack of nerves. They would do what they had come to do, and the odds, anyway, were in their favour. Odds, he thought – a lesson for his future career – were usually in favour of attacking commandos.

They knew their drill. There were no sentries outside Sharafim Field Detention Prison. Why should there be? Who on earth would try to break into a Glasshouse? Sentries are always within prison walls, for they are there to keep men in, not out. And all knew the scene beyond those high wooden double doors let into the high barbed-wire topped mud walls.

The guard-house was built against the wall just by the main gate. Inside the guardhouse the gate-guard, five privates kipping down against their two-hour turn on the gate, or bulling already shiny toecaps and Brassoing brasses in case of a mean turn-out by Sergeant-major Fry – 'Call me Killer. That's what I am, you 'orrible shower.' With them would be their guard-commander, a staff screw.

Offer didn't know which screw would be unfortunate enough to have that night's duty, and it didn't much matter – they were all rotten bastards, a pleasure to hammer into pulp. The only thing certain was that it would not be Staff Milkin. Reports along the Naafi grapevine said he was in hospital and likely to be there a long time, and might never be of use for prison work again. Naafis brightened all throughout Egypt when the griff came through.

On duty before the gate would be the sixth sentry, a man immaculate in blancoed gaiters and webbing, rifle smartly handled and a pounding heel-stamping drill that would have done credit to a Guards' sentry outside Buckingham Palace. There was no mercy on prisoners inside Sharafim, and no less mercy on unhappy privates detailed for guard in the desert jail.

Detached from the wall but only thirty yards from the gate was the Armoury. Here were housed a further twenty men, from whom were drawn the guards and admin personnel for the rest of the jail. Well, *they* couldn't do much good if the plan went well that night, thought Offer, and was suddenly feeling very comfortable, very confident that everything would go sweetly and they'd cock a snook at military authority with a vengeance that night – a broken snoot, he thought, and the thought brought his hand up to rub his flattened facial adornment.

Walker brought the Dodge to a halt twenty yards from the big prison gates, headlights bright upon them, revealing the bold-lettered proclamation of identity – H.M. FIELD DETENTION PRISON SHARAFIM, and the yellowed notice that had once borne terse instructions to visitors on whatever business to the jail.

Sergeants Offer and O'Keefe de-bussed, their prisoner obligingly dismounting without orders or prompting. On the ground, Cruiser put his big hands together as if handcuffed. He was properly dressed for the occasion, gaitered, webbed, and with full accoutrements of pack, kit-bag, side-pack, and water-bottle. The two sergeants took up positions on either side of him. Walker leaned over his wheel, very tense, eyes on the little door let into the main gate. Their headlights would have announced their arrival to the sentry on the gate.

Behind them the second vehicle, the Chev, was indulging in a minor bout of turning and reversing, all designed to bring it back on to the road facing the way they had come, ready for a quick getaway.

Sergeant Offer did the shouting, the usual sharp, hating injunctions to 'Get fell in.' 'Get into step, soldier.' 'Come on, smartly now, lef' ri', lef' ri'.'

He was reproducing the pattern that occurred hundreds of times every year outside those grim gates, though not so often after dark – a pattern every inmate knew well, just as they knew every detail of action and reaction around H.M. Field Detention Prison. The alert sentry – Glasshouse sentries were never anything less than alert – would call out the guard commander. In fact as they got into stride they could hear him shouting beyond the gates. Two yards from it Sergeant Offer gave the command to halt, and they came to ramrod attention and waited. His body was throwing a shadow across the little door, and Offer shuffled slightly to one side so that the headlights of

60

the Dodge would beam straight into anyone's eyes if the gate opened.

It did open, though no one stepped out. Blast! Though Offer's plans provided for this eventuality, hence the Dodge waiting there.

Staff Anacard came into view, framed in the small doorway. Instantly his hands went to cover his eyes. 'Put those bloody lights out!' he roared, and Gunner Walker obliged but for seconds afterwards Staff Anacard's vision would be impaired. 'What you got there? A flamin' bastard prisoner at this time of night?'

'No. Betty-flamin'-Grable,' retorted Offer, enjoying himself, because if one sergeant talked tough, so could another. 'Come on, Staff, we don't want to be here all bloody night. We've had this sod on our hands all the way from Mersa.'

Anacard bridled at the way this sergeant stood up to him, and snapped and snarled at the sentry to cover his annoyance. It was an order to throw open the gates.

The gates opened outwards.

That was something that had occurred to Offer when he lay on his camp bed going over his plans the previous night. Sharafim's gates swung outward and could not be opened into the prison compound because of their design. A memory highly important to Offer and his comrades this night. The Dodge began to crawl slowly forward, Walker unable to restrain himself.

They saw the big, heavy doors swing back flat against the thick walls of the prison entrance, pushed slowly open by the sentry, rifle slung over his left shoulder. They saw a man step out between them, the lean hated figure of Staff Anacard – 'the thick 'un,' as he was often known.

He came out belligerent, wanting to beat down this lippy sergeant who talked back to him before his sentry. 'This is a soddin' fine time to bring a prisoner in. You been layin' about with Cairo bints all day?'

Startled, he saw the stiff little group of men disintegrate. Simultaneously the Dodge engine revved into a roar calculated to drown, say, men's voices shouting. Sergeants and prisoner went leaping away from each other, and out of the path of the Dodge.

Sergeant Angus O'Keefe, the leanest, quickest man in their mob, leapt at the ears of Anacard and had them before the screw knew he was moving. O'Keefe, exulting, kept on running and swinging his body as he ran. Anacard came with him because he had to go where his ears went and his ears were firmly gripped by O'Keefe's savage hands. Anacard came – actually his body lifted off the ground and went flying through the air, dragged behind his pain-racked oral appendages. It crashed, as O'Keefe intended it to crash, against the thick mud wall of the prison.

A startled sentry saw it happen then swung his eyes to the sergeant and prisoner. Offer got his shoulder to the left door and hurled it shut. Cruiser swung his door and it hit the unfortunate guard flat on the face and sent him stunned and reeling and with no thought to unsling his rifle and give warning fire. Those seconds were highly important.

The doors were closed, but there was no way of bolting them from outside. But the Dodge could do that. It drove up, not too hard, and rammed against the gates before the engine was switched off. Handbrake on, leave it in gear, hurl the key far into the desert, and Gunner Walker was out of his cab and leaping to where Anacard was taking the chop.

O'Keefe, exulting at having One Of Them before his fists, went driving in as Anacard slid down the wall. He hacked hard at the neck and back of the head. Break the bloody thing. Smash the head like an eggshell. One, two, smash and swing.

Yet Anacard, hard man, came rolling to his feet, swaying away, the instinct of a hard-pressed boxer under pressure. His foot came round and the steel-capped toe got O'Keefe in the left groin. And as O'Keefe went reeling, Anacard, face lighting with fierce joy, came erect and faced the next of his attackers. He had guts and didn't think – or was he too thick? – to shout out for help.

Cruiser got him. A flurry of big bodies, the stab of solid bony fists against hard faces, the lift and smash of heavy boots, Anacard almost recovered from first shock and holding his own. And only about twenty seconds left to do the job, according to Offer's plans.

Offer went in this time, swinging and catching Anacard a dizzying blow on the side of the head. Then Walker was there, hurling Offer aside in order to get at the screw. Walker chopped him to his knees. Too late Anacard saw the strength of the opposition and opened his mouth to shout. Cruiser gave him the old one-two across his face, sending Anacard's head jerking madly first one way, then the other. Walker put the boot into Anacard's crotch, and after that there was nothing much left in the screw.

Offer pulled out of the fray. He didn't need to do the thrashing himself in order to satisfy his need for vengeance. Just watching the screw get what he had given so many helpless others was enough. Besides, he had to maintain his sense of timing.

Inside the prison compound the sentry would be gathering his wits. Any second now there'd be a yell or a rifle shot. That would bring out the guard. But they wouldn't get past the gate – not even through the little door – with the Dodge solidly jammed against it. The big danger came from the wall. There were places where riflemen could mount to platforms high up the wall, quelling possible prison riots, safely beyond reach of vengeful hands. From those high platforms, though, riflemen could also fire out across the desert.

'Ten seconds,' thought Offer. That was all the time they could devote to Anacard now.

But ten seconds are a long time, a long time, that is, for someone taking the hammering of his life. Cruiser did for Anacard's face, while Walker, who had a particular hatred for Anacard, put in a boot that made a mess of the screw's ribs.

Suddenly there was a wild shout beyond the doors, then a response. Offer snapped, 'Enough!' Cruiser hit Anacard a last time, the hardest blow yet, but the face was already pulped. Walker, so good-tempered with his oppos, drove one final merciless boot into the ribs, but, perhaps fortunately, the screw was now past consciousness. Then they ran.

The Chev was revving up. Offer leapt round to the passenger seat. Lean O'Keefe, a satisfied man for all his pain, was helped over the tailboard by Cruiser and Walker. The truck went lurching away.

It seemed to get into speed with agonising slowness. God, God, why was the thing crawling so slowly! Back of them they'd have found the prison gates jammed against opening. They'd be leaping up the wooden steps to the firing platforms. Rifles would be lifting and taking aim at the clumsy receding vehicle, an easy target with its bulk – soft transport incapable of protecting human flesh and bone against high velocity bullets.

Their nerves screamed in agony as the Chev bumped and lurched, engine revving flat out and yet the road speed not seeming to match the roaring sound. Gathering speed, yet never going fast enough for them. The moonlit sand crawling by. And every man taut, rigid, holding himself in, waiting for the bullets to rip through the canvas, chew through the woodwork, and tear a way through the thin metal plating. And then into them. Any moment now. A bullet in the back. A lot of bullets in the back. A fusillade from the high wall. A volley that would halt the Chev and leave them writhing and moaning in their blood. Or dead.

Yet it didn't come. Not one single shot. No rifleman reached the platforms in time to spot the truck and open up on it. Panic lost time for H.M. prison guard that night. Too many men, bemused by recent sleep, spent too much time vainly trying to shove open a main gate which refused to budge. Too many men and not one leader among them for vital minutes. Their commander, Staff Anacard, was on the wrong side of the gate. Anyway he was out, cold out, on the sandy ground beneath the high prison wall.

In the Chev, when they realised they were safe, the tension began to drain from them, to be replaced by an elation as near to a hysteria as big, solid, unimaginative men can attain.

Offer realised that he had stopped breathing, holding in his breath. It was painful – nearly two minutes. Now, he let it out in a great gasp and panted for a second, then looked at Busker, face still strained as he leaned over his steering wheel as if urging on his vehicle.

'Easy, now,' Offer said, and began to laugh. 'We made it!' Two minutes. From a standing start, probably half a mile away now; and bright though the moon was, a truck wouldn't show up at that range. 'We made it, d'you hear?'

Busker's flattened face seemed to relax slowly, as if it took time for a thought to percolate through that thick skull. Then a grin began to develop, bigger and bigger, and finally the ex-fairground busker began to laugh and to shout, 'We did it!' and banged on the back of the cab and shouted so that the men behind would hear. 'We did it!'

Then a swift, almost savage turn upon his officer, almost a snarl: 'But next time, I want to beat up the bastards. No more bloody truck-driving for me!'

'Next time,' Offer soothed, 'it'll be your turn.' At the moment he felt inclined to promise anything, to give anything out of gratitude for the successful accomplishment of another commando raid.

In the truck behind the men were shouting their heads off with joy. Probably thumping each other with friendly blows that would knock out more ordinary men, Offer thought, banging each other on the back and cheering and feeling good, better than if they had had a skinful. Well, they'd soon get a skinful, a big skinful, he'd see to that.

He settled back, watching the track spin into the light of their twin beams. The tarmac Canal road, and the Chev swung obediently on to it. Five minutes and they'd swop over to the utility. Offer began to slip out of his sergeant's bush shirt.

And a thought was coming to him, a thought so glorious it dazzled him with the grandeur of his vision.

If they could do it once, they could do it again.

And again.

The unbalanced hatred of the Glasshouse drove him on, his thoughts racing, seeing pictures in his mind. Pictures of more commandos, more daring next time. Pictures of him and his men stealing silently from the desert to strike at the hated places. They could get the whole prison system in turmoil, he thought, and the idea was intoxicating. Put the fear of God into the screws and maybe they'd go a bit easier with the poor bastards who came into their calloused hands.

They were heady thoughts, marvellous thoughts, but on that ride back to pick up Pom, Offer's future began to take shape. Now he knew how he would ride out the war – by getting his own back in a way no man had ever imagined. By having fun with bastard authority, he thought grimly. The plump little man's idea of fun was going to be painful. And he'd have the whole of the

British army rooting for them, he knew, and perhaps sometimes in time of need the ordinary British Tommy would become a useful ally ...

Bolder, next time, he kept saying to himself. Bigger villains than Milkin and Anacard; for though it had been Milkin who had bust his nose Offer knew it was higher ranking men who created the brutal system. The Killer – R.S.M. Fry – and Major Tulloch, the bastard Scotsman. But even beyond them, who stood higher in the punishment industry? Who was the big man of the Prison Service? A general, a brigadier? They must find out who he was, and he must know what it was like to work on the Wall and be alone in a windowless punishment cell with two sadists to break bones and bruise and bloody flesh.

Offer's thoughts raced on and on, planning as the wheels brought them into the village where they'd left the utility. It was one of the most marvellous nights in his life. Be audacious, plan carefully, and commandos could get away with murder ...

Pom was not there, the utility had vanished.

When the Chev came bumping and grinding off the road to skirt the back of the village, the headlights revealed only blankness where the small truck should have been.

Offer heard big Busker curse, then bring the Chev to a halt. Behind, voices were raised in startled question. Offer swung down and walked into the light of the beams. The elation had gone. What was that he had been kidding himself about careful planning? First operation, and now this! Had Pom taken fright at being left alone and scampered, leaving his mates in the lurch? Offer began to curse the rat-like Pom, then checked himself. If anyone was at fault it was he. They all knew how undependable Pom was, all mouth and no guts.

He stood, indecisive, wondering what the devil to do

now. A swift chain of thoughts. Forget the original plan, stick to the Chev and hope to make it back to camp? But they'd be using the telephone now at Sharafim; within minutes the M.P.s would have road-blocks all along the Canal road. And there was only one road across the desert. If they bluffed past one road-block, Offer was sure they wouldn't bluff past the lot.

The trouble was, they were without their final disguise. Offer's captain's bush-jacket was in the utility. An officer with a party could get away with it. Scruffy O.R.s even with sergeants would be under suspicion. No, their truck was a trap.

So? His eyes peered into the darkness. The other men had alighted to stand with him. They could hear the life of the village beyond these hovels, for it was still very early, and Egypt only really comes to life after dark along the Canal. Someone – some dark shadow – came momentarily into the light of their beams, then fled. Someone wanting to use the communal toilet, this waste of land that stank to high heaven.

If they took off on foot, going out into the desert, far from sight from the road, could they make it back to camp? How many miles? Twenty at least. They'd never make it. No water, no food, little knowledge of direction. A group of men would somehow be spotted, perhaps from the air. No, that was no go.

Walker said, 'Someone coming, sir.' Sir, even then.

A shape emerged, someone running. A short man became revealed in the headlights.

'Pom!' they all said, but it wasn't a glad, welcoming sound for the distraught Pomegranate Face. Where was the utility, their precious vehicle? 'Where the hell have you been?' – ex-Sergeant O'Keefe, voice snapping with old authority.

Pom said, 'Sir!' very breathless, even coming to salute in his agony. 'Oh, Christ, it's been fuckin' awful! Christ,

68

am I glad to see you!' He was babbling, almost raving. That time alone there on the dark wastes beside the village had sapped him of all nerve, and Pom never had much, anyway.

'Stop that silly chatter!' snapped Offer, as Pom babbled on. 'What happened? Where's the truck?' He wanted to shake the stupid little bastard.

'It's gone!'

'We know it's bloody gone!' O'Keefe, losing his temper.

Offer quietened him. 'What do you mean, it's gone? How?'

They got it out of an almost incoherent Pom. Quarter of an hour after they'd left, Pom began to notice shapes flitting about the wasteland, tall whitish figures. Pom, petrified with fear, realised there was a gathering of many men, Egyptians, and before he could make up his mind what to do, they came closing in on the small vehicle.

'Why didn't you start up and drive off?' – O'Keefe again. Pom could have driven a short distance away, and waited there, or kept moving until he saw their Chev return.

'I did, sir. But the truck wouldn't move when I shoved it in gear.'

'Wouldn't move?'

'No, sir. Some of the bastards had lifted the back wheels off the ground.' So they'd spin futilely, without traction. An old trick.

'And then?'

Pom's nerve had snapped at that, and he'd gone rushing out of the car, to flee headlong across the wasteland. He thought someone began to follow him, but if so it didn't last long. The booty inherent in the army utility was too strong for possible pursuers. When his breath gave out, Pom halted and looked back.

'What did they do with the car?' It wasn't there. They must have driven it away ...

Pom said, 'They pushed it in among them bloody houses.'

'Pushed?'

'You don't think I left 'em the fuckin' key, do you?' An indignant Pom, and it surprised them that a panicky little man like Pom should do such a thing at such a critical time.

'Then it's not far away.' Offer swung round. 'How long since this happened?'

'Five minutes ... six ... I don't know.'

If they were lucky, the Gyppos wouldn't have had time to remove the wheels and tyres, the booty from stolen cars that brought most price in wartime Egypt.

Offer snapped, 'Come on, let's find it,' and began to run towards a shadowy alleyway.

'The Chev –' someone called.

'Forget it!'

They all ran together, a silent vengeful bunch. The sounds of village life grew louder, and ahead was a glow from oil lamps. Abruptly they came out along the Canal edge. Here was the usual scene of a small Egyptian village. A broad space fronting the water, gleaming white in the moonlight, a space turned into the inevitable evening market, with vendors squatting beside sacks and trays of fruit and seeds, and tiny charcoal fires where squatting men cooked little bits of meat on spits watched by hungry-eyed children. On the edge of the open space the principal buildings in the village, but none of them more than a two-storeyed mud-brick affair. Some shops, naphtha-lighted, and a lot of small open-fronted workshops where carpenters, cobblers, and metalworkers plied their trade in full view of the passing public. Everywhere people, men women and children, strolling, talking, or squatting and talking ...

Sharp-eyed O'Keefe snapped, 'There!' He'd spotted the utility.

There was a crowd outside a bit of a garage. As it milled around, glimpses could be obtained of the hood of the utility. Then they saw the bonnet was up.

Offer thought, 'Oh, God, what have they done to her!' If the truck had already lost its wheels or been immobilised ... But they'd only had a few minutes, according to Pom. 'Come on!' They swung round and began to race for the truck.

Someone in the crowd saw them coming and gave warning. Offer, leading his men, saw them turning, mostly men but also some small excited boys. White galabias – and some not so white. Turbanned or skull-capped heads. White eyes in features almost coal black in that light. A lot of them, Offer thought, and they looked ugly and menacing as they seemed to draw up around the vehicle.

'Keep going!' he shouted. The hell with it, everything depended on that truck.

When they came up to the crowd it began to scatter, especially the small boys, leaping away in alarm. But not all. A group momentarily held their ground, bold men who knew their strength on their own territory and were prepared to fight to keep this wonderful prize that had been delivered by Allah right into their lap. And how few swaddies there were, too.

Offer felt a surge from the rear. Busker passed him. He was a fight behind the others that night. Yet it didn't begin as a fight.

The crowd standing their ground allowed themselves to be jostled to one side by the burly Busker, then by the others, but the natives were mutinous, only yielding at the last because Egyptians have always found it painful to cross the aggressive white peoples from the North. Walker shouldered his way to the bonnet. A quick look inside. 'Seems okay, sir.' He slammed the bonnet.

Offer was watching the Egyptians. He knew there was going to be trouble. Right at the last, when they saw their booty about to be driven away, they would turn nasty.

'See if the engine starts.'

A frightened Pom shot into his driving seat, key out, at Offer's sharp command. Offer and his other men faced about, backs to the utility. The engine started. 'Thank Christ for that,' Walker said, and then the crowd came at them.

They had been silent people up to this time, but now they began to shout in that high-pitched manner of excitement so typically Egyptian. They came in wildly, a flood of men, a flutter of robes; and as they shouted other men began to race towards them from all quarters of the Canal side. The British soldiers were vastly outnumbered.

'Get moving!' Offer called, and Pom slipped it into gear.

Busker swung and knocked the nearest Egyptian flat on his back. They had courage and came on. Cruiser leapt to meet them, one-two, one-two, a couple of Egyptians reeling and Cruiser back against the car, just beginning to move.

'Inside!' shouted Offer, swinging open the passenger door. Walker was within reaching distance, kicking out and holding back his attackers. Offer dragged on him and sent him toppling back into the passenger seat, then Offer fell on top of the gunner, and two pairs of kicking boots stuck out of the moving doorway.

O'Keefe gave a yell and dived headfirst over the low tailboard. Cruiser turned as the van went past him, tried to do the same but got stuck, stomach across the tailboard. Busker couldn't get in but grabbed one of the canvas supports and started to run faster than he'd ever done before, dragged by the accelerating utility through the scattering crowd.

When they'd gone fifty or sixty yards, Offer gasped, 'Halt! Quick!'

Pom stepped on the brake. The lurch threw Cruiser over the tailboard. Offer struggled out. They couldn't go far like that. Besides, were all his men with him? That was his first thought – his men.

A quick glance round as Walker hauled himself outside. The mob hadn't given chase, perhaps too astonished by the unorthodox departure, but the nearest Egyptians weren't more than a dozen yards away, and already beginning to run towards them. And Busker was between them and the truck, losing his hold just before the brakes were applied and falling on a face that had had much worse treatment in its life.

Offer shouted, 'You okay, Busker?'

Busker came on to his feet with the celerity of a ballet star, for all his bulk. He began to run.

'In the back!' Offer to Walker, who swung round and was inside the utility in a flash. The crowd was racing towards them, a great flock of screaming, thwarted, long-suffering people. Busker began a headlong dive over the tailboard. Offer hoped the others inside didn't get in the way of that massive projectile. He slid into his seat. Pom didn't wait for an order but had the nimble little vehicle leaping into speed before Offer's backside even hit his seat. The door swung shut.

One Egyptian grabbed the tailboard. Cruiser gave him a casual clout that sent him spinning and no one could catch up with the truck after that. So the Gyppos threw things – sticks, mainly – and it was then that the commandos suffered another casualty. O'Keefe, struggling clear of Walker's and Busker's bodies, lifted his head just in time to stop a stick with his mouth. It knocked one front tooth out and chipped another. O'Keefe had suffered more than anyone on that night's party.

But they were away. Even O'Keefe didn't mind losing a tooth, spitting blood and watching the village recede behind them. They had finally pulled it off. There'd been a bit of a bodge with the planning, but overall it had worked out right. Everyone began to feel cheerful

73

again and Walker for some reason began to sing he was the Cock of the North, until the others couldn't stand it and told him to shut his something mouth. But amiably. Friendly men with each other that night.

Offer saw a string of red lights ahead, as if a column of vehicles were stationary, or nearly so. 'The road-block,' he said to his driver, and felt Pom quiver with apprehension. 'Now, don't get worked up,' he said kindly. 'Just leave everything to me.'

He'd struggled into his officer's tunic and now flashed his torch on his face scrutinising himself in the mirror. They slowed, drawing on to the last-most vehicle in the queue. Offer called out to the men in the back, 'I think this is a road-block. Don't panic. I'll do the talking.'

The column before them – mostly Allied army vehicles but with a few civilian cars interspersed among them – kept moving forward jerkily. After a few minutes they saw waving lights ahead and Offer said, very calmly, he thought he'd get down and stretch his legs.

He did, strolling beside the line of trucks as they moved to where a barrier had been placed half across the road. Offer saw men with torches who mounted trucks and flashed lights within – men with white blancoed webbing and gaiters, the Military Police, nobody's friends.

There was an officer at the barrier supervising proceedings. Offer strolled up to him. 'Flap on?' The Military cop was a two-pipper.

The lieutenant hardly bothered to look at him. Every bloody officer came up to ask that question, stupid buggers. Would they be there if there wasn't? 'A flap,' he agreed.

'Enemy activity . . . sabotage?' said Offer, hinting.

'No.' Very short now. 'Trouble at the Glasshouse.'

'Oh,' said Offer, letting his voice go flat, then walking a yard or two away to await his truck as if he'd lost interest in the business. His utility came up. Offer went and stood by the open passenger door as an M.P. approached. Perhaps the fellow had seen Offer talking to his own officer and felt reassured, for he hardly bothered to look inside the tiny utility.

'Okay, sir,' he said and went off to look into a more interesting Matador gun-towing vehicle.

Offer didn't hurry, but slowly lowered himself beside Pom and equally carefully closed the passenger door. Then he said, very calmly, 'Home, Pom, my boy, and please don't start off in a hurry.'

So a meek Pom moved gently through the gears and away they went scudding up the moonlit Sweet Water Canal road, all at peace with the world. Two more road-blocks, but now neither was terrifying. Offer strolled about and looked very calm and nobody really took any notice of a small party of troopers in the command of a very amiable, slightly portly officer. Not once did Offer have to show his identity documents brought with him for such an emergency – Field Salvage (Forward Area) Coy.

Well before midnight they rumbled over the desert to their camp and the men they'd left behind them. Well after midnight they were still drinking, even Offer having rather more than he normally took.

It was a wild, noisy party, getting more uproarious as time went on. The men who had not been on the operation drowned their envy in buckshee ex-Naafi liquor, and the heroes who had done up the old enemy on his own doorstep more than kept pace with them ...

It was curious, their reaction to John Offer. He sat at a trestle table away from the crowded little bar, a benign smile, a smile of infinite toleration and good-humour, on his broken-nosed face, and one by one his men came across as if to do homage to him.

Sometimes they asked if they could get him a drink; others simply walked unsteadily across with glasses containing everything from beer to the best cognac and slapped it before him, then stood back and grinned the big grin of alcoholic good fellowship.

They stayed for little chats, and they flattered him, telling him he was a great guy and they'd go anywhere if he led them. Flattery, but they meant it, and they would follow him, too. It was all rather moving, and it stirred Captain Offer and had the effect of making him think, 'I'll show 'em. I'll give 'em reason to like me.' He'd have to, anyway, he knew. And quickly; for admiration and good fellowship swiftly die if the winning streak isn't maintained.

Lean, hungry-looking Angus O'Keefe came over once in the evening. Offer noticed that he was still wearing his tunic with the sergeant's stripes. From that day on he always wore those stripes, assuming his previous rank without asking anyone's permission, and it was accepted by the men as of right and no one – not once – ever questioned it. Sergeant O'Keefe was reborn that evening they picked up Staff Anacard and carted him to hospital to lie alongside a battered Staff Milkin.

Without his front tooth, O'Keefe looked more wolfish than ever, giving a sinister quality to the smile that had always looked taut and mirthless anyway. But he was cordial towards his leader.

'Sit down, Sergeant,' invited Offer, and that seemed to set the seal of approval on O'Keefe's resumed rank. 'It's quite a party.'

'It was quite a night, sir.'

'A good night. Though I thought once it wasn't going to come off.'

O'Keefe seemed to shrug carelessly. The old L.R.D.G. man was a commando through and through. Nearness to death and disaster seemed to leave him unmoved – only screws and M.P.s got him going.

'You can never plan right down to the last detail. It's a

risk you always take on an operation.' He drank, his eyes seeming to shine softly over the beer he preferred to other drinks. 'It's always worth the risk.'

Offer said, 'It is,' his thoughts back to that excitement during the raid. Nothing on earth was like it, neither women nor drink; nothing could compare with a gamble such as they had pulled off.

And then he said abruptly, because now, of course, O'Keefe was a sergeant and therefore his second-in-command, 'I've got something bigger in mind. Next job will be a shaker.' Already his racing thoughts were beginning to shape a new commando raid.

O'Keefe said, simply, 'They can never be too big.' And then he said something that Offer never forgot. 'The bigger they are, the more likely they are to come off. It's when they think that no one in their right senses will have a bash at them that it's all made easy. But that's commando work, of course.'

'Of course,' said Offer. He looked at the lean red face of the ex-L.R.D.G. man, now beginning to run in sheets of sweat because of the humidity in that overcrowded tent. An interesting man, this O'Keefe. Plenty of intelligence; all the courage in the world when it was needed. A hard commanding manner when giving orders, yet in conversation his normal voice was somehow thin and immature. Offer wondered about the sergeant's background, and why M.P.s in particular sent him berserk. Working class, he thought, life uncomfortable for him. And a father with a buckled belt to thrash him for nothing in particular? Did he see his father in those stern, hard Military Police?

O'Keefe rose, as if feeling he'd had his ration of his commanding officer's time. 'Make it soon, sir,' he said, and grinned a gap-toothed grin that wasn't pleasant and seemed to tell of a hunger for violence inside the man.

'Soon,' promised Offer, and around two in the morning

the party broke up, though a few were already sprawled in drunken sleep on the sandy floor of the tent, and Captain Offer retired to his neat little cot.

Within forty-eight hours the Military Police had found them and were on to them.

Offer maintained only the mildest of discipline within his camp. No one did anything unnecessarily. True, there was always one man now on piquet duty, night and day, comfortably seated under a shade on top of a sandy hummock that gave a clear view all over the camp and right across to the main road. He could smoke and was plentifully supplied with char, so it wasn't a bad turn of duty.

There were no parades, and a minimum of fatigues, and every late afternoon, when the sun was beginning to cool, a leave truck bowled into Cairo taking with it any personnel aching for the fleshpots of that smelly but exciting city.

The day after the thrashing of Staff-sergeant Anacard everyone wanted to go off on a binge, the ackers in their pockets burning through their KD linings. Everyone lay abed until late in the morning; then breakfast was prepared for those whose stomachs could take it; an afternoon's snoring kip in their E.P.I. tents, brailings removed to give maximum draught, and by five o'clock every man was ready to take on another load of liquor.

Offer watched them go from his tent. He'd even dispensed with a piquet for the night. He wasn't leaving the camp, and Sergeant O'Keefe, very bruised now where Anacard's vicious boot had caught him, wasn't taking the leave truck, either. So a sentry hardly seemed necessary.

After the truck had gone captain and sergeant were alone in the camp, but neither bothered the other with his company. O'Keefe lay on his blankets, an oil lamp behind his head, happily reading some four months' old *News of the World*s that had been picked up in some foray. John

Offer simply sat at his table in his tent and thought.

The idea that had germinated on the ride back from Sharafim seemed irresistibly to be taking form. It was so breath-takingly audacious that Offer's brain was inspired by it and his excited thoughts ran on and on, meeting doubts and matching them with plans. That day he hardly ate but seemed to have an insatiable thirst; it was as if the fires of inspiration within him raged and even grew as the hours of planning passed.

Finally he began to draw a diagram and to make notes alongside the carefully penned sketch. About midnight he was satisfied. It was as O'Keefe said: when the thing seemed impossible it was so easy to knock 'em off. The bigger they are, the harder they can be made to fall, he found himself quoting, tired but triumphant. And by God this was big, and by God what a fall it would be for prison authority. There'd never been anything like this since the Roman Spartacus.

He was a long time falling asleep. He heard the leave truck rumble in well after midnight, and he had a feeling that the leave party seemed curiously quiet and restrained in seeking their beds.

Next morning he began to understand why. Gunner Eddie Walker gave him some hints. Walker still seemed to regard his captain as a special buddy, and loyalty this day brought him trudging over the hot sand to Offer's tent before most of the camp was astir.

'Morning, sir.'

'Morning.' A smile up at the big ex-palais bouncer. Captain Offer was neatly reducing to shreds the plans and notes he had made the previous evening. He no longer needed them. They were dangerous lying around, and anyway every detail was now firmly planted in his memory. 'Good leave last night?' Very genial this morning. The future looked good and exciting to Captain Offer.

79

'Well –' said Walker, and the way the word came out reluctantly removed the smile from Offer's face.

'Any trouble?'

A nod. Walker's face showed the struggle within him. Loyalty demanded silence where erring comrades were concerned; good sense and equal loyalty to his old cell-mate dictated frankness at this moment. Offer waited, knowing the gunner would talk. Wasn't that why he had trudged across the sands to see him, anyway?

'We had a shindig in a canteen, sir,' he began to tell about it; after a while, confident in his superior's sense of justice, very openly. They'd all got to drinking too much and it had become another celebration party. Then some of them had got cocky and talkative, throwing their weight about. They'd begun to boast that they were an élite unit, hinting at cloak and dagger work, the best fighting mob along the Canal. All the usual stuff designed to make ordinary infantry wallahs feel humble in the presence of bold buccaneers.

'They were talking about the G.G.C.U., openly, sir.'

'Oh, Christ,' said Offer. That was damned stupid – full of drink and in a service canteen where rumour would pick up and in no time spread to every unit along the Nile.

Walker looked guilty. 'Sir, someone was also shooting off his mouth about –' He hesitated.

'Go on.' Offer knew this was the serious bit.

'Well, about beating up Old Knackers last night, sir.'

'Someone said that?' Offer was incredulous. 'Someone was daft enough to talk about *that*?' Christ, this passed all belief! He thought, 'Pom?' but didn't put the name to Walker, knowing he'd get no answer.

Some damned idiot had told the world that a commando unit, even giving the name, by the sound of it, was responsible for the assault on a prison staff-sergeant.

Almost he or they had left their address – somewhere along the Canal.

Warning bells were whirring frantically in Offer's brain immediately. No good staying here. Must get the men up and moving. But where?

'What happened?' Walker had spoken of trouble.

Walker looked a bit dispirited. 'They were Jocks, there, sir. Fifty-first Highland Div.' Offer realised now that Walker was looking sore. 'Bloody Scotch buggers,' said the gunner feelingly.

'You met your match?' Offer was ironic. Telling one of the 51st they were inferior soldiers was tactless. 'They beat you up?'

Walker said, 'They beat us up.' Then he brightened. 'But we almost held our own, sir. Just too many of the bastards.' He became subdued again. 'We smashed up the canteen pretty awful, sir, and in no time the place was lousy with Redcaps.'

'Oh.' Another shock to come. 'Did they pick up any of our boys?'

'Wise, sir, and Crookshank. And some Jocks.' But in the face of a common enemy, Jocks and G.G.C.U. had combined forces, driven off the M.P.s, and rescued their men. Well, that was a relief.

But the M.P.s had been called in, and there was always someone to remember boastful conversations, always someone to squeal to questioning authority. Offer thought, 'They'll be searching every camp along the Canal for a commando unit.'

'Gunner, get every man out of bed. Tell 'em to pack. Tell 'em we're moving from here in half-an-hour. Oh, and send Sergeant O'Keefe to me – *jildy*!

Walker, startled, went off at the double. He was back in the tent within seconds, his eyes wide and shocked. 'It's too late, sir. They're here, the M.P.s.'

Offer picked up his hat and stick, his face resolute.

'Not too late,' he said determinedly. 'Go, get everyone moving.' But he'd thought of one more thing. 'Oh, and tell everyone we're Field Salvage today.' Commando units were unhealthy.

Captain Offer went out into the sunshine. A jeep was just coming to a halt by the empty guard tent. Offer strolled nonchalantly towards it. There was an officer next to the driver and two stiff-backed men in the rear. All wore the red hats of the Military Police.

Offer was hearty. ' 'Morning. To what do I owe the honour?'

All the M.P.s were dismounting. The action had an ominous look. They all had their eyes on him as he approached the jeep. Offer didn't like the look of the officer, a captain. He was so clean-looking, so pink and scrubbed, tall and thin, almost white-haired and with a professional manner of distaste and chilliness that hit home immediately. It didn't upset Offer.

The captain merely rapped, 'You've got no one on sentry.' He was hostile. His men ranged in line just behind him, hard men with nasty eyes that looked everywhere and disapproved apparently of everything they saw.

Offer sounded amused. 'Probably off for his morning char. We don't bother too much about discip –'

'Who are you?' No beating about the bush with this tall blue-eyed Redcap. A gesture. 'I see no regimental signs.'

Offer extended upon his amusement. 'We don't bother about such things. We're always on the move.'

The M.P. merely held out his hand. Captain Offer went into his breast pocket and brought out some sweat-stained papers which he handed carefully to the M.P. 'We're a Field Salvage Unit –'

'Oh.' Disappointment apparent in the other officer's voice. His eyes looked from the papers to the short, plump-ish captain. He was looking for a nest of commandos.

Field Salvage sounded noncombatant ... scruffy. The slackness in discipline hardly appeared to be what they were looking for.

Out of the corner of his eye Captain Offer saw movement. The men, roused, were coming into the open. He approved; they were doing it well, not revealing that they had been locked in sleep, most of them, only seconds before. Now they were marching around as if intent on camp fatigues, doing things with brailings, picking paper up off the desert, or simply walking with something in their hands, tools, cans of water, oil, or even – Weybright's inspiration – a load of blankets on his head which he solemnly dumped in another tent.

Offer's eyes came back to the M.P. He had finished studying the Field Salvage (Forward Area) Coy documents. He'd never heard of the outfit, but there were so many small units doing something or nothing towards winning the war for the Germans, he thought, and Field Salvage anyway had a vaguely familiar ring. He handed back the documents. They were in order. His disappointment grew.

Offer, greatly daring, said, 'You're looking for someone? A deserter?' Making it sound very small ...

There was a Redcap behind the M.P. captain whose head was turning slowly, his eyes following someone moving. Offer found his attention riveted upon the fellow. What attracted his gaze to the M.P., though, was the sharp frown behind the stare, the puzzled, questioning look.

'As if he's seen someone he thinks he recognises,' Offer thought, and his head moved slightly taking in a wide vision. He saw who the M.P. was frowning at.

Sergeant Angus O'Keefe, late of the L.R.D.G.

'Oh, Jesus wept!' thought Offer in anguish. Of course he'd told Walker to send O'Keefe to him, but that was before he knew the M.P.s were paying them a call. Why was O'Keefe marching straight towards the group? Didn't he know? Walker must have rushed on, not warning him.

Him. Angus O'Keefe, a man probably known and cursed by every Military Policeman in the Canal Zone. That chap had spotted him and thought he recognised him.

Out of the corner of his eye Offer saw O'Keefe abruptly make a smart turn to his right and go between two tents. He'd spotted the danger and hopped it, but was he too late? Had the damage been done?

Offer's eyes swung back to the M.P. The Redcap was frowning, his face puckered. Offer recognised the expression. It was: 'Now, where the hell have I seen that face before?'

The M.P. captain shoved the documents back at Captain Offer, his voice was ungracious. 'We're looking for someone. Someone we don't like.' His tone was thoroughly nasty.

Offer waved vaguely towards the tents. 'Well, look as much as you like. I don't think you'll find your deserter here.' Again making it sound very pedestrian. And then he became effusively hospitable. 'I say, why not all come in and have a drink? I mean, it's hot, so damned hot.'

He was throwing a bluff, making it sound as if he really wanted them to linger, and using his light-coloured, just-out-of-OCTU voice that hard fellows like M.P.s detested. For one terrible moment he thought the M.P. captain was going to accept his invitation. Certainly he hesitated; a cold drink was welcome even so early in the morning. Then he turned away.

'Thank you. Not today. Another time.' He gave a salute that was an insult to Forward Base noncombatants. 'I've another five miles of Canal to search.'

'A pity,' said the two-faced Offer heartily. 'If you get time ... on your way back ...' Though we won't bloody well be here, he was saying to himself, fervently.

The other captain just nodded and climbed back into

his jeep. Offer's taut attention swung to the Redcap, getting in last. The fellow was still puzzled, still frowning, still trying to remember. The jeep started up. Offer thought, 'You'll get ten miles down the Canal road, then suddenly you'll snap your fingers and say, "It's that bastard O'Keefe, that's who it was. What's he doing wearing sergeant's stripes, and in a crummy outfit like Field Salvage?" And they'll be back here before you can say Glasshouse.'

The jeep went off in a wide turn, throwing up the usual cloud of dust, and Offer saw the Redcap's head turning to look back. A very unsatisfied man, that M.P. Thank God his memory was a bit deficient so far as faces were concerned.

Offer shouted, 'Come on, come on! Everyone out! Here, here, here!'

The cry was taken up and from every corner of the camp his men came running. O'Keefe was the first there, however, in spite of the handicap of a bruised groin. John Offer looked at him, shocked. 'Christ, sergeant, I thought you were going to do for us that time.'

'That bloody Walker –' ground O'Keefe. He was just getting over that startled moment when he found himself walking on to a posse of his bitter enemies.

'He didn't warn you?'

'Just shouted you wanted me and ran on.' O'Keefe shook his head wonderingly, as if no one could account for insanity. 'Stupid, stupid bugger!'

Offer said, his voice quick with anxiety because seconds were precious now, 'One of 'em spotted you but couldn't put a name to your face.'

'But he will.' O'Keefe was sweating on the top line.

'He will.' Now Offer's men were there. He lifted his hands. 'Listen. Listen carefully. Any minute the balloon's going up. Any minute your friendly M.P.s will be back here to march us all of to Sharafim.'

He saw shock register at his words, men suddenly growing apprehensive, men suddenly worried by the thought of more time in the brutal Glasshouse. They began to talk. Offer shut them up.

'I told you to listen, not talk. Now, look, I'll give you five minutes to get your kit aboard a truck. That's how long we're staying in this camp now.'

'The tents, sir?' someone called out as the men began to scatter. Offer told him what to do with the tents. There was no time to take down E.P.I.s and pack them on to a truck . . .

'Hold on, sergeant.' O'Keefe had been leaping away with the others. Offer held him back. 'I want you.' O'Keefe was an important man in the plans simmering in Offer's mind. O'Keefe came to a halt.

'You know what our position is if that damned Redcap does remember you? We've only one road out from here, east or west along the Sweet Water road. They'd nab us within minutes if we tried to escape either way. So, sergeant, we're going to take to the desert, and that's where you're going to come in useful.'

O'Keefe's eyes seemed to begin to glow. 'The desert!' Some men were a little mad when it came to deserts, Offer knew – a love-hate relationship – and his sergeant clearly was one of them.

'We've got to disappear – fast.' How many men did he have now? Fourteen altogether? With trucks and all their kit, and every road blocked in Egypt, their descriptions well circulated. The desert, that was the only place left to them. 'So, we've got to take to the desert.'

'It's a hard place, hard even here within miles of the Canal.'

'I am sure you're right, sergeant, but you're the man of experience, and you're going to reduce the hardship. Right?'

'Yes, sir.' O'Keefe was raring to go. Couldn't get into his

bloody desert fast enough, Offer knew.

'So what do we need to keep us alive in a desert?' Not too far in; they had business back here along the Canal.

'Water,' said Sergeant O'Keefe simply. 'Water, water, water, and water.'

'And?'

'Shovels, sandtracks, camouflage nets, sun-compass, plenty of petrol, food—'

Offer cut him short. 'You're in charge. Organise it. I'll still give you only five minutes. What trucks do we take? The utility?'

A shake of the head. O'Keefe was already beginning to leap away. 'All Chevs. Thirty-hundredweights, sir. All alike.' So that any spares carried would fit any vehicle. 'Lots of spares.' He was away, a whirlwind organising a move at very, very short notice.

Captain Offer saw the scurrying figure of Pomegranate Face. Pom had a kit-bag over his shoulder and was belting across to the vehicle park. Offer shouted, a right stentorian command: 'Hold it, Driver!' Pom stopped, startled. 'When you've disposed of your kit, into my tent and pack mine! You've three minutes. *Jildy!*' Pom ran off, very *jildy*.

Offer ran up the sandy slope where the look-out was normally posted. The jeep was still in sight, but maintaining a steady pace along the Canal road. He gave a sigh of relief, though he knew there was still no safety for them, none until they had disappeared into the vast desert that encroached so close towards the Nile and its canals. And any moment now that ᵇlasted M.P. might remember...

He raced over to the vehicle park. His men were crowding there, tossing their kit-bags over the sides of the open trucks. Packing hadn't taken them long, but then so soon after release from the Glasshouse they hadn't had time to accumulate much in the way of personal possessions.

Blankets and eating utensils made most of their load.

O'Keefe was doing a mighty job of organising. 'Camouflage nets – some on each truck.' They were taking four Chevs and leaving the rest for anyone who wanted them. 'They might be needed.' Offer had a feeling the sergeant was playing a great and much loved game, revelling in this move.

Men were running to and from the mess and cooking tents. The bar was receiving thorough attention, and cooking equipment and all food was being distributed among the trucks.

O'Keefe snatched a moment to say, 'We're taking the water tanker, sir. Small enough to go where we can go, and it solves our water problem.'

No time to fill jerricans, thought Offer. Good man, O'Keefe. O'Keefe was now supervising the loading of all the petrol in camp. They had plenty for four vehicles. Guns and ammunition were hoisted aboard.

Captain Offer looked at his watch. 'That'll do!' It would have to do. Every minute now brought them into greater danger. 'Sergeant, you take the lead truck; we'll follow. You know what to do – just lose us, get lost.'

'Will do.' O'Keefe swung himself into one of the trucks. Drivers climbed up in a hurry. Pom came staggering up with Offer's kit. There was more of it than the men had, but the silly little sod needn't have brought his camp bed.

'Come on, Driver, get cracking!' Pom was probably the reason why they were having to move in a hurry, the big mouth. Strangely, though, Offer didn't feel any animosity towards his batman for putting them to this trouble. Of course if it didn't come off and they all ended in the infernal Glasshouse he wouldn't think so tolerantly of Pom's garrulity. As it was the move was exciting, thrilling, and the prospect of taking to the desert seemed at this moment a marvellous adventure.

The other trucks swung after O'Keefe. Pom got behind

the wheel of the fourth Chev and started up, the sweat pouring from his furrowed brow on to the steel rims of his glasses. He was one man who was certainly not enjoying this moment. Captain Offer took the passenger seat beside him. If he couldn't lead, he would bring up the rear.

The way those Chevs skipped across the desert towards the Canal road told its own story. Every driver was in a damned great hurry to get away from this unhealthy neighbourhood. Still, one thing in their favour for a quick getaway was that the Chevs were lightly loaded. The men not driving were all on the back of the first truck – just six of them. The other vehicles merely carried kit. Just in front of Offer's Chev was the little water tanker.

As they came bumping up to the Canal road Offer leaned out of his cab and stared down the way the M.P.'s jeep had receded. There was quite a bit of traffic on the road, so there was no knowing how far away the Redcaps were by now.

O'Keefe pulled east along the Canal road and drove at a spanking pace for quarter of an hour, then swung south down a sandy track between cultivated fields. Inevitably, as he had guessed, the track ended in a tiny village consisting of half a dozen rude hovels. O'Keefe drove through, scattering scrawny hens, naked children, and black-robed women as he did so. The cultivated land ended. There was a tiny cemetery, sited on barren ground beyond any possibility of irrigation; for the dead do not need to occupy soil that can support life. And then they drove into the desert.

Within two minutes they were in a sea of quite golden sand, beyond any sight of human activity. Immediately the heat of the late morning rolled upon them, the sun reflecting suffocatingly upon the bright desert and making them gasp as the hot air currents enveloped them. Only the draught created by their movement seemed to keep them from frizzling to the marrow, and more than one man thought, aghast, 'Christ, I think I'll take my chances with the Redcaps in Cairo rather than hide out here!'

But they were committed, and on they drove, mile after mile, the sun ascending until dead on midday O'Keefe finally found the place where they could hole up.

Captain Offer heard brakes going on and woke out of a half-doze induced by the heat. 'Now, why are we stopping?' was his first thought. The trucks halted in line. Offer swung down and trudged through sand that lapped over his shoe tops and into his socks, and it felt burning hot.

O'Keefe was down from his cab, standing in the little shade it gave. He looked very red-faced in that light, but still seemed to be enjoying himself.

'Why have we halted, sergeant?'

'No need to keep going further, sir. Here's as good a place as any to hide up.'

They'd already climbed and crossed one bit of a rocky escarpment, and now they were facing another, rather more rugged. O'Keefe was pointing towards a narrow defile between high eroded rocks of reddish stone. 'If we tuck ourselves in there, sir, and spread the camouflage nets – I'll show 'em how to do it – no one'll spot us.'

Offer thought, 'You're playing a game, laddie.' The game he used to play with the Long Range Desert Group. But then the L.R.D.G. had operated in hostile territory, where the danger was real. Offer was amused. Where was the danger for them here? Curiously, they were too close to civilisation for anyone to suspect their presence. Right now, if that Redcap remembered where he'd seen Sergeant O'Keefe's face, the M.P.s would probably be scouring every brothel and bar in the Nile Valley. But not the desert. 'Camouflage nets?'

The gap-toothed face turned upon him. The immature

voice spoke tolerantly. 'You always take full precautions, sir.' Then gently: 'You die if you don't.'

Offer said, 'Yes. Yes, I'm quite sure you're right, sergeant. Good work. ' But he thought O'Keefe was overdoing it.

They made camp in the desert, and slight though the effort was, it was a gruelling experience. The vehicles were driven into the rocky cleft and unloaded. Blankets were stretched from the sides of the Chevs to give shade. Over all were the camouflage nets, stretched and pegged out to break the angular lines of their vehicles.

That done, the men drank their fill, then crawled into the shade beside their trucks and cursed the flies that came from nowhere to torment them. They didn't want to eat, didn't want to move another inch until it grew cooler.

Offer felt the heat no less than his men, but preferred to sit in the shade of the cab with both doors wide open to let through any draught. There wasn't much wind stirring, and what there was was bitingly hot. He was interested, though, to see how O'Keefe reacted to this return to the desert.

Satisfied that their camp was well concealed, O'Keefe had trudged off through the heat to a break in the escarpment where he could climb to the top. It was not a great height – probably fifty feet at the most – but Offer didn't envy him.

On top, O'Keefe was obviously reconnoitring the terrain around their camp, and doing it with great care. Offer saw him turn slowly, time after time, hand shading his eyes when he looked towards the sun, clearly mentally assessing the hot wasteland for possibilities unguessed by his captain. In a vague way John Offer thought he would be reccying the land for its possibilities for cover for any enemy, or maybe looking for safe lines of retreat if an attack was threatened.

The amusement continued within Offer, watching the

indefatigable O'Keefe. Still playing. But what a man to be able to stand this heat, seemingly unaffected by it, unlike the rest of the men. That came of long training with the L.R.D.G., of course.

O'Keefe was still on top of the escarpment an hour after he'd first climbed there, and Offer realised that for the last ten minutes or more he'd been facing one direction only — north, the way they had come. Abruptly the sergeant turned and looked down towards the camouflaged camp.

'Sir!'

The call floated down to him. Offer sat up immediately. There was something urgent about that call.

'Sir!'

Again the call, and now more urgent than ever. Offer's instinct for danger was roused immediately. He dropped to the ground and shoved his way out under the scrim.

'What is it, sergeant?'

Offer looked up to where O'Keefe was silhouetted against the horizon. The L.R.D.G. man gestured to him to come up, and Offer did not feel affronted by that imperative command. Something was decidedly worrying O'Keefe.

So Offer made the climb, very nimbly in spite of his round, soft figure, though the effort made his head spin in that great heat, and his eyes were swimming before he came up gasping beside the sergeant. O'Keefe unceremoniously hauled him up the last yard of climb, then stood him beside him and pointed. 'See that?'

Offer followed the direction of the nicotine-stained finger. Before him the desert danced under shimmering waves of heated air that rose continuously from the sun-drenched sand. It took him seconds to adjust his vision, and then he saw it. 'It' was a black speck scudding close to the ground a few miles north of them.

'An aeroplane?'

'A Dragon Rapide.' What sharp eyes this L.R.D.G. man had to recognise the type at this distance and under such distorting conditions. A Dragon Rapide: Offer tried to spot the spiky wings of this biplane and its small, underslung twin engines, but his eyes were still not up to it.

'Well?'

'Sir, that plane is on a search.' O'Keefe was emphatic. The words roused Offer. Search in this context could only mean something to do with them.

'Sure?'

'Certain.' Offer wasn't going to raise any doubts. This man knew his stuff and would know if a plane was on a search. A Dragon Rapide, that all-maid of the services, air-taxi, sleeve-tower for ack-ack target practice, reconnaissance plane and artillery spotter, was just the sort of plane they'd use if they were looking for a commando believed to be in the desert.

The thought jolted Offer. How could anyone suspect they'd taken to the desert? Because they hadn't been picked up by a road-block? Thin, that theory; must be more to it than deduction based on such a slender premise. Because they'd had rotten bad luck, someone spotting them turning down a native track and wondering at it and speaking aloud his wonder at a road-block? Maybe another observant Military Police patrol. And someone later following it up would talk to the people in the tiny hamlet and they'd point and anyway their tyre marks led south out of the village and into the desert. So then they'd called up a Dragon to recce for them.

Tracks. Offer's eyes fell to the lower ground and saw their tyre marks leading into their hideout. For all his expertise Angus O'Keefe hadn't been all that smart.

As if divining his thoughts, O'Keefe said, 'We've got to get rid of those tracks, sir.' He turned his thin red face upon his officer. 'We wouldn't have covered up like that in the L.R.D.G., sir, and left tracks to show where we were hiding. But the men aren't used to the desert – this heat at midday – so I took a risk.' It wasn't an apology, just a tough, taut explanation.

'And now what do we do?'

The aircraft had banked and turned and was flying back on a parallel course, only now it was half a mile or so nearer. O'Keefe was right: that plane was on a search. It mightn't be for them, of course, but they'd be fools to take any chances.

O'Keefe started to run down the escarpment. 'We do what I should have insisted on, heat or no heat. We obliterate those sodding tyre marks.'

Together they ran into their camp. O'Keefe called through the camouflage netting, 'I want one man, just one man.' A face peered out, very battered. It belonged to Private Charlie Crookshank. 'You'll do.' And to Offer – 'Two of us can do the job. We don't want lots of bods tramping around in the desert if that shufti kite comes flying over.'

'No,' agreed Offer. So O'Keefe was going to do the job himself, along with Charlie Crookshank. He was a little bewildered. 'You can't wipe out our tracks all the way back to the Canal road.'

O'Keefe was dragging feverishly on two spare camouflage nets. 'Don't need to,' he jerked. 'We were running on hard ground right from that last escarpment to within half a mile of here.'

The sergeant was quite right, Offer remembered. It had been a bit rocky and rough all over the escarpment and down this side. 'You'll not be able to wipe out half a mile of tracks and get back here before that Dragon comes over.' And two men running across this desert were as much a giveaway as parallel tyre marks.

The big grin on the lean red sweating face. 'He won't see us.' He jerked on the camouflage nets. 'When I hear him we get under these. Done it more than once and got away with it, sir.'

Offer thought, 'These boys are bright,' and stood and watched O'Keefe and Charlie Crookshank go out dragging the camouflage nets over the tyre marks. The weight seemed sufficient to smooth out the impressions.

Captain Offer watched for a while right until the sound of the Dragon Rapide became audible, then he retired under the camouflage netting, ordering everyone to remain under cover.

So they squatted there, two o'clock in the afternoon now and very, very hot, and they heard the plane more distinctly each time it made its run across the desert. There'd be the loudening sound of it, then the diminuendo as it went to the far point of its beat, and then the crescendo again with its approach towards where they were hidden.

Offer, waiting there with the flies dancing annoyingly round him, pictured the scene out upon the open desert. O'Keefe and Crookshank dragging their nets behind them while the plane was on its outward run, then halting and getting under cover when it banked and came back on its tracks . . . not quite back on its tracks, each time that much nearer their place of hiding. Under their camouflage nets O'Keefe and Crookshank would appear like some grey bush or patch of stones, Offer thought, that is if they were distinguishable to the pilot and observer under such circumstances.

He thought, 'God, how they must be sweating!' It was no fun dragging a quite heavy camouflage net behind them over that hot, soft, yielding sand, and though the camouflage protected them from sight when they crawled under the scrim it would be of little use as a means of shade against the torrid sun.

Once O'Keefe had set off, though, Captain Offer never had a moment's worry about him. The L.R.D.G. man knew what he was up to and would be more than a match for a Dragon Rapide pilot. Offer wondered how often O'Keefe had lain under camouflage nets and listened to the throb of aircraft engines searching for them . . .

The plane was getting very near. Now all the men were standing against the side of a truck, unable to remain cooped beneath a blanket. Offer felt they were nakedly exposed because they could see through the scrim so easily, yet he knew their camouflage was pretty perfect.

The Dragon was now coming in quite close, probably passing in line overhead of the track sweepers, Offer thought. It was low flying and seemed very noisy. Every man there grew increasingly tensed as the sound rose to a bellowing crescendo, then once more it began to die away.

'Nearest yet,' he heard Art Weybright; the radio operator, say, then – 'Gawd, how I could do with a swaller!'

'No smoking yet,' Offer told them, but knew Weybright, an intelligent man though he did look as shapely as a sack of potatoes – old ones, his comrades told him – wasn't likely to light up.

And then they all grew taut again. The sound of aircraft engines hadn't receded to the distant murmur as on previous runs. This time it died somewhat, true, but the noise appeared to maintain a certain intensity and a degree of loudness that said it was fairly close at hand. Again Weybright spoke, interpreting the sound. 'It's circling, coming back.'

It hadn't continued its usual distance this time, as if something had attracted it and caused it to start to turn. Offer's heart did a bound. Did this mean they had spotted the pair outside?

The Dragon came roaring back, right overhead this time, and everyone held their breath as if fearing they would be heard if they kept on breathing. Through the scrim they could see the plane, and it was banking *and flying right up the obliterated tracks.*

'They've spotted something.' One of the men, his voice aghast. Could only be their tracks, Offer thought – what else? Even at this critical time, though, he was interested in the reaction of his men to the imminence of danger. Sure they got tense, but it was like the keying up of a man's nerves before he went into a fight, and there was no hint of panic or desperation about them, only from Pom, but he hardly counted.

So they stood there, the sun beating through the camouflage upon them, the irritating flies unheeded, watching and listening. The Dragon Rapide never left the area. Time after time it came banking round, flying so close to the desert that several times it sent dust spirals cavorting upwards. So close they saw it and even made out the pilot and observer in their seats, but they were never seen, down there in the rocky gully.

Ten minutes passed. Twenty minutes. Art Weybright once growled, 'The soddin' thing's a fixture. It's never goin' to leave us,' and though he was widely read and perhaps the man with the highest I.Q. there, he followed up his prophecy with a lurid mouthful of army obscenity, all directed at the R.A.F. types turning the silent desert into noise-filled Bedlam.

But finally it did clear off. All at once, as if satisfied, the Dragon tilted its spiky wings and resumed its steady patrol across the desert. Half-an-hour later it was only a distant buzzing in the far distance. And half-an-hour later still a tooth-gapped grinning Sergeant O'Keefe came tramping in, dragging his camouflage net behind him to obliterate tell-tale footmarks. A long way behind the sergeant came Charlie Crookshank. The heat had nearly done him in. This man who could go fifteen rounds in a professional boxing ring collapsed when finally he reached the trucks. When they had poured water over and into

97

him and he was at last able to speak, all he said, feelingly, was, 'Fuckin' desert. Let's get out of here,' and Offer noted the words and knew he had to give them great consideration.

O'Keefe, too, drank a couple of quarts that refreshed him instantly, though in temperature the water was well over 70° Fahrenheit. He seemed quite cheerful, as if he'd enjoyed the recent danger and had hardly noticed the discomforts that had knocked out his comrade.

Offer said, 'They spotted you?'

A shake of the sweating head. Another copious drink, followed by an intense sigh of pleasure. 'Not a chance.' He wiped his streaming forehead with a bare, hairy forearm. 'It came over a bit too quick. There were still some tyre tracks in patches before the rocks began.'

So they'd taken to cover, he and a moaning Charlie, and watched the light aircraft drift over and hoped the R.A.F. wouldn't spot the few remaining tread marks But it had, and they'd realised it when the damn' thing didn't go away.

'We managed to wipe out the last bit of track before it came back,' O'Keefe continued. Only just in time. Then they'd lain for an uncomfortable half-hour under the gruelling weight of an almost unbearable sunshine while the Dragon made pass after pass over them, looking for tyre marks which no longer existed.

That toothless grin. 'Must have puzzled the buggers.' A final, satisfying drink. 'Bet they couldn't make it out. One minute they thought they'd found our tyre marks, the next there weren't any.'

In the end the Rapide had flown off probably thinking they'd made a mistake, that there weren't any treads on the desert, or they had failed to find the place where they had first seen them. Now they were extending their field of search, perhaps hoping to pick up the trail again.

'Think they're likely to have called up a land patrol?'

– Art Weybright. All the men were listening in.

O'Keefe shrugged. 'Could be. But they won't find us before dark, that's for certain.'

'So we'll have to move tomorrow,' was Offer's thought, and where the devil could they move to safety if they were known to be roaming the desert?

He went over to resume his seat in the cab of his Chev. There was a lot to think about, and not much time to do the thinking. A red, sweaty face shoved into view round the corner. It jerked to where the other men were now lying under their shades.

'Give me three months and I'll have them swaddies loving the desert.'

'Three months?' Offer had to laugh. 'Even Charlie Crookshank?'

'Charlie-boy's all right. Good lad, our Charlie. It was lying up out there all that time that did for him. In the L.R.D.G. we never got ourselves into such a fix; we did everything so that we didn't have to lie up in the full sunshine in the heat of the day.'

Offer could believe him.

A pause, then O'Keefe came out with it. 'Three months is a long time. You know what I think – sir?' A shake of sir's head. 'By the end of three days there'll only be you and me left if we decide to hang on in the desert. They'll all be back in Cairo, even if they've had to walk out.'

Offer said, 'I know you're right.' Just one more day of lying up in this inferno would have them mutinous, and what was to hold them back? 'You L.R.D.G. could stick it, though.'

A nod. 'But we were volunteers; we wanted to go into the desert. We had training, getting used to it. And anyway, the thing that kept us in the desert was that we had a job to do. What are we doing here? Just running away.'

Running because someone had opened his blasted mouth too much. Now, if they could have marked time in their comfortable camp along the Canal the rest of the war would have been a piece of cake, and they could have done it, too, Offer knew. Instead, big mouths, sending them fleeing into this desert. But where now was there safety, anywhere along the Nile or Canal?

Offer said, thoughtfully, 'I can give them purpose.' His mind flitted back to the plans he had made before the M.P.s turned up to queer everything. No reason why they shouldn't go through with them, and anyway it would take them out of the desert.

O'Keefe pricked up his ears hopefully. 'Purpose, sir?'

Captain Offer said calmly, 'I intend to knock off Sharafim Glasshouse.'

John Offer outlined his plans to his men later that evening. He picked that moment carefully, for he wanted a good hearing, and men don't think straight in the heat of the day. But when the sun had gone down and darkness was upon them, when a cool breeze came up across the desert and soothed and brought relief and everyone felt relaxed and comfortable, then he brought them together. They'd eaten and were now happily knocking back canned Canadian beer of great strength – hot beer because there'd been no way of keeping it cool, and when they stabbed the lids gas hissed out and froth foamed but still it was highly acceptable. Some of the men were even skylarking, brawling on the soft sand. They soon forgot, Offer thought ironically, but they'd soon remember when the sun came up next morning...

When they were ready and listening, Offer opened up with the same remark that had had Sergeant O'Keefe almost shocked out of his mind.

'Tomorrow, gentlemen, we go out of this hot desert and knock off Sharafim Glasshouse.'

Dead, dead silence at that. Perhaps they thought he was joking. So Offer went on talking, very calmly, very concisely, so that even the thick Busker could see the plan and knew what it was all about. When he had finished, Offer, whose hatred of the Glasshouse system would someday get him into dire trouble, knew he had them. They went crazy with delight. It was a plan so reckless, so imaginative that the appeal was irresistible to their ruffianly minds. There wasn't a man there who wouldn't take appalling risks in order to even scores with the Glasshouse – not a man there who hadn't suffered so much under prison screws that he'd ever forgive or forget and forgo a chance of vengeance.

They would back him to a man. The ultimate consequences of their daring exploit? None of them, not even Offer, ever gave a thought to that.

'We'll move at daylight,' Offer announced.

'Sir,' interrupted Sergeant O'Keefe, 'let's move while it's still dark and cool.' And that was the first lesson they all had in desert tactics from the L.R.D.G. man.

'Okay.' Offer accepted O'Keefe's suggestion gracefully. Someone asked about weapons. 'We take them, but unloaded.' Offer hadn't many scruples, but he didn't want someday to find himself, back to a wall, facing a firing party.

They were in position for the attack on Sharafim before daylight. There were no road-blocks but plenty of military traffic in the early hours, and no one had taken any notice of the small convoy of four Chevs and one water tanker which bowled steadily along the Sweet Water Canal road while it was still dark.

When they reached the track which led across to the grim Glasshouse, they turned right, and when they came to the dip in the road they turned right again, bumping across the open desert until Offer was satisfied they could not be seen from road or track or Glasshouse.

Like many other things necessary to that morning's

planning, Offer had remembered the dip in the Glasshouse track. Here, he remembered, a man could be out of sight of the Glasshouse, a man stopping a vehicle, for instance. Not far from this point, and also hidden from view of any long-sighted prison screw, were the high poles which carried a power line into the Glasshouse. They also carried the telephone cables.

The previous night, after the men had got to drinking to the success of their next day's exploit, Offer had spoken thoughtfully to his sergeant. 'You know, what we need tomorrow is a Trojan horse.'

O'Keefe had looked blankly at him. 'Trojan?'

'Forget it.' Offer knew where he could find his Trojan equine – the only vehicle that could enter the prison without fuss was the early morning bread truck.

They had a brew-up and breakfast shortly after the sun rose. They felt quite safe, surrounded by low, hummocky sandhills, and got their fire-cans burning, tea brewing, and bacon sizzling in short time. But already it was hot, too hot, with that flaming sun swiftly climbing into the cloudless sky. Not long to go, though, Offer reassured his men. The balloon was to go up about seven-thirty. They began to black up.

At seven-fifteen a black-masked Offer, O'Keefe, and three of his men tramped back along their tyre marks to where they joined the Glasshouse track. Offer looked round. His memory certainly was good. Here in the dip no one could overlook them. They laid their weapons carefully down beside them, then squatted in the sand and prepared patiently to wait.

Bread was brought daily to the Glasshouse in a civvy truck. An Egyptian transport company held the contract, and it probably also held some sort of record for the ancient vehicles they used for their deliveries. The bread van was an ancient hard-tyred Scammell which had arrived somehow in Egypt circa 1924. Its top speed was about twenty-five miles an hour, granted good road conditions and a following wind, but what it lacked in speed it made up for in noise. Offer and his men knew they would hear it long before it crested the rise leading into the dip. They also knew it would arrive almost dead on time, ancient crock though it was. It was rarely more than fifteen minutes out, and though it always seemed on the point of collapse it never missed a run. This was their Trojan horse.

When they heard it, they rose without hurry, dusted off, then grouped on both sides of the road. Of course their presence would attract attention, here where men afoot were never seen, but their British uniforms would hardly alarm the Egyptian driver or his mate.

So it was. The box-like vehicle began to appear above the crest. Groaning, it gained the summit and then, still protesting, began its swifter descent. Captain Offer stood in the middle of the road, hand raised against the Scammell. The driver obeyed the order to halt because there was no reason why he should not do so. Anyway, he, like most Egyptians, believed it wiser always to do as the British officer-types ordered them. He clapped on the brakes in good time, and in less than fifty yards had brought the vehicle to a quivering standstill.

Offer strolled up, very calm. He looked up at the enquiring brown face and ordered, 'Get down.' To assist he opened the door. Two of Offer's men came and stood beside him. With their black faces and hands on tommy-guns they looked thuggish and scaring. The driver obliged by getting down. His mate, a galabiaed and tarboshed youth, fell out of the cab in his haste to descend on the other side.

No orders were given. Offer's men knew what to do. Gunner Wilborn raced back towards where their trucks were standing and when he came into view he put both hands above his head. That was the signal. Four trucks and the water tanker started into movement, the remaining personnel aboard. They came down to the bread truck to find everyone, driver and mate included, hurriedly removing the trays of loaves from the back.

'Shove some on board each Chev,' Offer ordered. 'We'll need fresh bread before the day's out.'

They'd need all their trucks, too, if Gunner Walker's prophecy was right. When Offer had outlined his plan to an enthusiastic audience the previous night someone with a flash of doubt had said, 'But there's only fifteen of us, you included, sir.'

And what was it Walker had said? 'The moment we get through that gate we'll have another couple of hundred.' What if all two hundred wanted to go on the run with them? Four trucks and one water tanker mightn't be enough...

One Chev was manoeuvring under the power lines, though it was the telephone cables that interested Tiffy Jones, clambering on top of the cab. Offer saw a flash of metal-cutters – and then the telephone cable parted with a snap and recoiled down to the desert below. Sharafim Glasshouse was now out of touch with the rest of the world, the telephonist probably not even realising it yet. The second stage in his plan had been successfully accomplished.

The Scammell empty, all spare personnel clambered in where the sweet-smelling bread had been and the doors closed against them. The young tarboshed Egyptian was also shoved into the back, though Offer first thoughtfully helped himself to the tarbosh.

Offer ordered the driver back into his seat, climbing up beside him and donning the tarbosh. Offer had a pistol – empty – across his knees. 'Now, my friend, drive into the prison just as you would do normally. Any funny work and –' He tapped the pistol ominously. 'Understand?'

The Egyptian understood. To show how friendly he

was towards the black-masked Captain Offer, he smiled hugely, showing flashing gold teeth, and declared, 'I understand, sir. I good bugger.' His English was perfect.

The Scammell resumed its way. The Chevs let it get out of sight over the hill, then followed cautiously. The orders were for the Chevs not to show themselves until the bread truck had entered the prison, then they were to come up at a rush, the vehicles being parked for a quick getaway, and their drivers racing in to give a hand inside the prison.

Captain John Offer saw the Glasshouse come into view. This time there were no doubts within him. True his stomach was so tightly drawn he could not have eaten a mouthful at that moment. But he felt quite calm and reassured. Nothing would go wrong. On their side was the biggest asset anyone could have demanded – surprise. No one in their right senses would credit what they were about to do.

'It's going to come off,' he told himself. Before the shock of seeing them had evaporated, Sharafim would be in their hands. Anyway, he reminded himself, they had several hundred allies inside those grim walls.

They came winding across the dusty desert, the old truck announcing its approach from far away. The gate sentry would hear it, would recognise the sound because every day it came, and probably would not even bother to peer through the grilled observation port in the big gate, so sure it would be the bread van. He would, of course, call to the guard commander, because that was routine, and theoretically the guard commander, a corporal, would march smartly from the guard room, solemnly peer through the grilled opening, then if satisfied would order his sentry to unbar the doors.

But Offer knew how the drill varied. If no nosy screw was around the guard commander would remain in the shade of the guard-room doorway, and the sentry, *the only man with a rifle inside the prison at that moment,* would begin to swing open the big gates without any order from his superior. Familiarity bred, if not contempt, at least unmilitary ways. And the guard-room was on the passenger side of the Scammell truck.

The gates began to open. Offer thought, 'Too late to turn back now.' His nerves were tingling, his heart suddenly racing as the moment of action came swiftly nearer. He saw through the opening space, and it was a familiar sight, one he had never thought to see again as long as he lived. Squads of heavily burdened swaddies being doubled frantically up and down the sandy parade ground. Truculent, cocky staff-sergeants strutting and bellowing – he could hear them above the groan of the Scammell engine. And the Walking Wall. There it was, and poor sods were already stumbling frantically across the length of it, sandbags in their aching arms, praying for a moment's interruption so that they could rest.

'You'll get your moment!' John Offer told himself grimly, and the gorge rose within him at what he saw, as the remembered torment and torture flooded back to him. If he had had any doubts about this plan of his before, John Offer had none from that moment. No matter what happened to him as a consequence, he was going to make every screw in Sharafim pay for what he had suffered at their hands.

John Offer, it must in honesty be acknowledged, was not concerned about other men's sufferings; all he remembered were his own, and the score to be settled was his personally.

The sentry stood to one side, hardly glancing into the cab. That casual glance would see a tarbosh on a shiny black face. If he had bothered to look a little more closely he might have wondered at a bread van's mate who wore a British captain's bush-jacket.

Offer said, softly, 'Halt!' and obediently the Egyptian

driver put his sandalled foot on the big brake pedal. Offer swung open the door. Right before him was the corporal guard commander. Behind the truck Offer's men would be pouring out and taking care of the sentry.

Offer saw startled wonder on the corporal's young face. A strange black-masked man wearing a British captain's jacket had stepped down from the bread truck. Offer raised his pistol. 'Move and you're dead.' A very cold statement. The guard commander never moved.

Offer saw his men come running along the side of the truck. All knew what to do. Sergeant O'Keefe would take charge of the guard-room and then capture the armoury. If it wasn't done expeditiously, their number would probably be up. As soon as O'Keefe was alongside him, Offer stopped bothering about the guard commander and started to run. He raced across the corner of the parade ground to where the broad wooden steps gave access to the second floor of the admin block where the O.C. had his office. Behind him, he heard feet pounding. That would be the two gunners, Walker and Wilborn. There was so much noise and shouting on the parade ground that no one seemed to notice their three running figures...

O'Keefe snapped, 'Inside!' and shouldered the young corporal into the guard hut. Cruiser and Busker padded in behind him, tommy-guns ready. Most of the guard were lying on their beds, asleep. The only one awake, seeing them, nearly fell off his chair where he was bulling his boots.

Busker scooped up the rifles, then backed out. That was the gate guard disarmed. There was a big key on the inside of the door. O'Keefe removed it. 'I'm locking you in,' he told them. 'If you so much as shove your head out of the window you'll stop a bullet, so use your loaf.'

He went out and locked them in. Twenty-two seconds. The plan was going to time. Over to the armoury, all of them, leaving Pom, who had just run in from his truck, to pose aggressively outside the guard-room window, empty gun looking very threatening.

O'Keefe kicked upon the armoury door. Men turned at the noise and sat up in the long hut. When they saw a crowd of black-faced British commandos in the doorway no one moved, such was the power of shock. Theoretically these were fighting men, who would come into action in case of riot by the Glasshouse inmates. In fact they were the usual assorted lot who gather round every HQ – telephonists, orderlies, medical personnel, clerks, and so on. There never was any emergency within the Glasshouse that the brutal staff-sergeants couldn't quell, so when O'Keefe burst in upon them, tommies threatening, the occupants of the hut did not know how to react. All of which the shrewd Captain Offer had anticipated.

They froze, and the commandos slipped through the doorway, most of them big, powerful-looking men, intimidating with their bulk. The door leading to the armoury was open. Some sound must have attracted attention. Sergeant Palmerston suddenly appeared in the doorway. In his hands was a pull-through with its four-by-two dangling at the end. He must have been cleaning the rifles.

Staff Palmerston was neither better nor worse than any other screw inside the Glasshouse. Just a first-class, right rotten sadistic bastard, as every inmate there agreed. He was young, new to prison service but learning fast and was an eager beaver for promotion. That meant he always put up a good showing with his boot and fist, while his voice never let up on any poor sod in sight of him.

He had two complexes. One, he had an obsession with mothers. He never let up on a man's mother, detailing all the possibilities of sin, disease, and sexual proclivity any woman could be capable of. Sometimes it stung so badly that a man retaliated verbally – on fewer occasions, physically – and found himself in the punishment block as a consequence, with young Staff Palmerston coming at midnight to scare him and tell him more about his mother and give him a beating if he felt like it.

His other complex was guns. He loved smooth, shiny metal, the slightly oiled surfaces and the silent sliding action of parts lovingly designed by gun-makers to ensure the killing of other men. His idea of peaceful relaxation was a few hours of devoted care and maintenance of the rifles stacked in the armoury. Because of this enthusiasm, Staff Palmerston became the first victim of the Glass-house Gang that morning.

He said, 'What the bloody hell!' his voice stentorian, incapable of sensing danger because this was his midden where staff-sergeants were gods and all-powerful. 'Who the bloody hell do you think –'

Cruiser, light as a ballet dancer, seemed to slide across the bare wooden floor before Palmerston realised he was moving. A black, sweating face was suddenly close to his own; he saw teeth showing in a snarl. Then a fist got him just under the ribs, right in the solar plexus. It was a paralysing blow, and Staff Palmerston started to go down. Cruiser slammed him twice before he hit the floor, and Palmerston fell back inside the armoury. Busker and two other men leapt into the room behind Cruiser. All kicked hard at the writhing, gasping Palmerston on the floor. It was vicious, more than anything convincing the men in the hut that this wasn't a game. They kept quiet.

O'Keefe covered them while a human chain swiftly ferried all the rifles out of the armoury. Two minutes eight seconds and it was done. The plan was working smoothly. Every weapon inside Sharafim was now in the hands of the commando; the Glasshouse had been disarmed in a swift and simple coup.

The lean sergeant was the last to back out of the hut.

This time there was no key on the inside of the door. O'Keefe altered his plans accordingly. In the doorway he paused for a moment, then addressed the silent, shaken men.

'Listen, you dozy shower, listen to what I've to tell you so that you won't get hurt. We've no quarrel with you. It's the staff-bastard-sergeants we're gunning for. So just stay put and keep your noses out of it, see?'

He was tossing a grenade in his left hand.

'I'm going to leave the door open. Ernie here's going to stand guard with this grenade.' He tossed it to Private Ernie Wise, making every man there go apprehensive as Ernie, not expecting it, fumbled the catch but finally held it. Though it wouldn't have gone off if it had fallen, they realised immediately, because it wasn't primed. 'Ernie, just one move out of this shower and you let 'em have it, see?' And a grenade going off in a crowded hut would do some terrible damage.

O'Keefe ducked away, satisfied that no one was going to indulge in heroics inside that hut.

The only enemy still left to be dealt with were the staff-sergeants. They, oblivious of everything except the daily routine of giving men hell, were still bawling their heads off and putting wretched men through their paces.

It changed when a black-faced commando ran on to the parade ground to where Staff-sergeant Knottley was trying to break all hope, faith, and physical endurance of a squad of prisoners. They'd had an hour of it and still had a long way to go. He had them drilling at the double, laden with packs, up and down the parade ground, about turn, on the spot mark time, up with them fuckin' knees – up, up, up, up – for – ward, about turn, about turn, up with them, smarter now or you'll be 'ere all fuckin' day. Their limbs felt rubbery, without strength. Their shoulders were raw from the rubbing of webbing through thin shirts. They breathed in great, painful gasps, their tortured lungs on fire from the relentless exertion. The sun fried them, there on the exposed parade ground, and the sweat poured from them though their desiccated bodies cried out for water. It was torture, the daily torture that all Glasshouse prisoners had to endure, and men kept at it and didn't fall out because then it was much worse for them.

Every Glasshouse inmate develops a particular hatred for one screw more than another. Art Weybright's had been Staff Knottley. And the reason? Each staff-sergeant always seems to single out one prisoner as the particular target for his invective and sadism, and Knottley had picked on the unsoldierly-looking Weybright as his butt during the radio operator's time of sojourn in the prison. Knottley had given him particular hell, a torment only to be wiped out some day by physical means.

Weybright forgot all his orders when he heard that evil bellowing voice across the parade ground. He began to run towards it, hatred building up to murder. Knottley's back was towards Weybright, so he didn't notice his approach, but his squad did.

They saw a big, heavily-built man with commando-blackened face, sten gun in hand, come lumbering up behind their staff-sergeant. It was so fascinating, so unexpected, that their drill faltered and went to pieces, and that was Knottley's first intimation that something untoward was happening.

He began to shout even louder, furiously, filled with indignation and wrath. 'Come on, pull yourselves together, you whores' sons, you poxed-up, useless –'

Some instinct made him turn. Weybright was right behind him. Weybright saw the hated face, the big, marble-hard eyes, the brutal contours, the wicked, snarling mouth. He hit him. He put behind the blow all the pent-up rage and despair of those pain-wracked months while under the hands of this sadistic monster in the pay of

His Majesty. He hit him between the eyes, because Weybright was no skilled man at fighting, and the blow was terrible, like the pole-axing of an ox.

Stunned, Knottley began to spin round and fall, hands out blindly to save himself. So he fell on all fours in the sand, and his squad gasped in horror but yet joy to see him down, and then, chests still heaving from their exertion, they watched fascinated the next move from this big, shapeless commando.

Weybright, not satisfied, that terrible rage still consuming him, grabbed Knottley by the hair and jerked back his head. Knottley was dazed but instinctively began to struggle. Weybright's vengeful fist came swinging up and smashed into Knottley's teeth. Some broke and he bled, and then the fist came in again ... and again ... and again. Weybright who had gone to the Glasshouse for being found asleep over his set while on duty; dead-tired Weybright who hadn't slept for close on thirty-six hours while a disordered army fled before Rommel, and had been unlucky in being found by his colonel who was nowhere near as tired – Weybright was a man quite mad at that moment, wanting only to kill this evil man who had terrorised him for the sake of his own enjoyment.

Some in Knottley's squad began to cheer. Astonishingly more took it up. Then it became a full-throated roar of sadistic approval, and the men broke ranks and started to crowd round the pair. That was when the entire parade ground took notice of unusual events within the Glasshouse.

Staff-sergeants suddenly realised that they no longer had the attention of their victims. Other squads drilling also became ragged as heads turned to look towards the unusual disturbance. On the Walking Wall men came to a halt, holding their sandbags and staring across to where an undisciplined mob was milling around some centre of activity, all shouting and cheering.

R.S.M. Fry, the Killer, happened to be on the parade ground that morning, keeping his hand in at adding further to the torments of prisoners. 'You're not giving 'em enough hell,' he had told his sergeants at breakfast that morning. 'When these fuckers leave Sharafim I want every bastard's spirit broken. I want these 'orrible things to say never again, and I don't even want 'em to have any guts left to be villains. I'm coming down to show you how to break the hearts of that 'orrible shower,' and down there he was, loving every moment of it, doubling the men faster even than his sergeants and making the workers on the Wall go so hard at it, two had already stumbled and fallen, one smashing his kneecap, the other twisting his back, and both going into hospital, but the R.S.M. not for one moment reducing the pace for the others.

'Expendable, that's all you are,' he told them, and he told them more, much more about themselves and their ancestry, and he knew there was murder behind those strained sweating faces, and that's what he loved about this job, being hated.

Now, seeing the commotion, R.S.M. Fry immediately flew into a mighty rage and began to run towards the scene of it. Sergeant O'Keefe, coming away from the armoury, saw the Killer on the rampage and said, 'At the double!' Mustn't let any of these bastard staff even for a moment get the upper hand. He took his men across the parade ground as fast as they could run, but Fry got to the brawl ahead of them.

Fry came up behind the mob of milling men, his stick lashing out. They scattered, the instinct of self-preservation instantly restored at sight of purple faced authority. He saw one of his sergeants having his face beaten in by a big, black-faced soldier, and the surprise rocked him back on his heels for a moment, then he went in, boots flying, stick lashing down on the unready Weybright. The radio operator let go of Knottley and grappled with the

113

R.S.M. This was another much-hated enemy.

'You bastard!' Weybright was yelling, then the R.S.M., a better man at rough-housing, did some awful damage to Weybright's privates with a bone-hard knee that came up and up. And when Weybright collapsed, an exultant R.S.M. gave him the boot on the side of the head.

O'Keefe, lean, vengeful whippet of a man, saved Weybright from being damaged for life. He swung and hit the R.S.M. over the ear. Fry turned, snarling, seemingly unaffected by the blow. Busker and Cruiser backed up their sergeant. They got the R.S.M. between them and chopped and jabbed and swung and battered him so that he reeled like a shuttlecock from one to the other.

And again the crowd of prisoners went mad with delight. Again they crowded round, roaring ferocious approval. And now other squads broke ranks, because their staff-sergeants were running in every direction. From the Wall, those with strength enough tottered towards the astounding break in their morning's torture. Whatever it was, the interruption had their complete support.

Staff O'Dwyer went streaking over to the wooden stairs that led to the O.C.'s office. That was instinct: hand over to a superior in an emergency. And the sight of R.S.M. Fry engulfed among a horde of howling prisoners constituted an emergency to O'Dwyer's way of thinking. He went up those stairs three at a time, head down, not looking. When he was six steps from the top a boot took him in the face and sent him crashing down the stairs. Captain Offer had stationed Gunner Milborn at the head of the steps for just this possibility. Staff O'Dwyer, breaker of hearts on the parade ground, was a hospital case from that moment. Nobody wept.

Staff Furnival, one of the two South African sergeants, who took care of coloured prisoners, went running towards the guard-room, but saw O'Keefe and his men in the way, changed his mind and ran for the emergency siren. Lashley, an Australian milkman in civvy street, and thus used to running, for Sydney milkmen always run with their deliveries, a race against the dawning sunshine – Lashley saw the danger and left O'Keefe's party. He brought Furnival down with a flying tackle before the staff-sergeant's hand could grasp the switch. Then they began fighting like cat and dog in the sand.

Offer's party now recruited their first ally. One of the prisoners ran across from the Wall. He could see that Lashley would get the worst of it, tackling the tough South African alone, and he came in with fists flying to help the Australian.

That appeared to be a signal to other prisoners. All at once some changed from the role of spectators to that of instruments of retribution. Staff-sergeants, running up to help their R.S.M., found themselves facing men who did not now yield to their shouted threats. Some continued to throw themselves at their prisoners, and they suffered quickly in vengeful hands. Other staff-sergeants, a little wiser, tried to bolt for it, but were pursued and hunted throughout the prison.

Now little bands of men, quite out of hand, began to roam this terrible jail. They raided the cookhouse, and drank and ate their fill. They went down into the punishment cells and found two screws there enjoying themselves with one bloodied sobbing youth. They half-killed the screws, then locked them in the cell, an excreta-filled bucket rammed over each head. Dazed solitary prisoners were released and helped out by comrades fiercely compassionate, who took them over for the food and drink they needed more than anyone.

Then the mob stormed the sergeants' mess and wrecked it and got at the bottles, and after that they began to destroy everything within the prison walls. It was a riot such as no Field Prison of His Majesty had ever witnessed before.

Not all men took part. The broken, the apprehensive, the creepers to established authority tried to keep apart from the ravening mob, and even more, tried to let the staff-sergeants see that they were not of it. It did them no good. No one there had time to notice the goodies in such a turmoil.

In eight minutes Sharafim Prison was in the hands of the invaders.

Captain Offer was a satisfied man. He had gone up those steps two at a time, Walker and Milborn pounding after him. Still no unusual sound from down below. So their arrival was going to be a complete surprise for Major Tulloch.

It was. Himmler was at his desk. With him was a lance-corporal who did all his paperwork. In the adjoining room, door wide open, would be the telephonist. Offer and Walker just burst in on them, Walker with a tommy swinging nastily to cover the room.

Unoriginally the major said what every staff-sergeant had said: 'What the bloody hell –' In fright his clerk dropped his papers to the floor. The telephonist leaned back on his chair legs and glanced into the room. Next minute he was trying to use the telephone. Offer knew what he was up to but wasted no time on him.

Offer snapped, 'Come on, Himmler, out from behind that desk!'

Tulloch roared, 'Like hell I will! R.S.M. – !'

Walker brutally hit him across the face with the butt of his Thompson submachine-gun. Offer pitched in for a moment, too. He was soft-looking and not very big, but there was a fierce tigerish quality to Offer's character, and sight of the prison commandant brought it to the surface.

There was no time, anyway, for half-hearted methods. Any relaxation and the boot would be on their neck, and Offer knew it. He grabbed Tulloch's head while the major was still dazed from the wicked blow, then rammed it face down on the table before him. Then he chopped three times to the unprotected neck, and even tough men like prison commandants don't easily survive such treatment.

Offer, like a coiled spring of fury, now hauled on the commandant and brought him toppling to the floor. No angel in a fight, not after the treatment they'd given him here in Sharafim, John Offer went to it with his boots. When he had finished there wasn't, for the moment at least, much fight left in the most evil man in the Glasshouse.

Meanwhile Walker stood and covered the clerk, an unnecessary proceeding, and ached to put his boot into the bastard, too. When Offer thought Tulloch had had enough and couldn't do much damage now, he told the terrified lance-jack, 'Get him out on to the balcony.'

They could hear the telephonist whirring away at his instrument. Offer looked in on him and said, 'You're wasting your time, mate,' and went out of the office just as he began to hear a swelling roar from down below.

He stood against the wooden rail, one floor up above the parade ground, and looked down. He saw frantic activity below, a big group of men almost in the centre of the parade ground, smaller groups pursuing once-powerful staff-sergeants. Himmler was dragged out and draped over the railing for all to see. But he was recovering, beginning to get his senses back and trying to haul himself erect. Walker stood behind him, hoping he would make some untoward move. It was at that moment that Gunner Milborn settled the hash of the fleeing Staff O'Dwyer, and looked very satisfied when it was done.

Captain John Offer was now in command of the Field Prison which so recently had provided him with hospitality. The burning, vengeful fury that unbalanced him when he thought of Sharafim in no way abated at the thought. There was more, much more he wanted to do, he thought, and the thought was like fire to his brain. Nothing would satisfy him but to humiliate and torment these staff-sergeants the way they tormented the poor bastards who came through their merciless hands.

He shouted down to O'Keefe: 'Sergeant, round up the staffs! Get 'em on the Wall!' They must get a taste of their own medicine before Offer was to be satisfied, and the dreaded Wall would give them that.

The mob took up the cry, and it delighted them. Word spread, and now everywhere staff-sergeants were dragged forward and brought to the Wall. It must have been a chilling experience, even for hard men who didn't frighten easily, to find themselves surrounded by their former victims, every man with a special score to settle. But by this time they were so battered and bruised the screws hardly seemed to know what was happening to them. Their world of cruelty had toppled in on them.

Offer said, 'Get him down,' and brought the telephonist out to help the lance-jack support the evil Himmler down on to the parade ground. When the mob saw the commandant, their anger rose to new heights. Screws like Anacard, O'Dwyer and Oddine might do the actual bashing, but everyone knew where the torment started – higher up.

It was here that the pattern of suffering was established, by the prison commandant. He could, if he had wished, have made it easier for the men to serve their sentences. If he had been of the right mind he could have said, 'Be firm, but no sadism.' But he wasn't of that mind, which is why Military Authority, all that hierarchy that stretched up to the Commander-in-Chief in Whitehall, and even into Downing Street, had carefully selected him for this place of power over unfortunate men.

If Major Tulloch, the Scotch bastard, as he was known even more frequently than 'Himmler', had wanted he could also have reduced the suffering in those punishment cells. But he was the one who gave out the sentences, and gave them on false and cynical evidence, they all knew; vicious, terrible sentences, which included brutal games for sadistic sergeants, there in the solitary cells, and nasty things to boys who were good-looking. He knew it all went on; he knew and approved and encouraged every brutal excess, and every man there knew it and knew that Tulloch was finally responsible for the awful excesses they suffered.

So now they wanted his hide. They wanted to kill him, men not right in their heads; because no man can stay really balanced and sane and be an inmate of a Glasshouse, prisoner or staff.

Offer stopped them. Killing was too good for the bastard, and he told them so. 'The Wall!' he shouted. That was the cruellest thing on the Sharafim parade ground. They bundled Tulloch over towards it.

He fought. He had guts. Strength returned with his appreciation of danger. He was a hard man from Glasgow, and he showed no weakness now. Tulloch snarled and lashed out, and when they struck back – a hundred fists – he seemed to take it without feeling it, though his eyes began to disappear in the folds of bruised flesh, and his mouth was pulped and his cheeks were swollen.

They got him to the Wall, along with the other staff-sergeants. The screaming horde of prisoners surrounded them, trying to force them to climb up and lay sandbags, but Tulloch snarled and refused to play. Neither would the sergeants for a while. Then one of them broke. Or perhaps he had sense and thought, 'If I don't, it could mean curtains for me.' The mob would stop at nothing. Stay alive and get your own back later, when help arrived.

Staff-sergeant Culpepper, not too long in the service, suddenly stooped and picked up a sandbag. The act was greeted with a great roar from the crowd. Hard, jabbing fingers got him moving towards the ramp, and some men followed him all the way across the top, keeping him at the run, until he was down the far ramp and made to lay the bag in neat position. Then they had him racing to the start again, a gauntlet of painful fists and boots having to be run to get to the ramp and another heavy sandbag.

Sergeant Oddine couldn't stand the screaming hatred and the buffeting, either, and he, too, stumbled over to pick up a sandbag. Then one by one the other staff-sergeants joined in. Finally, even Major Tulloch, sure he'd be torn limb from limb if he didn't co-operate, joined the staggering line on the Wall. That was the height of triumph that morning in Sharafim. The Wall was being made to walk by the prison screws.

It was also being made to walk faster than it had ever travelled before. The exultant prisoners, lusting to get their own back, saw to that. Every staff-sergeant was harried by a little group of men who kept at him, boots and fists going, driving him on at a pace that was killing. Any unfortunate who stumbled or went down from exhaustion was kicked erect again and made to run on. Which, as more than one man pointed out, was no different from what it had ever been, except that the positions were reversed.

They watched the bloodied, ragged staff-sergeants, for their uniforms had been ripped to tatters by grasping, vengeful fingers, toiling away in the awful heat on the Wall, and the sight was fiercely satisfying. Offer looked at his watch. He wanted to stay, wanted to have his fill of this reversal in barbarism, but time wasn't altogether on their side. Somewhere someone might be trying to telephone, and if they found they couldn't get through, some bright spark might send signals down the wire to find the break. The sooner they got away, the better. If they were to follow Sergeant O'Keefe's suggestion they needed two clear hours, anyway, before the hunt began. Even that wasn't too much if this time more than one aircraft came looking for them.

He beckoned towards his sergeant, who came running across to him a very satisfied man though his knuckles were swollen and sore. 'Time we left, sergeant. Let's slide away.' They could leave the Wall and its staff workers to the milling prisoners, many of them reeling drunk by now. They'd keep Tulloch and his bastard crew at it for hours, or until authority stepped in and quelled the riot with military force and then started asking questions: 'Who started it?' Then the hunt would be on.

Slide away. 'We don't want them to see us go.' Or they might all want to come.

Sweat ran off the sergeant's thin nose in an almost continuous stream. Offer thought, 'You've been having fun.'

'Sir, there's a few chaps I'd like to take out with us. You'll know 'em all. They're in for long stretches and they can't take any more. Good lads, and we might need 'em.'

Offer was saying, 'Not too many,' and then his gaze, travelling round, saw a sight that brought an exclamation to his lips. 'Great Jesus Christ, look! We've got visitors!'

Pom, still covering the guard-room with his empty gun, watching the crazy brawl on the parade ground and viciously wanting to put his boot in too, was the first to spot the car. It passed him, unheard in that din, making him jump out of his cowardly skin as he caught the movement from the corner of his eye.

A big green-camouflaged Humber staff car had driven through the conveniently open gates. Pom caught a glimpse of big brass inside and quaked and nearly ran. Ernie Wise, on guard outside the armoury, saw the staff car and never thought of running. Instead he raised his tommy to cover it and wished it was loaded.

The car halted just inside the gates. Doors opened. A tall officer stepped out, a brigadier-general, the observant saw at a glance. A captain alighted, too, and stood dutifully one pace behind his master. The brigadier was looking towards the noisy, brawling mob with astonishment on his pink, well-shaven face. It was probably only at that moment, when he was well inside the prison, that Brigadier Thorbry realised that these men milling about were Glasshouse prisoners and he had driven innocently into the midst of the biggest riot ever known in a Glasshouse. But by then it was too late to turn back.

Brigadier Alexander Montbrier Thorbry was as fine a man as ever stepped into an officer's mess. Every junior officer in the Middle East who came into contact with him would, in varying terms of fervency, corroborate and even enlarge upon that statement.

He had the advantages, of course, of being highly personable to look at, tall and soldierly in bearing, handsome too, warming men to him by the perennial smile of good nature ever on his moustached face. Thorbry had charm, as much charm as any man could ever hope to have, and undoubtedly this aspect of genial good nature had assisted in his rise to general by the age of only forty-four.

A benevolent, good-hearted man, and sometimes strange officers in a Cairo club or officers' mess would be asked, generally by some enthusiast a little bit cut by too many Tom Collins', 'Now, you try to guess what sort of a command the brigadier holds. Go on, try! Bet you don't guess in a thousand years!'

And if he was listening, Brigadier Thorbry would look humorous, as if he too found the situation a bit droll.

When the young officer, no doubt awed by the presence of the great man, friendly though he seemed to be, admitted he hadn't a clue, they told him.

Brigadier-general Alexander Montbrier Thorbry was officer-in-command of all His Majesty's Field Prisons in the Middle East.

Thorbry, no different from so many other officers, had no time for Other Ranks. To him they were 'they' and 'them', not really acceptable humans like officer ranks. If they did as they were told, that was fine, and indeed he could appear to be thoughtful and generous to those serving his needs close to him. His batman, for instance, and servants in the several establishments that his wealth maintained, respected and even adored him. But outside this personal group, and especially if men erred or transgressed even slightly, he could be merciless in a manner unrecognisable to admiring officers in his mess.

Beneath that veneer of geniality, Brigadier Thorbry was a cold man, a man ever calculating the chances to his benefit and heedless of all human rights and dignity so long as he came out on top. He had always been on top.

This, then, was Brigadier Thorbry who found himself, quite dazed by the situation, on the parade ground at Sharafim that riotous morning. Offer's wish had come true. The big man, the man nearly at the top of the pile that thought they came out better for men's suffering, had chosen this day of all days to make an inspection of the Glasshouse along the Canal. This was his idea of keeping his staff on their toes. He found the prisoners were doing just that, and he did not know how to react to the situation, not with a black-faced fellow already covering him from the rear with a nasty looking Thompson sub-machine-gun.

Few there, turning and seeing him, knew who he was. A few did. That was sufficient. The word travelled swiftly. 'It's the big bastard! It's the man himself!' No one, except perhaps Offer, saw higher than a general at that moment.

So they did terrible things to that brigadier on that sun-drenched parade ground that morning, and when they heard of it, officers throughout the Middle East were turned against those men. 'They did that to poor old

Thor?' It was unbelievable. 'The swine!' they growled. And indignantly, 'Why, old Thor wouldn't harm a flea! Why did they have to do that to him?'

The men, crazed by violence, knocked him around so much that he lost some of his good looks for ever. In fact the big difficulty was in keeping him alive so that their fun could be extended. He lost all his clothes, and a man has little protective dignity when they go; and then, bruised and battered, he was driven to work on the Wall. Brigadier Alexander Thorbry suffered many hells that day, just as he had been responsible for the many hells inflicted on thousands of men of lesser rank.

Offer said again, 'We're getting out of this.' And O'Keefe went round quietly pulling their men out. Even so some of the prisoners followed them, so that in the end Offer found himself with thirty-four men, not including himself and Sergeant O'Keefe, perched on their open Chevs.

They took to the desert again, though this time in a totally different direction from their first run to cover. They went south, along the Nile, then took off on a track which Sergeant O'Keefe, navigating for the column, said would lead them through el Faiyhum to Siwa.

Siwa. That, O'Keefe had said, was *the* place for them. No other place for it, he gave his considered opinion when Offer put the question to him the night before.

'Sergeant, you're the expert. When we've done our stuff at Sharafim, where do we go from there?' No good this time hiding in the desert close to civilisation; as for civilisation itself, crowded though Cairo was, there'd be no safety there for any of them, either. So where could they find safety?

After several moments of deep thought the ex-L.R.D.G. man came out with the word. Siwa.

'Isn't that an oasis?' Offer was very vague about the place.

It was, and as Sergeant O'Keefe told him about Siwa his tone became increasingly exultant. The place sounded as near to perfection as anywhere could possibly be.

To start with, it was about four hundred miles south-west of Cairo, deep in the Libyan Desert, and wasn't that something to dwell on, O'Keefe's expression asked. Offer reserved his opinion until later. And later he was to learn that Siwa was tucked uncomfortably close to the Great Sand Sea to the south with the Qattara Depression a few miles westward. Both were terrible killers of men, but that night O'Keefe made light of them.

The oasis was out of this world, the ex-L.R.D.G. man assured them. It was quite big, stretching for miles, a freak of a place where water came bubbling up from the desert, almost icy cold and in any quantity that man could want. Palm trees flourished, and there was fruit and vegetables in abundance. As for flowers, apparently the annual show at Chelsea just didn't get a nose in.

In Roman days Siwa had been a place of great importance, and still within the oasis were the ruins of a great temple. The Romans had created a number of bathing pools at the spring, still in use, the one most popular with the L.R.D.G., O'Keefe said, being the celebrated Cleopatra's pool, romantically and coolingly overshadowed by tall palm trees.

Offer said, ironically, 'Of course there are no flies in this Vale of Paradise.'

O'Keefe's tongue explored the gap in his teeth with thoughtful deliberation. He couldn't really remember, he said finally, but he supposed there'd be a few. He also uuld there wuu a desert tribe who lived there, and it wuo on a caravan route from Benghazi to more distant oases such as Farafra, Dakhla and Kharga, so there were plenty of goings on.

He clinched it, though, with an argument directed to safety. Siwa was a place of call for all the roaming cloak-

and-dagger units of the desert. The Long Range Desert Group, for instance, had a headquarters there, in a modern building put up by someone, probably the Egyptian Government. The Special Air Services came and went constantly on their maurauding expeditions. And others, less well known, drifted in and out of the place.

'That's why it'll be safe for us,' O'Keefe argued. 'No one ever asks questions there. We'll just be another bunch on some operation, and if we don't talk about it, that's to be expected.'

The more he thought of it, the more sure Offer became that O'Keefe was right. Siwa offered the perfect hideout, and by the sound of it, a comfortable one. Anyway, what was the alternative? Captain John Offer, agreeable man, bowed to the better judgment of his sergeant.

By the time they went into action the following morning everyone knew about Siwa, and everyone couldn't wait to get there. This was *the* place to sit out the war. Do up Sharafim, and then they could retire from the fray with good heart and easy consciences ...

At Faiyhum they knocked off a lot of jerricans and filled them at the army water point there, abandoning the water tanker when they took to the deseıt trail again.

It turned out to be anything of a picnic, those hundreds of miles across the oven-hot desert, rounding the great Qattara Depression with its almost unscalable cliffs and, there beneath, a treacherous area of marshland, far below sea level, which could engulf a vehicle in a minute. Long before the journey was over men cursed the day they ever heard of Siwa Oasis. Not O'Keefe, of course. He just looked surprised when men moaned and said they wanted to pack it in. The journey didn't seem to worry that lean man.

Day after day they toiled, sometimes not making thirty miles after the most searing, prodigious effort. That was when they ran into soft sand, and wheels spun and dug themselves down to the axles. Then men, tired from hanging on to a bumpy, unyielding truck, bone-weary from the exposure to that awful sun, had to tumble down and dig away sand and insert sand tracks, then get their shoulders to the Chevs and manhandle them on to firmer ground, where perhaps only fifty yards later the things got stuck again.

Digging and shoving, a raging thirst upon them, their eyes aching from the glare of reflecting sunshine, it was a nightmare of a journey. Then tyres punctured so easily, and massive tyred wheels had to be replaced. Fan belts went and engines overheated. Always there were stoppages, and the worst of it was, all had to stop when one was in trouble. 'Never split in the desert,' said the master, O'Keefe, wisely.

Yet there were moments of compensation. Some days they ran on to sand that was hard-packed, and as level, as everyone was at pains to point out, as the proverbial billiards table. Then drivers put their feet down, and the Chevs went stampeding across the desert sand like a herd of joyous buffaloes. Those were the times the men enjoyed themselves, when Siwa seemed, after all, worthwhile. If only they could always have travelled on like this, racing each other, and cheering on their respective drivers. But it never lasted, though one day they notched up the better part of a hundred miles.

Finally the weary convoy changed course, now travelling on a bearing north-west of their point of turn. O'Keefe, very busy with his theodolite and sand compass told them that day, 'We've turned the Qattara Depression. Siwa's not far away.'

That cheered them, though when they looked round and saw the endless monotony of parched and eroded hills they wondered how far 'near' was. Some time later there was another change of course. Now they headed due west. This time O'Keefe said they had rounded a sprawling treacherous corner of the Great Sand Sea, and Siwa mightn't be more than a day ahead. Nobody questioned the expert. To them all the land looked alike – awful. But if O'Keefe said that one bit of desert was more deadly than another, they believed him.

To Captain Offer, whose plump body took to the desert travel better than most men's, O'Keefe also gave other news. 'We're on the caravan route from Mersa to Siwa.' Mersa Matruh was due north of them, on the coast of the Mediterranean.

Offer stared around. He couldn't see any trail. He said so.

'Oh,' said O'Keefe indulgently, 'you won't get a trail here. Too much drifting sand.' Besides which the camel trains just headed across the desert making their own trails over land perhaps as wide as twenty miles apart. But they could expect to see Arab caravans along this route, O'Keefe threw in, which was the reason why he had mentioned the subject.

To everyone's disappointment they failed to make Siwa that night. Everyone's dream of coming out of the baking hot desert, of plunging into a deep pool of clear cold water and having a good meal for a change, instead of this severely rationed hard-tack, faded with darkness. Sergeant O'Keefe said the going had been slower this last day than he expected, but Offer thought he might have erred in his calculations.

How far were they from Siwa, he asked, just on night-fall. O'Keefe said perhaps twenty miles, though the going, so far as he remembered, from here on was quite good. He and a few others were all for going on through the night, but most of the men had had enough, so Offer said, briskly, 'No, sergeant, we'll camp. A few more hours out here won't do us any harm.' They would waken at three in the morning and with a bit of luck would hit the oasis before the heat of the following day was upon them.

It was a weary and somewhat depressed bunch of men who finally made camp that evening. Camp? You made fires in cans and stirred hard biscuits and bully into mush with part of your ration of water. You pulled a couple of blankets on to the sand and that was home for the night. This night there was little of the jubilation that had attended their first desert camp on this journey, even from the prisoners just released from the Glasshouse.

'By Christ,' Offer had heard one of his new recruits moaning at an earlier camp, 'don't I miss my cosy, comfortable cell at Sharafim!'

'And a nice cosy staff-sergeant to tuck you in,' Offer had said gently, and the man grinned. None of them, they all knew, would have changed the rigours of desert travel for the pit of pain that was Sharafim Glasshouse. Still, in the British army a man had to have his moan.

Sergeant O'Keefe came over after his meal to have a word with his captain. This was a nightly ritual, when they made plans and discussed events of the day. O'Keefe got down in the sand beside Offer. He was still drinking his tea, hugging the battered enamel mug as if loth to absorb its precious contents. It was dark now, serenely, beautifully dark and still comfortably warm. No moon, but stars in plenty to give them some light. A perfect night, but none of the men seemed to be appreciating their luck.

Offer said, 'They've had enough.'

O'Keefe surprised him. 'Oh, they're not as far gone as you'd think. They're beginning to adapt to desert life. Next time we take off they'll be like old hands.'

'You really think so?' That was interesting and could cause Offer to revise some of the planning he had in mind.

O'Keefe was quite sure. He had seen the miracle before. 'Don't take any heed of their bloody griping, sir. That doesn't mean a thing. You watch 'em, and you'll see there's more kick in 'em now than there was after we left Faiyhum.'

'I hope you're right.' Well, that was a bit cheering. They sat in silence for a while. A sentry on patrol – O'Keefe always had one posted every night in the desert; one was quite enough, so far from the enemy lines, he argued – came closer. His bulk obscured some of the stars, and that was all they could see of his presence. Then the piquet drifted away.

'Sergeant, we've got a few hard cases among these new men we picked up at Sharafim.'

'We're all hard cases,' O'Keefe's voice came drily through the night.

Offer laughed at that. 'But some are harder than others.'

O'Keefe said, 'I know who you're thinking of.'

The Bombardier. Another gunner. Offer had known him in Sharafim and hadn't taken to the man even there. McTone was big and vicious. He had, to Offer's way of thinking, the unpleasant eyes of a fanatic, never showing the softer emotions of human life, but always fiercely hard, truculent, seeming to seek a quarrel that could end in a fight. McTone was in Sharafim for striking a new young lieutenant who had just joined them in the desert. 'He got on my tits, the fuckin' nance,' was how the Bombardier explained the incident in the Glasshouse, but apparently it had been a very violent assault, with the second-lieutenant in hospital for months.

McTone was no longer a bombardier, but was still known by that title because he used it in the boxing ring.

'I wish he hadn't joined us.' McTone promised nothing but trouble.

'You're dead right.' O'Keefe's voice was unexpectedly fervent.

'You've had trouble already?'

'Well, let's say I've only just avoided it. But I don't like walking away from the bastard just to keep things quiet.'

'As bad as that?' Already?

'What's this rank I've got over him?' O'Keefe spoke with a touch of bitterness, then finished his tea noisily and cleaned out his mug with sand. 'It's not real, and he came out with it when I gave him orders, right in the beginning.'

'Well, my rank's not approved by Higher Command, either, so what will he make of that?'

'He'll tell you to stuff yourself if he doesn't want to do what you order him to do.'

'Yes?' A very quiet little word came to O'Keefe's ears. 'I think the bombardier will find himself being stuffed if he does.' And O'Keefe cheered up, because though Offer was so much smaller than McTone he was most resolute and resourceful. Sitting there in the dark O'Keefe had a sudden, happy feeling that the fellow would meet his match with their leader.

Offer spoke again. He was looking fixedly across the desert, as if something had attracted his attention. His ears, listening, realised that the sentry wasn't moving now.

'You said they were all good lads, coming with us from Sharafim, but it's not just McTone.' True, most of his men were okay, ordinary chaps who had got on the wrong side of military justice, but just a few of them were real bad eggs. He had no illusions about Cruiser and Busker, for instance, towers of strength though they had been in Sharafim — how long ago was that now? Nearly two weeks? How time flew! They were brutalised, conscienceless men, and it was interesting to see that already they were on good terms with the angry-eyed McTone. But there were others.

Offer rose, again staring out over the desert. The sentry was still not moving.

'How'd you like promotion, sergeant?'

'Would it bring more pay?'

'While ever we can knock off Pay Offices.'

'I'll take it so long as I don't have to wear shoulder tabs.' O'Keefe wasn't officer material, not even in Offer's mob, and he knew it.

'As soon as you can win an R.S.M.'s badge of office, the job's yours. And I'll want stripes, too. I'm going to make up several sergeants.' Walker, faithful Walker would be one of them, though he'd probably make a lousy sergeant.

O'Keefe said, 'Oh? and his remark was a question that invited an answer. So Offer gave it.

'There's going to be trouble – that blasted bombardier. We can't have him telling us to get stuffed and do just as he pleases. That could be dangerous if we ran into trouble. So I think a bit more rank around the place, now we've got more personnel, might keep McTone in line.'

Make a man a sergeant, even in this Comic Cuts outfit, and he'd live up to his stripes – that was human nature. With an R.S.M. and three or four sergeants supporting him, Offer felt sure he'd be able to handle McTone and any other truculents that had joined them. Men did obey authority – Offer stiffened. He hadn't been mistaken. Now he saw it again. He began to say, 'Sergeant, there's some-one out there. I just saw a light –' when an alert sentry called out, 'Sir, there's a light across the desert.' He kept his voice low, as if not wanting sound to travel. So he'd spotted it, too, and had been watching for it again.

O'Keefe came up on to his feet in an instant. Other men rose from their blankets and clustered round the sentry. All stood and watched. A few minutes later they saw momentarily a red speck of light, and almost im-mediately another and then another.

'Someone's smoking,' the men began to say, but O'Keefe would have none of it.

'They're fires. Someone's brewing or cooking, and they're sitting round them, and when they move we can see the flames.'

'How do you know they're not cigarettes?' An obstinate challenge from McTone.

The sergeant's explanation was devastatingly logical. 'Men who smoke talk. If we could see cigarettes they'd be near enough for us to hear 'em talking. Sound travels easily across this desert.' O'Keefe's instinct said they were fires, and as always Offer took his word for it.

'How far away, sergeant?'

'Could be two or three miles.' It was very difficult for them to estimate distances. 'Perhaps more.'

'They weren't there when we halted.' That had been with some daylight lasting, and they would surely have seen any other party across that flat desert. So someone must have caught up with them and gone into camp after dark.

'Are these your Bedouin?' Offer remembered O'Keefe's talk earlier that day.

Offer felt rather than saw the sergeant shrug in the darkness. 'Could be. Could be anyone. Free French, Popski's Private Army, S.A.S., L.R.D.G. – could be any of those.' And then, thoughtfully, 'Of course they could be Eyeties or Bosche.'

That shook them. The enemy out there, so close at hand? Offer said, 'What are the odds on that, sergeant?' but O'Keefe wouldn't like to guess.

Siwa was close on four hundred miles from the coast where the armies of several nations were locked in bloody contest, and neither the Germans nor Italians showed much inclination to wander deep into the desert, as the British did. Still, now that Tobruk had fallen a second time and Rommel's army had reached Mersa Matruh – the last news they'd had of the fighting – the Axis commander might want to capture this strategically situated little oasis, which gave so much advantage to the desert guerillas who were a thorn in his side. Yes, they could be enemy patrols out there.

'We'll assume then that that is the enemy,' Offer said briskly. 'No sense in taking risks. Good job we'd done our cooking before they came up.' There were a lot of assumptions behind that statement, and of course this might only be an Arab caravan, after all, or a friendly mob of British desert warriors.

Still, Offer wouldn't change his plans. They all needed rest.

'We'll rise and shine at three o'clock, and hope those buggers aren't doing the same.' Not if they were enemy. 'So get your heads down, chaps. Don't make any loud noises. No more open fires.' In the morning they'd be able to brew up safely with a fire-can down a hole in the sand. 'And be careful if you smoke that your match is well-shielded from that direction.'

They understood and drifted off. Ten minutes later someone lit up from his blankets, and the flare of the match seemed intolerably bright under the circumstances. O'Keefe's voice rapped, 'Go easy with that light, you there!'

A crude voice roughly advised O'Keefe to go and commit an improper sexual act upon his own person. It was McTone.

Offer's voice rapped out instantly, as it were coming between the bombadier and his sergeant. 'Less of that, McTone! Just be careful what you're doing – and saying.'

They heard McTone growl a bit in the dark, and he continued to smoke, as the swelling light showed when he puffed on his fag, but that was all there was to the incident.

The sentry on duty woke the camp dead on three. Offer gave them fifteen minutes for breakfast and packing. The sentry had put in his time usefully by scooping out a pit and having all four firecans on the glow. Tea was ready for them as they crawled, shivering in the cold night air, from their blankets.

The men mounted their vehicles, very cold leaning against the metal sides, hands deep in pockets and wishing they'd never seen a desert. 'Roll on Siwa,' said many a mournful warrior, and the sooner they got to that earthly paradise the better.

The engines started, the sound terribly loud in the silence of that early morning. O'Keefe said, 'That'll waken 'em.' If, as Offer pointed out, they weren't up earlier and now already far away. They would soon see, when daybreak came.

Away they went, and this morning Captain Offer sat in the cab of the leading truck with his sergeant. 'I'd like to be alongside you if there's any trouble,' Offer explained. He was very uneasy about those lights they'd seen in the desert last evening. Be damned to O'Keefe and his tales of Arab caravans and returning S.A.S. In his bones Offer was sure those lights came from an enemy.

On they rumbled, hour after hour, a small sliver of a moon up now to give aid to the starlight, though it wasn't much. Men dozed fitfully, swaying in unison as the trucks lurched or bumped. Then dawn made its presence known, a lightening of the eastern sky, a light which grew steadily more and more yellow until finally it burst into vivid orange upon a high layer of thin clouds, and the sun's rim showed; another day of heat had begun.

Men came to life as dawn broke and all looked round for sight of any other party. But the desert seemed to be without human life, save for themselves, and with some relief the four Chevs chugged along.

The going was quite good, and O'Keefe grew more and more optimistic. 'We'll be there by midday,' was his prophecy now.

'We'll halt for a brew-up,' said Captain Offer, and his driver slowed and halted, and the others pulled up behind them. 'Breakfast!' called Offer, and with that everyone tumbled down to the ground and began the usual swift drill for preparing a meal.

Watching them, Offer thought, 'You were right, O'Keefe.' The men were showing greater alacrity than he'd noticed earlier in their travels. They must indeed be getting hardened to desert ways, he thought, and realised that he himself didn't feel as jaded as he had done on other mornings.

He also noticed ex-Bombardier McTone. The big chap didn't help in making the fires, but was there with his mug when the char came up. He was also there when the food was dished out, though he made no attempt to give anyone a hand.

'Wants waiting on, this bastard,' Offer thought. Well, McTone didn't have any stripes in this outfit, for all they still called him Bombardier. There was going to be trouble but Offer wouldn't hold back when it came. 'Just let us get off this desert,' he told himself grimly. Then he'd settle McTone's hash. Or McTone might settle his, the thought occurred to him but it didn't persist. Captain Offer felt a match for any man, even one as big as their new recruit.

They had hardly started on their breakfast, when the look-out, chewing on cold bacon with hard biscuit, from his vantage point seated on a Chev cab roof, called out, 'Convoy approaching, sir.'

His finger was pointing. Everyone wheeled instantly, tension rising, alarm within them. Coming up on a parallel course with them and just a few miles to the north was a long cloud of desert dust.

Offer said things in annoyance under his breath. Those vehicles were uncomfortably close; they ought to have been spotted long ago. Damn the sentry. Probably too bothered about his two, fat-congealed rashers of bacon to have been keeping a proper watch.

Offer said, 'Here, hold that,' and shoved his tea mug into the nearest pair of hands. He climbed up beside the sentry, withdrew his binoculars from their leather case, and trained them on the distant column. Objects leapt into vision instantly. A familiar marking was clearly to be seen on the leading vehicle.

Offer's pulse jumped and his heart skipped a few beats. This was the first time he had actually seen the enemy, and by God they were uncomfortably close. He called down, 'They're Germans,' and dropped to the ground.

O'Keefe still put up an argument. 'Don't you be so sure, sir. L.R.D.G. and S.A.S. sometimes use jerry trucks as disguise. The S.I.G.' – a reckless band of German Jews who operated behind the enemy lines – 'always do. So it mightn't be the Bosche.' Germans had never been seen so near to Siwa, and O'Keefe still couldn't imagine them being there now.

Offer was blunt to the point of coarseness. 'So far as I'm concerned, brother, anything wearing a swastika is a bloody German. I'm not staying to find out. Everybody aboard, and bugger your breakfast!'

There was a pause even so, everyone swilling back their tea ration, too precious to throw away even under such circumstances. Offer all the while eyed that distant dust cloud. It was coming up fast, and he knew that glasses had spotted them as easily as his had helped him identify the oncomers. 'Wonder what *they'll* make of our Allied markings,' he was thinking, when McTone spoke.

'Runnin' away?' There was a depth of nastiness in the tone. The bombardier was directing his question at Captain Offer. 'Not going to put up a fight?' The question was a dirty sneer.

'Don't be silly. Who wants to fight? We might get hurt.' Offer made light of it, treating the questions with humour, but he knew, and some of the others must have known, that McTone was beginning a challenge for his leadership. He also saw how McTone's pals, men as crude and treacherous as he – Privates Sibrett, Skipper and Dodge –

were standing close to the bombardier, like men giving support to a leader, their jeering smiles adding to McTone's. *They* knew McTone was deliberately out to make trouble, and that was something of appeal to them, even at this moment.

O'Keefe saved the moment with some very caustic remarks. 'Fight? You dozy bloody clot! What have we got to fight with? Tommies and rifles? If they're Jerries they'll have heavy machine-guns, Schmeissers and Spandaus. You know how long we'd last against them? Just long enough to die, mate! So on those trucks, and don't talk so bloody daft in future!' He was being deliberately rough with McTone because the gunner had to be taken down a peg in public, just as he'd tried to take Offer down a peg a moment before.

McTone had to save his face with a show of obstinacy. While everyone else clambered swiftly on to their Chevs, McTone took his time, swigging his tea and only slowly moving towards his truck. O'Keefe wasn't waiting for the bastard. Wickedly he ordered, 'Get moving! Fast!' It was big, lumpy, Art Weybright's turn at the wheel, and he understood and gave a grin and got the Chev into quick motion. McTone found himself being left behind and had to run and catch up with his vehicle and then had to be dragged over the tailboard, which didn't put him in good-humour. He had hardly won that round.

He'll have another try, was Offer's thought, up in the cab alongside O'Keefe and Weybright. Most of life was a struggle between men trying to land the other fellow's job, and if you were a McTone you went about it crudely, without finesse. McTone was going to spell big trouble for him. He had no capacity for leadership, just bullying strength but that wouldn't deter him. McTone, unpleasant man, always had to try to be top dog. Even in the Glasshouse he had exerted his presence in his cell, Offer had heard, dominating his fellow prisoners, though

God knows there was little to gain by being cell-leader in Sharafim.

McTone would go on trying to topple him and take over leadership of this small mob – that was McTone all over. After all, he, Offer, wasn't a real captain, just another ex-Glasshouse swaddy to McTone, so why not grab for top job? Sitting in the cab, watching the scrub desert flit by under their long-suffering tyres, Offer quite coldly decided to get rid of the fellow. He knew how he would do it, too, spectacularly and with a ruthlessness to match McTone's. It didn't pay to use kid gloves with a bastard of McTone's calibre.

Weybright, nearest that other column, said, 'They've changed course, sir. They're heading for us.'

'They're either friendly types trying to catch up, or Squareheads out for our scalps. Driver, can't you put your foot down any further?'

'Only if you move the floorboard.' Weybright grinned. He was a man Offer could count on in any struggle for power with McTone. The wireless operator had been a mighty sore man at the beginning of their journey, the battering by R.S.M. Fry during the prison riot showing for many days afterwards. But he too seemed to have recovered now, and certainly was in better physical shape than when they left the Nile Valley.

Both Offer and O'Keefe leaned forward to look beyond the driver at the distant column. Not so distant now, thought Offer uncomfortably. O'Keefe lost his illusions about that moment, he too accepting that Germans were coming across the scrubland without friendly intent. A race had begun, and in the next hour it became apparent that part of the German column at least had the heels on the Chevs. A small group had detached itself from the main column and seemed to be coming full pelt on their trail.

O'Keefe, expert to the last, said, 'In half-an-hour they'll

be in range. Spandau range, anyway.' Then comfortably, 'No one's going to hit us at this speed.' The uneven desert was now in their favour. Still, in time they were bound to catch up. What were they, these faster vehicles? German patrol cars? Then they'd have mounted machine-guns...

Only a few minutes later O'Keefe said, 'There's Siwa.'

Through the place where there should have been a windscreen, only desert-going Chevs didn't retain their glass, O'Keefe pointed. There was a smudgy line on the horizon. In the refracting air currents above the desert the smudge kept detaching itself and rising like a stratus cloud above the land.

'Palm trees.'

Quite quickly they began to resolve into familiar shapes. Within half-an-hour they became trees with feathery heads, still on that windless day. About this time someone in the back yelled to Offer, 'They're opening up on us, sir!' The pursuit was as close as all that now.

Offer calculated their chances on getting to the oasis ahead of the Germans. He looked back at the Afrika Korps vehicles. They looked ominously close now. Half a mile away only? Black, seemingly turreted vehicles at that distance, throwing out a long slip-stream of dust that rose and dispersed and lingered for a long time.

And Siwa? The thought beginning to obtrude equally uncomfortably was, would they find sanctuary in the oasis? Was it, in fact, in friendly hands? If not, if it had been taken by the enemy, a deduction not difficult to draw with a Panzer column romping across a once friendly desert, then all they were doing was racing on to disaster.

Offer spoke his thoughts aloud. 'I'd like to know what's happening in Siwa.' It was drawing very close now.

Two minutes later O'Keefe told him. 'It's being bombed – by Stukas.'

*

From nowhere half a dozen specks had appeared high in the brilliant blue sky. There was a lazy circling, like vultures making sure of their target, then one by one they peeled off and came hurtling almost vertically earthwards, in a power dive that must have been terrifying to those beneath.

They saw smoke rise from among the trees, and seconds later the deep crump-crump sound of high explosive came to their ears even above the rattle and roar of their hard-pressed vehicle.

'Well,' said Captain Offer cheerfully, 'at least that proves one thing. Our people are still holding the oasis.'

He told Weybright to steer a southerly course, the bombing occurring more to the north of this many-mile-long Siwa Oasis, and unexpectedly they ran on to very smooth sand and for a few minutes actually gained on their pursuers. Behind them this was noticed, and ever-ready to cheer, the men banged on the cab roof and said crude but complimentary things about their comrades' driving. To their relief the Afrika Korps now seemed to lose interest in them, and sheered off northwards.

So they ran into the palm trees of the oasis, their eyes gladdened by the sight of so much greenery after such a time in the monotonous grey-yellow desertland. Everyone sat up as their progress fell to a more comfortable speed. There was a bit of a track running through the palm trees, and the drivers took to it and instantly found themselves running in shade and the coolness was almost like ducking under a shower.

'Let's stop,' ordered Captain Offer. 'We deserve a drink and a rest.' He must also consider their next move, and work out the implications of that distant bombing. They could still hear it occasionally. Some of the men also said they could hear gunfire.

The gallant, over-strained Chevs halted, dispersing for safety under O'Keefe's directions beneath the palms. The sergeant then threw out patrols far distant, while the others stretched and lay gratefully in the shadow of the graceful trees. They drank from their water-bottles – no time for a brew-up – and ate squashy bully beef that almost ran out of the cans as they opened them. And rested.

After a time one of the sentries sent back word that he could see a lot of natives heading out of the oasis on the open desert. There were whole families, men, women and children, taking with them their camels, horses and livestock.

'They're getting the hell out of it,' said Walker. 'And I don't blame the poor sods, a war going on right in their backyard.'

Art Weybright was lying beside him. 'You know, Walky, we've got a bloody nerve. We come thousands of miles to have a barney on other people's property, and we don't give a damn what destruction we cause, and how many Arabs get killed or wounded.'

Offer heard them but didn't join in the conversation. This was no time for philosophy. He was having to make decisions. That decision, once made, committed them to driving on to where they'd heard the bombing, though now it seemed to have ceased. 'Probably gone home for more bombs,' Offer thought. Stukas had such limited range they wouldn't linger after laying their deadly eggs.

They rested for fifteen minutes, then Offer got them back in their trucks. This time McTone gave no trouble. At first they drove west deep into the oasis, then turned north. This was to ensure that they didn't run into their German pursuers, also probing into the oasis. All the time they drove, everyone remained in a state of high alertness, eyes searching the distances between the avenues of trees, hands holding rifles and automatic weapons, but seeing nothing hostile.

They did, however, cross a broad, well defined track, one that had been beaten hard by thousands of hooves and bare feet over a time of many centuries. O'Keefe said it was a trail that led south to Kharga and the other oases. And that broad track was solidly crowded with fleeing people.

Their four Chevs had to cut through them, a long procession of laden camels and other quadrupeds, but even more people on foot. They looked down into brown anxious faces, into big eyes that spoke of fear – veiled women, children frightened and scurrying to their mothers when they saw them, and men apprehensive at sight of their war-like appearance.

But they did not turn on the invaders of their land, only collected themselves and hurried along the faster. Seeing them go on to the harsh open desert, turned from their homes into a time of suffering, Captain Offer remembered the words he had overheard from Weybright during their recent halt. Yes, it was a crying shame that Europeans had to come deep into the African desert just to kill each other, turning out the inhabitants in the process. Bloody silly Aryans.

'Damned if I want to kill anyone,' Offer thought. Not even a Bosche. Only screws and McTone.   –

What impressed the men about Siwa was its size. Only O'Keefe had made deep desert travels before, and all other men's vague ideas about oases were of a few palm trees and an odd well. But this palm-covered depression in the desert covered tens of square miles, and contained many villages with cultivated areas. The 'wells' were great sheets of water, tantalising them as they were glimpsed under the palm trees. O'Keefe said the population of Siwa was probably ten thousand or more Arabs, and then added that if they thought this oasis big they should take a dekko at Kufra. Now, that was something to see!

They were following a well defined trail that ran north. Now they began to hear the sounds of fighting, the thudding of high-explosive shells, though muted by the serried ranks of palm trees. Mortars, said the knowledgeable among them. Offer didn't like the sound, but they had to go towards the fighting if they were to make contact with any British within the oasis. That was logic, unhappy though they might be made by it.

Another bit of village, deserted. Cultivated plots. A great hedge of prickly pear cactus. Then trees and trucks and men moving about.

Offer began to say, relieved, 'We're there,' and then he heard Weybright, quick man though he ran to bulk, yell, 'Oh, sodding heaven, the bloody Bosche!'

The markings on the trucks weren't familiar Allied roundels; the desert uniforms of these soldiers had a tinge of green.

The big boot nearly went through the floorboards this time. Offer hoped that the following trucks would follow their example. The engine roared into frenzy and the Chev tore along the dusty trail. Offer saw startled German faces some no more than fifty yards away. What saved the British, in fact, was suddenly appearing right in the middle of the enemy force. It took seconds for the Germans to appreciate that this revving truck was indeed British and not one of their own. Then they opened fire.

The leading truck – Offer's – skipped out of sight round the prickly pear hedge almost as the first shot came after them. The second truck got through, hard on the heels of the first, without damage, either. But the third truck took a lot of lead and had bullet holes through the metal sides to prove it – too many to be comfortable, yet astoundingly no one aboard got a scratch.

The fourth truck caught the full weight of the cross-fire. It struggled on gallantly, the men in the rear trying to stand erect and use their weapons but probably doing no damage. Then everything seemed to hit it at once. Lashley, the Aussie, glimpsing the moment from the back of the third truck before it ran out of sight and into safety, saw it all.

His comrades from the Glasshouse started to topple from the speeding Chev, shot from the back of the truck, to fall out sometimes writhing when they landed in the dust, more often quite still. Then the Chev began an erratic course, as if the driver had been shot and control lost. It careered off the trail for no more than twenty yards, though, then ran into a palm tree. Even then the Germans kept up their fire on the stricken vehicle.

'Don't reckon anyone came alive out of that flamin' wreck,' was the Aussie's opinion when reporting to Offer later. So a quarter of the Glasshouse Gang Commando Unit were wiped out in their first encounter with the enemy.

Almost at once they found themselves running among buildings, mostly mud, but some starkly new and made of concrete. O'Keefe afterwards said fire was opened on them by defenders inside the buildings, but it stopped as abruptly as it had started as if they had been recognised as Allied.

Weybright, with some instinct for safety, drove close up behind the most solid building there, then dragged on the handbrake and halted. They were all breathing hard, as if from some recent exertion, though no one had done anything energetic. But running an unexpected gauntlet of an enemy trying to kill them did things to their pulses and hearts, and their laboured breathing showed it.

Looking beyond Weybright, Offer found himself staring into the building. There were bars to a glassless window, and beyond, the room was dark with shadow. A face lifted into view. It had the whitest beard Offer had ever seen on a man, yet a young British voice spoke from behind it when he saw them.

'Hello, you chaps. Where've you sprung from?' Nobody told him, a bit too startled by recent events. A hand came into view and a good part of the beard was sliced away. The beard was lather; the owner was shaving.

'If I have to run for it,' the calm voice announced, 'I'm going to start clean-shaven.'

Captain Offer came to his senses. He smiled. 'What's the score, old chap?'

'You've just arrived then?'

'From out there.' A vague indication that embraced a whole lot of desert. 'Had to fight our way through the Jerries to reach you.' That made their entry sound more satisfactory than the truth.

'Did you, by Jove.' The last of the lather went. The man behind the bars introduced himself. 'I'm Edwardes, Jack of that ilk, lieutenant.' He could see the pips on Offer's shoulders. 'You're Captain –?'

'John Offer. G.G.C.U., you know.'

Lieutenant Edwardes didn't know. There were so many initials around. But he didn't pursue his ignorance. 'We're L.R.D.G. here ... Haven't I seen you somewhere before?' His sharp eyes were on O'Keefe.

'Former L.R.D.G., sir,' O'Keefe told him proudly.

But Offer had had enough of preliminaries. This was too civilised. Only three minutes ago they had been very near to death. 'You haven't told me the score.' He threw just that shade of iron into his voice to remind the lieutenant of the difference in their rank.

'We're on our way out. The Bosche arrived in force during the night, and has been doing some softening up with his Stukas.'

'We saw that.' And Offer's mob had arrived just ahead of German reinforcements.

'We've no garrison here – can't hold out. We're just putting up a delaying action while we get our trucks loaded for a run to Kufra. That's the better part of a thousand miles away.' He spoke gloomily, as if even the L.R.D.G. didn't relish that journey.

Offer was impressed. He knew where Kufra was, even deeper into the heart of the Sahara than Siwa. Drying his face, Lieutenant Edwardes told him that the L.R.D.G. had a good well-established base there, and while the Germans occupied Siwa they would operate from that more distant and even more inaccessible oasis.

'Hear that?' Captain Offer turned to his sergeant. 'No picnic for us in Siwa, after all.' No bathing parties in clear cold water, and lovely days doing nothing in this desert paradise until men stopped fighting in Africa. If they didn't get out pronto they might never get out. 'You'd better fill up with petrol and water, food and anything you can lay your hands on.' As an afterthought, remembering the helpless feeling they'd had as they were pursued across the desert, he threw in: 'And see if you can get us some MGs with mountings – Lewis, Bren, Vickers.'

Sergeant O'Keefe said, 'I know my way around.' Offer alighted, responding to an invitation to join Edwardes in a drink in the mess – a meal was almost ready, too. O'Keefe drove off with the other trucks on a scrounging expedition.

Offer entered the building just as several machine-guns opened fire from the flat roof overhead. Edwardes met him and took him into a large bare room where some sweating, bearded L.R.D.G. and other officers were making a hurried meal and getting outside a lot of very cold bottled beer. They greeted the clean, fresh-shaven Edwardes with much badinage, then were introduced to Offer. No one seemed interested in Offer's outfit, just as O'Keefe had prophesied, but they commiserated with him over the loss of one truck and its personnel.

They all seemed very much at ease, even though the situation was undoubtedly tight. Their sandbagged gun nests on the concrete roofs gave them a commanding field of fire which had so far daunted the enemy from making a very serious attack on their position. The dive bombers had missed their targets, for all their frightening effect, and some inspired work by the roof-top machine-gunners had put out of action the first of the mortars that had opened up on them. Now, doubtless, they were trying to find a more suitable place for the mortars to lob their explosives on to the concrete building, but it seemed to be proving difficult. Too many close-pressing palm trees, someone opined.

Offer, knocking back the cold beer as if he could never stop drinking, told them about the reinforcements. 'Quite a strong force,' he said. Perhaps this was why, so far, no major attack had been mounted; the Germans were waiting for the laggard column to join them.

His thirst temporarily satisfied, Captain Offer dug into the food available. There was a great bowl of stewed meat, very delicious, and other bowls of cooked vegetables, with native bread, warm as if just from an oven, and plenty of fresh fruit. Looking round, Offer thought, pity the Bosche had to get interested in Siwa just when the G.G.C.U. had come there. What he had seen of the oasis satisfied him. He could have played for time comfortably here until they were able to go home to a country at peace once more. Maybe he would put in a claim for his war medals, when he got back, he thought good-humouredly, then decided not to take such risks even out of a sense of fun.

Something hit the wall of the building with an almighty wallop and dust lifted and filled the room and things showered to the ground. Offer noticed that though the bronzed and bearded warriors of the L.R.D.G. ducked instinctively, not a man was so far moved as to spill a drop of his beer. He also thought how dashing they looked, those who wore the *kefir wa aghal*, the headrope and kerchief that was the Arab headdress. But he was thinking of the headdresses more in practical terms than for their swashbuckling appearance. He was also, up to the moment of that explosion, visualising in his mind a map of the area around Siwa, and already beginning to develop startling ideas.

'Mortars,' someone remarked laconically, when the reverberations had subsided. 'Back in business.' A slow satisfying drink of the beer. 'That's our number up, and it's time we hopped it.'

It appeared to be the unanimous conclusion. Offer's tale of reinforcements, and now the mortars ranging on the building, said they'd lingered long enough.

'Anyway, were probably well stacked up for the long run to Kufra by now,' a black-bearded L.R.D.G. captain said, smiling in friendly fashion at Offer. 'That's all we've been waiting for ... What are you going to do? Come with us?'

Offer's sense of theatrical timing was too much for him. He had to deliver a line that held drama. 'Not so sure.' A drink – he'd match any of them for coolness; wasn't he a professional actor? 'No, I think we'll just hang around and keep Jerry on his toes with a few night actions.' His imagination got the better of him. 'Can't let the old Hun just take over and do nothing about it, y'know.' He made his voice sound good-humoured but just that trifle plaintive, appropriate for a man showing a hint of strong emotion.

How the actor in him loved the effect of his words upon those hardened warriors of the desert! They gave him respect with their eyes, strong men acknowledging gallantry beyond the normal call of duty. The effect was somewhat spoiled by another mortar shell trying to knock a hole through the solid concrete. This time they went, the L.R.D.G. captain snapping out orders.

'Get cracking. Out the back way. Joe, bring the machine-gunners down with their MGs in five minutes – that'll get us clear. Have a truck waiting for them, the 15-hundredweight.' More orders. Then he saw Offer again, very negligently strolling out after them into the sunshine. 'Keep in touch with us at Kufra by radio. Hope we're not long before we're back ... Best of luck, old chap.'

Offer waved acknowledgement and wished that he was a pipesmoker, so that the last they saw of him was of a lone figure calmly lighting up, oblivious to the shells now falling with greater frequency in the area. But he didn't smoke; silly habit and anyway it didn't do any good to an actor's voice.

When they'd all raced away to where their vehicles were ready for boarding, Offer skipped off nimbly, too, in search of his own party. They weren't hard to find. Behind a long shed that had been a vehicle maintenance workshop there were again four Chevs. O'Keefe had knocked off another vehicle. 'The L.R.D.G. didn't want it, and you never know ...'

His men were still running up with all manner of supplies, though the vehicles seemed already well-loaded with jerricans of water and petrol, interesting-looking crates of canned foods and bottled liquor, and more vehicle spares than Offer had seen in a long time. O'Keefe had done a good job, especially in piling up spare tyres. They'd need them.

'Good show, sergeant,' Offer approved, and O'Keefe responded by lifting a bony hand and scratching his red beak of a nose, his face unsmiling. Captain Offer saw a leather strap around O'Keefe's wrist, with a very shiny metal badge upon it. Offer's eyes flitted to the sleeve of O'Keefe's bushshirt. His sergeant's stripes had gone. So he corrected himself. 'I beg your pardon, Regimental Sergeant-major O'Keefe, and my congratulations on your promotion. Well deserved, I am sure.' He wondered where O'Keefe had knocked off that R.S.M.'s wrist strap, but tactfully refrained from asking.

There was a lot of noise now, and bullets were spanging uncomfortably against the concrete wall of the building they'd just vacated. But they were not in direct line of fire. More mortars were in action, still interested in the main building, fortunately. Offer saw small figures on top, scurrying across the flat roof, machine-guns cradled in their arms. The MGs were withdrawing. Then a mortar shell landed plumb on top of the roof and exploded and they saw bodies flying, arms and legs seeming to disconnect. Almost a direct hit, and some of the machine-gunners, at least, wouldn't need that 15-hundredweight truck waiting back of the H.Q.

Everywhere under the palm trees trucks were roaring into life and moving, heading west along a dusty track. Offer said, 'No more. Time to move.' If they hadn't got everything by now they'd have to do without it. The furious hail of fire concentrating on the buildings, even to his inexperienced mind, suggested a preliminary to a storming attack, and they mustn't be there when it developed.

So they all swung aboard their vehicles and got moving, falling in with the L.R.D.G. column. Once they were started, however, no one seemed much bothered, and the withdrawal from Siwa was conducted at an almost leisurely pace. No one was going to come chasing them into the desert, all instinctively realised. The Germans would be too busy for a time cautiously taking over the built-up area before searching amid the palms and risking running into cunning ambushes. Even so their rear was brought up by an L.R.D.G. truck bristling with automatic weapons.

When they'd travelled two or three miles westerly, the L.R.D.G. took a trail going south across the oasis. Everyone was surprised, then, when Captain Offer, in the leading truck, held on along the track going west; but then he had been talking to O'Keefe, and everything his new R.S.M. said confirmed the idea that had been developing in his mind for the last half-hour.

Offer was, indeed, so confident of his control over events that when they came to a village, almost deserted, he ordered the trucks to halt. There was a bit of a bazaar amid the mud huts and Offer sent O'Keefe off with two men on a buying expedition. A startled Arab shopkeeper was delighted with the payment he received for what they wanted; for cigarettes and cases of food were better then debased Italian or Egyptian currency here deep in the desert.

What O'Keefe and his men brought back and piled into the trucks was so surprising that there were a few moved to say sadly that the old man was off his bleedin' nut this time. The bundles contained Bedouin robes and a variety of headcloths including the dashing *kefir*.

Offer drove on not a great distance from the village, then safely out of sight, had another halt. No tea this time, but beer while it was still nicely cold. And while they were slaking a thirst that seemed unslakable, Offer talked to them about their position and his plans for their future.

He said, 'I don't know how you feel about running on to Kufra. All I can tell you is that I've had enough of the desert for a while, and I'm damned if I'm going to have any more if I can help it.' There was a deep growl of approval at those words from men sitting round him where he leaned against a palm tree that gave them some shade. 'Kufra's probably a thousand miles away; *we* travelled less than six hundred from the Nile. You work that out for yourselves. Not a picnic.' Besides they'd had no time to rest and recover from the exertion of the past weeks.

'So what are we going to do? Now, I have a plan, and I've talked it over with R.S.M. O'Keefe –' He put emphasis on the title, and that had men jerking their heads up to look at their new warrant-officer. There were grins, but Offer was looking at McTone while he spoke, to see what reaction would come from the big man. McTone knew he was being watched and deliberately spat on the ground. All right, my beauty, thought Offer firmly. As soon as he could tackle Pom he'd deliberately provoke a showdown.

'The R.S.M. not only thinks my plan is practicable, but is in thorough agreement with it. Eh, R.S.M.?' O'Keefe obligingly nodded vigorously. 'Now, I'll tell you what it is.' Again the actor in him had to startle their minds with a dramatic statement. 'We're going to the seaside, and that's where we're going to hide.'

He had a map of the area and this he held against the palm tree. His men rose and crowded close so that they could look at it.

'There's the sea.' His finger stubbed a shaded patch. 'The Great Sand Sea!'

Someone said, 'Oh, Christ, for one minute I thought we were off to the bloody Med!'

Offer shut them all up and talked long and hard. When he had finished he had convinced them, and they were with him even if his plans did turn out to be folly. Anyway, the alternative was the thousand-mile desert journey to Kufra, and they were jaded and weary of riding in open trucks under the African sun, so there wasn't much real resistance to beat down, after all.

The basis of the idea was boldness. Boldness? Sheer brazen effrontery. By now Offer was convinced that the more audacious the idea, the more likely it was to succeed. Their attack on Sharafim Prison was convincing proof of this theory.

'So where's the safest place to hide from the Hun? Why, right here, in his own backyard ... in Siwa Oasis.'

The Germans wouldn't dream of such effrontery. By now they'd be sure that all Allied personnel had made a withdrawal from Siwa, and their scouts would report them as heading south towards other oases.

'They'll search around the old L.R.D.G. HQ, of course.' Thorough soldiers, the Germans would make sure there was no force under cover capable of mounting a counter-attack. 'But they won't waste their time combing the out-lying places, because Siwa's too big for that. No, they'll make themselves at home, and rely on Arab informers to tip them off if there are any stragglers trying to hide out in the oasis.'

'But won't they tip them off if we remain in the oasis?' – Weybright, very thoughtfully.

'A good question,' agreed Offer heartily, in his best officer-to-man manner. 'Not where we are going,' and that had them puzzled.

Driving into Siwa, Offer had noticed something curious about the oasis. It wasn't a neat thing, one moment desert, and the next ranks of palm trees springing out of the sand. No, there were scattered islands of palm groves, sometimes separated from each other by half a mile or more of sand. It was in just such a palm grove that Offer proposed to hide up and take the war quietly for as long as they could remain undiscovered. After their departure from the con-crete HQ, still taking such a battering from the German mortars, Offer had spoken about this germ of an idea to O'Keefe.

O'Keefe had given solemn thought to the plan for quite a few minutes. Even he was sick of desert travelling and had been wistful at the thought of leaving his beloved Siwa, so his mind did try to prove it practicable.

'You know, sir, I think you're on to something. And the best place to hide is west of Siwa.'

The depression in the desert which is Siwa is below sea level, comparatively narrow, and runs east to west at its greater length. Offer's impression was that there was a long underground lake beneath the sand, with the water quite close to the surface, certainly within reach of the roots of the palm trees. At the extremities of the lake were isolated pools, which provided sustenance for these small clumps of palm trees that fringed the main oasis.

'What we've got to do is find a palm grove that gives us shade and keeps us cool and is too far away to have Germans visiting us.' Of course there'd be an owner to the trees – there always was – but O'Keefe said it wasn't time for the date harvest, and until they ripened no owner would be mug enough to hike through the hot sun just to look at his trees. 'With a bit of luck we shall be able to sit it out in comfort until Jerry pulls away or is kicked out of Siwa.'

Offer was pretty sure that, like most of the desert war captures, this occupation of Siwa would be no long thing. Quite soon – it might be weeks only – Allied flags would be flying over the mortar-bombed HQ, and they could wander back beside those springs of clear water without having had to make the round trip of two thousand desert miles.

Of course the questions came fast at that. But was there water in these groves? A shake of O'Keefe's, the expert's, head. If wells could be sunk they'd have been dug and families would be living there. No families, no water. So how were they to survive without water?

'We'll come at night to the nearest waterhole and fill our cans. No one will question our presence, not with these on us.' He lifted one of the Bedouin robes, and now they understood why there'd been a mysterious shopping expedition on the way out.

'Sir, you said the best place to hide was west, but if we do get rumbled we'd be cornered, with the Sand Sea on two sides of us and Jerry blocking the other way out.' Another thoughtful man, Private Max Ward, staring at the map.

'That's one reason why R.S.M. O'Keefe and I have plumped for hiding towards the west. Because that's the last place the Germans will think of looking for us, and for the very reasons you have just so expertly propounded.' But the flattery did not completely still the doubts of a man made cautious by his examination of that map.

'You never know. Something might give us away. If Jerry surrounded us—'

'R.S.M.' Offer called his new warrant-officer into the debate.

O'Keefe cleared a throat that was already demanding further refreshment. 'There's a way across the Sand Sea west of Siwa. The L.R.D.G. found it, though I've never used it myself. It cuts across the neck of the Great Sand Sea and brings you out facing the Kalansho Sand Sea, though that's a long way westward. I reckon if I've a few days I could find that track, and if I do we'd have a back door through which we could slip if the Hun gets onto us.'

Later he said that anyway going via the trail through the Great Sand Sea would shorten the journey to Kufra by several hundred miles, and at that again there was a loud chorus of questioning voices. If the L.R.D.G. knew a shorter way across the Sand Sea, why had they taken the long way round?

'Because,' said O'Keefe grimly, 'by all accounts the Sand Sea way is bloody murder, only to be tackled in emergency. At least the long way round does have a couple of wells en route if you're running out of water, but there's none via the Sand Sea. Once you start on that trek you can only hope you'll get through before you dry up.'

He also told them of the terrible strain of travelling the short way. Even the trail itself was soft sand, so that vehicles drank up their petrol at an alarming rate, and it took a lot of muscle-power to keep their vehicles in motion. As for straying from the trail, which was quite easily done, if you did so you lost your vehicle if not your life.

'Much of the Great Sand Sea consists of sand so loose,

once you get on it your wheels just sink in to the axles, and the more you try to dig 'em out the deeper you sink in.' So you just write them off, he told them, and that wasn't a cheerful thought, not when your lives depended on a vehicle carrying you through.

'I know it doesn't sound at all inviting.' Offer broke into the talk. 'But that's the answer to your question. We're not trapped, here in the west of Siwa. There *is* a way out, across the Sand Sea, and if we're driven to it, well, those who want to can have a bash at getting across. Those who don't can go into the bag if Jerry doesn't knock 'em off before they've time to get their hands up. Personally I don't intend to go into the bag or try any rough crossings of the Sand Sea. I think if we just keep our heads down we'll spend the next few weeks quite comfortably here, catching up with juicy divorce cases back home by reading that damn' great pile of *News of the Worlds* someone's thoughtfully hoisted aboard. Who did it?'

It was Pom. He and a like-minded mate had picked up all the newspapers and magazines they could find in the L.R.D.G. camp. They were going to come in very useful, Captain Offer thought.

'So, my friends, that's the position. Isn't it worth some risk to avoid a desert journey of at least a thousand miles?'

They weren't the kind of men to look very far ahead. To that tough mob the idea of doing nothing for a long time in some isolated palm grove held much more appeal than desert travelling, so soon after their arduous trek from el Faiyum. Tomorrow could look after itself. There was a growling chorus of, 'Okay, us for the soft life,' and the journey was resumed in search of a suitable island of palm trees.

They found the palm grove and it seemed just about tailor-made for their requirements. It was almost the last grove of palms to the west. But this grove was quite luxuriant, and in spite of what O'Keefe said, Offer had a feeling there must be water in quantity below the surface.

They drove in amid the trees, eyes suspiciously watching, guns ready, but there were no inhabitants. It was about a hundred yards long and rather less than that in width. All agreed that if they kept right to the centre of the grove their presence would be undetected by anyone passing outside. What bothered Offer was their trucks.

Camouflage netting wasn't much good under the trees; their bulk would give them away. Offer, O'Keefe and Walker went out into the desert to scrutinise their hideout and weren't pleased to see how the vehicles showed up as large dark shapes between the tree trunks.

'That won't do,' said Offer. Besides, if the owner or any other Arab decided to drop in on the grove, men could hide, but trucks couldn't. Once seen the trucks would be a giveaway of their presence, which almost inevitably would be reported – for reward – to the new military masters in the oasis. They must do something better about hiding the trucks. O'Keefe also took one look at the tyre marks leading straight into the grove and told their new sergeant, Walker, to get them obliterated. Walker went off with reluctance to give his first orders to his comrades.

In fact finding a hide-out for their vehicles was surprisingly easy. Still further west of their grove the depression continued as a winding rift through sand dunes. They drove the trucks a couple of hundred yards out there, parked them neatly in line against a towering cliff of sand, carefully stretching the camouflage nets to break their outline, and unless one came quite close, four Chevs had been reduced to invisibility.

When it was done Captain Offer looked with satisfaction at their efforts. There was firm ground beneath, well matted with grass roots, still suggesting moisture below.

If they had to take off in a hurry, the going would be good, he observed, and R.S.M. O'Keefe nodded agreement.

The tall, spare ex-L.R.D.G. man looked round at the rolling, wind-shaped dunes, and there was love in his eyes. 'Just give me twenty-four hours to rest,' he promised, 'and I'll want to be off into the Blue. Anyway, I'll have to go, to find the back way out.'

'Yes.' That was highly important. The sooner they discovered their possible escape route, the better. The R.S.M. said it mightn't be easy, but he'd keep at it till he'd found the way, and they all trudged back into the cool, shadowed palm grove.

Sergeant Walker and his men brought up the rear, brushing out the tyre marks and footprints as they did so. Walker, the ex-palais bouncer, had been most reluctant to accept the honour of sergeantship in the G.G.C.U. In fact when the proposition was made to him he was quite appalled.

'But I don't like sergeants,' he argued strenuously. 'All non-coms are bastards.'

'Good job you said non-coms,' said the new R.S.M. ominously, but the big fellow wasn't intimidated.

'If I put them stripes up my pals will feel the same about me, that I've joined the bastards, and I don't want that.' He was a man who didn't want promotion and responsibility, but Offer finally cajoled him into accepting the post. Walker had a very soft spot for his old cell-mate.

'I'm asking you to do it for me, Walky boy,' Offer had almost pleaded. 'There's going to be trouble in this mob. Say what you like, even with this crew, I took him influence. I need Sergeant Walker to back me up when trouble starts.'

So Bouncer Walker took on O'Keefe's former sergeant's stripes and was a sick man when he showed his glory to his ribald and caustic comrades. As a sergeant he was probably about the easiest on discipline in the British Army, and for that his men tolerated and still accepted him.

Even so, Offer could not get anyone else to accept rank, no one having quite the same close loyalty to him as Walker. He offered stripes to Art Weybright, who merely looked amused through his steel-rimmed glasses and flatly turned them down. 'You wouldn't believe it, sir, but I actually volunteered for the army. That was at the time of Dunkirk. In those days I had ideals, and I thought the cause was good.'

'But now?'

'After the Glasshouse?' said Weybright roughly. 'I don't care who wins the flamin' war. They turned me, the British, when they slapped me into Sharafim. For what? For not being able to keep awake when we'd been shelled to hell for thirty-six hours.'

The British. Offer noticed the curious expression, and tucked the words into his memory for later examination.

'I won't do a damn' thing to help the war effort –'

'Who says being a sergeant with this mob will help the war along?'

But Weybright wasn't to be moved by any logic. He wasn't having anything to do with rank in the army he hated. Neither would Private Tulger, a sound, even-tempered Devon man, the other man to whom Offer brandished the stripes.

'Me a sergeant? You won't get me shoving my mates around,' and nothing Offer could say would change his mind.

Not that Tulger seemed to hold any bitterness against the army or even against established military authority, screws excepted. He was a good-natured, easy-going fellow apparently untouched by adverse experience which had included the Glasshouse.

According to him he'd been put away as an example

to others. His regiment had been warned that they were going up the Blue any day, and any man who missed the move – say, by overstaying leave in Ismaelia – would be for the high jump. Unhappily Tulger, like Walker and some others, was absent when the regiment abruptly folded its tents and set off to a hard-pressed front around Tobruk.

His story was that on evening leave in Ismaelia he'd found a dive which sold drink and they must have put a Mickey in it. All he remembered was coming to very gradually on the bank of the canal outside Ismaelia. His money was gone, and even his shirt and boots had been taken from him. He felt violently ill and kept vomiting. People passed him by – why should Arab citizens go out of their way to help yet another swinishly drunken Englishman? The hot hours passed and he lay in his misery without strength to move.

Finally some British soldiers saw him and got him out of the way of any reproving Military Police. They were good-hearted chaps, but so far as Tulger was concerned did exactly the wrong thing. They took him back to their camp and hid him in their tent for a few days until he was sufficiently recovered to report back for duty.

His story wasn't believed. Too many men had tall stories when it came to their turn to move to the fighting front. Yet in spite of all this, Tulger continued to be a nice, kindly Devon man, always helpful to his comrades, which was why he was liked.

But taking sergeant rank? Tulger just walked away from Offer at the very idea. So for the time Offer had to be content with one R S M and one sergeant.

They made a cosy camp in a shady hollow right in the middle of the grove. If they lay or squatted they could not be seen, but if they stood upright their heads showed, though even then one would have to be inside the trees to spot them. The trouble was that men could not always lie around in the hollow, and when they trudged among the trees – Nature demanding, for instance – Offer thought the movement might be detected from some distance off in the desert. He worried a bit over this weakness to their position, but found the solution unexpectedly.

It happened on their first day in camp, quite soon after they'd driven out their trucks to be camouflaged in the sandy defile. There'd been a brew-up and an issue of food quite luxurious after their hard-tack desert fare – flat *koubes*, the delicious native bread, steaks of meat, cans of Californian peaches and Carnation cream, and pots of strawberry jam for those still wanting bread to finish off the meal. Offer knew this standard of living would decline rapidly, with the L.R.D.G. gone, but while it lasted it was good and put them all in good heart.

Offer was drinking the last of his tea, belching gently and with satisfaction to revive the memory of a glorious feast. His eyes wandered round, seeing his men sprawling on their backs, some of them already comfortably sleeping. Two men would be on the alert, however, strategically posted on the edges of the oasis; for the others there were no duties.

To Offer's astonishment a tall Arab rose right from the midst of the men, brown-robed, *kefir* flowing under the glossy horse-hair headrope. Unbelievably, though he was within touching distance, none of the men seemed to be disturbed or even to notice him.

Offer thought, 'God, I've got a touch of the sun!' How on earth could an Arab be able to move right through the heart of the camp without being detected? He came to his feet with a swift movement, calling urgently, 'Stop that man!' and at once men wakened and began to move, danger bringing them to their feet, where they stood and stared and still made no move to apprehend the Arab, as if he were invisible to them.

So Offer, not far away, leapt across and grabbed roughly on a shoulder under the flowing brown robe. The Arab turned instantly, alarmed, recognised Offer and said, indignation high in his voice, 'What did you do that for?' Very much a British voice.

Captain Offer found himself looking into a familiar face under the *kefir*. It was Private Ward's.

Offer's hand dropped helplessly to his side. He had been startled and now it was his turn to be indignant. 'What the devil do you mean by dressing up? I could have shot you, thinking you were an Arab.'

Then Offer wheeled swiftly. The men had tumbled to their captain's mistake and were having a good laugh ... a good laugh, and not maliciously enjoying his discomfiture, either, all except McTone who let him see the contempt in his eyes.

The incident for some unaccountable reason – or was it McTone's faint gloating? – nettled Offer and upset him, and it was quite a time before his resourceful mind turned that moment into profit. But finally he did.

Ward. Now, there was a curious man to have in any outfit. Ward, ex-public schoolboy, was a Arab fanatic. Since his arrival in the Middle East he had fallen in love with the Arabs and the Arabian way of life. Every chance he'd had in his three army years in the Arab world had been devoted to studying their culture. It was said that he was fluent in Arabic, though he'd learned most of it in Iraq and said *nam* for yes instead of *ay-wah*, the word employed in most other Arab lands. And there were other differences, but Offer remembered how Ward had held conversations apparently with ease with Arabs along the Nile.

Ward, in fact, had gone to the Glasshouse because of his love for the Arab way of life. In Baghdad, where he was stationed, he'd heard of a caravan that was to go to Damascus, Amman, and finally Cairo. The journey would take something like a year. To Ward the temptation was beyond resistance. He had gone off with the Arabs, a welcome friend, and for months had lived a happy and contented life, just slowly moving over the desert, invaluable to his nomadic hosts and even their livestock with his knowledge of medicine – he had been a medical orderly.

As he said when the M.P.s picked him up in Cairo, what did he want with warfare? Why couldn't he be left to live the simple, satisfying life of the desert Arab?

They had one brutal answer to that. 'Because you're bloody British, mate, and there's a war on.' And he had been put into Sharafim with a sentence so long it would have destroyed most men, but not the gangling Ward.

When Offer got round to thinking of the incident dispassionately he gave an order. Every man there would henceforth wear Arab clothes.

In buying the clothing, Offer's original intention had been limited, just so that water parties could slip into the main oasis in disguise. Well, why not use the disguise here also, in their own little retreat? Suppose someone was seen from a distance walking through the grove, if he were in Arab dress it would be thought that some Arab was making a halt there. Perfect, thought Offer, and for the first time smiled indulgently at Ward, who hadn't been able to resist assuming the familiar Arab costume.

Later he called Ward over to him. 'Honestly, how well do you speak Arabic?'

Ward had blue eyes. Not many Arabs have blue eyes, but Offer knew there was a sufficient number, descendants of invading armies like Townsend's in World War I, and even way back to the Crusades, for the phenomenon to be accepted by the nomadic peoples. Ward, with his dark brown skin and black, pointed beard looked every bit an Arab.

Ward spoke earnestly. He was a very earnest man, anyway, lacking in humour and with an apparent simplicity which was contradicted by a vast storehouse of knowledge, to be deployed when necessary. Now he was modest but said that he had no difficulty in communicating in Arabic.

'But you'll have an accent?' Ward nodded, agreeing with him. 'Would that rouse suspicion if you went into Siwa and spoke with the locals?'

A shake of the head, the blue eyes expressing surprise at the thought. 'No. There are many accents in the Arab world. They will think I am Iraqui.'

Offer meditated for a moment, then said, 'I want you to do two things for me.' He was wondering why Ward, this passionate lover of the Arabian way of life, remained with them instead of taking up residence with the Arabs in the pleasanter Siwa oasis. Perhaps the thought hadn't occurred to him yet. Well, get as much use out of the chap as possible until he did wander off to join his Moslem chums.

'First, you know the idea is to have a nightly water party to go to the nearest spring and fill our jerricans?' Ward nodded. 'I want you to go with them. If anyone speaks to your party, you can do the talking.'

Ward simply nodded. So now Offer put the second proposition: 'I'd like you to go into Siwa and do a bit of spying. Keep your ears open and bring back any news you glean. Bazaar gossip might give pointers to our future survival.'

He was thinking that little news could ever be kept from civilian employees in any army. If the Germans had suspicion of any Allied troops remaining in the area, Arab servants would soon know about it and servants always talked. Ward nodded more enthusiastically this time. This was a job after his own heart. He could think of nothing better than to sit around in the shade and listen to Arabs gossiping.

No water party was necessary for a couple of days, but

Ward eagerly pushed off the following morning on reconnaissance. In camp, men luxuriated in rest, eating, sleeping, and gathering strength that had ebbed from their weary muscles in the trying days of the previous weeks. They were a perfectly contented bunch, but Offer wondered how long the contentment would last. They had some rum customers here, and anyway, even the placid-tempered men like Tulger would soon fret against simply lying around. And Offer knew what would come to disturb them most – lack of women. It would be so much worse for the men, knowing that within a mile were many, and that was going to get them very worked up in time.

The following morning the R.S.M. took a small party of volunteers out to the Chevs where they mounted an assortment of machine-guns, Vickers as well as Lewis. It took less than two hours, and only an hour after that O'Keefe took off in a truck with three men to recce for the trail across the Sand Sea. He was away for three days, arriving back at camp close on dusk. He was a dejected man. They had failed to find any signs which would indicate a way across that treacherous Sand Sea.

O'Keefe rested only one night, then again went off on search the following morning, taking a different party with him this time. O'Keefe's pride was at stake. As an ex-L.R.D.G. man he felt that he ought to be able to find an L.R.D.G. track.

There was nothing of incident in the camp during those days. True, the big bombardier ate and drank and did nothing to help with the work of food preparation. He also seemed at pains to let Offer see that he slacked with the work, as if wanting to rouse the officer into some sort of action. Offer evaded the challenge because he required something more serious to occur before chopping this big pro-boxer down to size.

Instead it reminded him and he went across to where Pom kipped on the soft sand under his own palm tree.

He made a request. He made it very firmly. Pom looked astonished, but dug into his dirty pack and amid some filthy shirts and long-used underpants found what he sought and handed it to Offer.

Offer put the object into the pocket of his shorts and told Pom he would have his guts for garters if he spoke to anyone of this moment. He meant it, too, and even the blabber-mouthed Pom kept his mouth shut after that warning.

On the evening at the end of their second full day in camp, Offer decided they must begin the nightly chore of fetching water. The Chevs were already loaded, ready for any emergency take-off, stacked with jerricans for long desert travel, as well as petrol, food, and spares. But camp supplies quickly ran low.

In that heat, he calculated, they needed a minimum of a gallon of water a day, and that wouldn't leave anything over for clothes washing and bathing. The worrying thing was the size of the water party. To satisfy the needs of twenty-eight men the water party would have to be large and therein was inherent danger.

Offer's first idea had been to send a very small party off with two jerricans each, but Ward, spoken to on the subject, was shocked. According to him, Bedouin of the desert would not be seen openly carrying jerricans – that was women's work – and the carrying party would therefore have to hold their jerricans underneath their robes and thus out of sight. But experiment proved the impossibility of a man carrying two jerricans under his garment, and even one was an awkward thing, getting in the way of knees. So in the end a party of eight set out, and one of them was Captain Offer.

Ward was a very thorough man, and had been highly critical of their disguise. At first he told them it wouldn't deceive the sharp-eyed Bedouin, because they walked like

Europeans, not Arabs. He showed them how they should walk.

They were told to get rid of their heavy boots. 'It makes you walk heavily, taking too long a stride,' Ward said, and they knew instantly he was right. 'You have also to learn to walk slowly, taking a great deal of time, and swing a little as you move, not be so stiff about it.'

From that day on Offer instructed the men to walk about the camp barefooted. It was healthier for their feet, for one thing, but also it would harden them and thus reduce the discomfort of walking over small stones when the water party went across the desert sands. 'Try and get us some sandals,' he ordered Ward, who obliged over the next few days.

Offer went with the party because he wanted to see for himself what problems attended such an expedition. He picked his men carefully, sound, unexcitable types and men who would respond to orders instantly. To his surprise McTone and his chums, Sibrett and Skipper, came up saying they wanted to go with the party. They put the request in a manner that was not very pleasant, almost as if trying to intimidate their officer.

But Offer was having none of their company. 'Sorry,' he told them, 'I've made up my party. Another time.' Over my dead body, he was thinking. He wouldn't have McTone and friends on such an expedition at any price. They might prove to be uncontrollable. Anyway, why did they want to go this night? Did they think they might slip away in the darkness and knock up some native woman while the others did the water-fetching? He wouldn't put it past them.

He heard McTone's growling voice as he went away with his friends. He was sure he said something about '... not a real fuckin' officer. Who the flamin' hell does he think he is!'

Offer grinned. Sticks and stones, he thought to himself;

McTone's words wouldn't do him any damage. As he walked off to join his men, feeling a bit ridiculous with the *kefir* trailing down his neck and the long Bedouin robe getting in the way of his stride, he also thought, 'But McTone will soon run out of words.' Then would be the time for action. Comforting him was the feeling of weight in the pocket of the KD shorts he wore under his Arab attire, that thing he'd asked for from Pom, astounding his inefficient batman and driver.

They took their way out of the palm grove in the brief time that was evening in this part of the Sahara, leaving a dubious and wistful Sergeant Walker in charge behind. Moving from the shelter of the trees that had been their home for nearly three days gave Offer a curious feeling, as if he had stepped naked into the open. Out there on the firm sand that stretched almost bare to the main Siwa oasis he felt very exposed, and his hackles rose, a response to an instinct for danger. He wondered if the other men had similar reactions, but when he glanced at them they looked a stolid lot in their Arab regalia. Still, one never knew what went on beneath an apparent mask of stoicism. Probably his expression gave nothing away, either, of the slight jumpiness he felt underneath . . .

He was tickled by the appearance of his comrades. Clothes certainly maketh the man, he quoted to himself, and by God these chaps looked more Arab than Arabs. Some, true, had shaved in their stay in the palm grove and this left their chins and cheeks pale, but a neckcloth could cover that and above they were burnt as brown as any desert dweller. Others, with scrub beards or even well-shaped and flourishing black ones, looked the part even more. Offer had selected only dark-haired men for the expedition, his blond followers hardly looking the part close to.

Ward, leading the way and keeping them to a gentle strolling walk, said the nearest spring was all of a mile off. Carrying a jerrican weighing well over thirty pounds under their robes wasn't going to be easy. Then Offer thought, 'But it'll be dark by the time we've tanked up with water.' It was only around the waterhole that they would have the inconvenience of carrying the clumsy jerricans under their outer garments.

With such thoughts in mind Offer walked sedately at the side of Ward, two Arab gentlemen enjoying the cool of the day with a short stroll and conversation. Behind them, in irregular groups, came the others.

They began to walk through the first of the trees of the main oasis. They were wide apart here, but grew more thickly together as they plunged deeper into the vast plantation. Ward led them on to a track which wound through the palm trees. Here there were also signs of cultivation, with plots of open land among the trees, and irrigation channels feeding them.

Then they began to come upon houses, poor-looking mud-walled dwellings, flat-roofed in Arab style. It was now fairly dark, though the moon was rising, giving more light than Offer quite wished for. They sensed, though, rather than saw, the dark shapes of people squatting against the houses, relaxing after their day's toil in the fields. They even heard the murmur of voices, but no one spoke to them. Offer breathed a sigh of relief. Their disguise at least was working.

After what seemed a very long time, the night now fully upon them, Offer heard Ward's quiet voice, 'Not far now. A few hundred yards.'

Very soon after that they began to see lights, then the sheen of water. A village had sprung up around one of the bubbling springs which gave life to this part of the desert. This was where their disguise would be tested.

But long before they reached the Arab village Offer began to realise that someone was keeping pace with them through the trees to their left. His eyes, adjusting to the curious light, intermittent because of their passage under the palm trees, began to notice a shape that seemed to glide parallel with them and no more than thirty yards away. That sense of danger immediately came upon the captain, and now he watched alertly, hand on the pistol butt at his hip, under his robe.

When he was sure his eyes were not playing tricks with him, and there really was some silent figure pacing them so close, Offer spoke softly, voices carrying far in such quietness. 'Some sod's taking an interest in us. What do we do?'

He gestured, and the tall Ward at his side followed the movement and saw the shadowy figure. Instantly, with startling loudness, his voice rapped out – no half measures about the former medical orderly. It had a hostile sound, as so often Arabic has. Offer, and no doubt the others behind them, had a tightening of nerves at that unexpected flow of words from Ward.

Back, equally hostile in sound, came Arabic from among the trees. But at that Ward seemed to lose interest in the proceedings and continued to stroll silently towards the lights of the village. So did the figure under the trees. So Offer finally said, 'What was all that about? Who's that johnny?'

Ward's surprised, innocent eyes came round upon him, the expression of a man who thought Offer ought to know without further telling. 'I just said, "*Mesakum Allah bil khair.*" That's an Arabic way of saying, "Good evening." '

'I see.' And their mysterious tracker had wished them, with equal energy, good evening, too. 'Next time you pass the time of day, Max, don't sound so cross.' But it didn't matter. Relief was upon him. Truly Ward was capable of handling all such situations.

Quite boldly now they moved into the lamplit area around the wide pool where a spring bubbled. This wasn't Siwa proper – quite a town, Siwa, according to their intelligence agent, Ward – this was just a bit of a village. But it had gaiety in that light, and even looked romantic, so that Offer would have liked to have looked around with leisure. Of course closer inspection would remove the romantic feeling, he knew, but still, there the emotion was and not without good reason.

As a backcloth to the village were the feather-headed palm trees, black silhouettes against a sky growing brighter with each minute as a brilliant silvery moon climbed the flawless expanse of sky. Before the village was the great pool, another silvery expanse but not still, for ripples stretched out from the centre where the bubbling, life-bringing water welled mysteriously from the desert sand.

There were hovels of houses clustered together, but also a few workshops and bazaars, a variety of lamps, some carbide, some naphtha, most of them oil, lighting them with unexpected brightness. Walking quietly and as if casually towards the edge of the pool, Offer and his men could see many people out at rest or at play. Dignified Arabs – no women, of course – sat outside barelooking cafés, sipping their *finganis* of strong distilled coffee, just a few drops in each tiny, delicate handleless cup. The womenfolk in their veils and dark robing shopped and gossiped and doubtless talked of pregnancies and scandal, while the product of both romped noisily and happily in and out of the water.

Ward gave his instructions. 'It is natural for those who have walked long and far to wade into such water and drink of it.' Even Ward's speech, Offer noticed, now had a stilted quality, as if he were translating from another language. 'See, you stoop and scoop up water in one hand, holding up your robe from wetting with the other.'

'And how do I hold my jerrican?' – Offer, good-humoured, the other men coming up and joining with them as if the meeting were accidental and unpremeditated.

'You don't. You let it drop, the cap open. It will fill and sink while you're drinking, and no one will notice it.'

And so it was. The steel jerricans filled themselves, their weight carrying them under, the air bubbling out of them with scarcely any sound. And when they had drunk the cool, deliciously refreshing water, their jerricans were ready to be hauled from between their bare feet, the caps clipped in position, and slowly they waded out from the pool.

It was awkward, here before the lighted village, having to walk with the cans hidden under their robes, but there was nothing else for it. Once they were through the village they were able to carry the cans openly, and then it was much easier.

A feeling of triumph filled the men, walking back to camp. Here was another operation successfully accomplished. There seemed little problem about keeping their camp sufficiently supplied with water, though Offer still had thoughts on digging to see if they could make a well.

All the same it seemed a long way back, the heavy cans dragging on their arms and making the muscles ache. 'We ought to make some yokes,' the Arabophile Ward suggested. 'Two cans at the end of a pole don't seem to weigh as much as one on one's arm.' He seemed to have practical experience. Offer thought they could experiment with the idea, bringing poles with them and hiding them on the outskirts of that village.

When they reached camp it was like a pleasant homecoming. Offer thought, 'I'm beginning to see why Ward's so struck on the Arab way of life.' These evenings were perfect, just gently warm. The soft stirring of dry palm leaves above, the scent of desert flowers, the moonlight over the intricately sculptured dunes around them brought a sense of peace almost unknown in their harsh, often brutal lives.

Fire-cans were on the go in the hollow. A radio, softly tuned, was giving them the Roy Fox band from home. Food was being energetically cooked. The odour of grilling onions, savoury meat and vegetables filled their nostrils and made their mouths water. Tea was up, someone called at sight of them, and within minutes they were all happily squatting round the fire-cans, knocking back the old char and demolishing vast quantities of food beter than most ever enjoyed in civilian life.

The one thing to mar the evening was the absence of the R.S.M. They weren't safe until they had found that back-door escape route. Offer found himself glancing round at the thought, though the firelight dazzled his eyes for the moment.

Uneasily he found himself thinking, 'Some day, if we stay long enough, we're going to have Jerries suddenly bursting into this hollow, machine-guns knocking the breakfasts out of us.' Then he dismissed the unusual pessimism. After all, they were living most discreetly here, and they had sentries on patrol night and day...

He found himself wondering who was on turn at that moment. Well, not McTone, for sure, he thought grimly. McTone was wolfing down the food he hadn't help prepare. Come to think of it, he couldn't remember McTone ever doing his share of sentry duty. Well, he would do nothing about it now, pretending he didn't know. When he had his showdown with McTone he wanted it to be over some major issue, so that McTone would seem to deserve the awful punishment he was to get...

Private Weybright came across to him. Watching him approach in the red light from the fire-cans, now burning out, Offer remembered that curious expression – 'the British'. As if Weybright wasn't.

Weybright carried a piece of paper with him. He came and squatted beside his captain, big hams bulging and threatening the stability of his shorts.

'Sir, I managed to contact the L.R.D.G. squadron on their way to Kufra.' Reception had been bad but somehow they had talked. 'They're at Kharga, resting for a couple of days before pushing on. Vehicle trouble, I think. Captain Leslie sends his compliments and hopes you are in good shape. I told him you were.'

Captain Leslie? Never heard of him, thought Offer, but guessed he'd be the black-bearded captain he'd met in the L.R.D.G. mess.

'Captain Leslie wants you to do him a favour, sir.'

'Oh? What's that?'

'I'm not quite sure. Reception really was bloody, sir. But I think he was trying to tell me they hadn't been able to contact one of their patrols which should have arrived at Siwa in the last days. He suspects they might have run into trouble with the Siwa garrison.'

'And he wants us to find out.' Had the patrol walked innocently into Jerry's arms and been demolished or taken prisoner? Well, that was a job for Ward. He called him over. Ward, he noticed, had even adopted the Moslem prayer beads, big smooth amber things, which he let slide through his fingers as he walked around or squatted Arab-fashion in meditation.

'Tomorrow, keep your ears open for any news of an L.R.D.G. patrol which might have had a brush with our German neighbours. Right?'

Ward nodded, then saluted his captain, only it wasn't a British military salute. Offer was tickled. 'God dammit, he's gone completely Arab,' he thought.

Ward had given the Moslem salutation, a smooth touch of the forehead, the lips, then the heart. All very gracious and expertly done. Now Ward *was* an Arab, and once again Offer wondered how long he would have the man.

Not long, he now felt sure, and when Ward finally decided to go and live native in Siwa how would the Glasshouse Gang get on without him? At the moment Ward was invaluable to them, their eyes and ears inside the enemy camp.

Two days later Ward came back with the news. He'd learned that an L.R.D.G. patrol had indeed walked right into the arms of the German occupying force at Siwa. There'd been a shoot-out on the edge of the oasis, with two of the L.R.D.G. being mortally wounded, three others so seriously hurt that they were in the German hospital tent, but four L.R.D.G. men had survived with little injury.

The big news, though, was that not all personnel in their own shot-up fourth Chev had been wiped out in that furious fusillade of crossfire. Again four had survived without much damage.

That astounded the Glasshouse Gang when Offer gave them the news. They had, of course, discussed the presumed deaths of their comrades several times while in the palm grove camp, mourning their loss though not very greatly because they weren't the mourning kind. The poor sods had got their chips, poor old bastards, was almost the limit of emotion displayed. But everyone had been certain that no one could have survived that concentration of fire upon them. Now they were being told that four had come out alive. Yet if some stupid Charlie accidentally let off his rifle in a tent, that one bullet was certain to kill instantly a comrade who happened to be passing outside at that moment. It gave the men more to talk about than the capture of the L.R.D.G.

Ward told his captain much more, though. The eight British prisoners could be seen if one went into Siwa. They were held in a barbed wire compound that had once guarded a great pile of tyres and other spares used by L.R.D.G. and other outfits. There was still some stuff in it, but it was pretty empty now because the departing L.R.D.G. and Offer's gang had raided it thoroughly before evacuating the oasis. A tent had been installed inside the compound, in which the prisoners lived, and the fence was constantly patrolled by sentries.

Listening to Ward, Offer thought even then that it didn't sound much of a prison. Resolute men could surely wriggle out of such a place. Then he thought, 'But having got out, where then?' The vast and terrible desert surrounding Siwa was a more formidable barrier to escape than any moats or high walls or locked and barred prison doors. Getting out of prison might be easy; getting away from Siwa without vehicular transport – which must first be heavily loaded with tons of petrol, water, food and car spares – seemed almost impossible.

So some of their comrades were prisoners-of-war, and quite close to them. Probably they would be flown out or taken out by truck in time, to end their war days in some P.O.W. camp in Italy or Germany...

Something stirred inside Captain Offer. It was the thought of men being held prisoner, just as he had been a prisoner in Sharafim.

He called to Ward, who had squatted down nearer to the fire-cans, and was brooding into them, the firelight dancing over his features, so much like an Arab's now, under the headdress he constantly wore.

'I'd like to go into Siwa with you tomorrow morning, Max.'

Ward turned to look at him. The private seemed to study his captain for a minute or so, then nodded as if in approval. 'You'll be all right,' he said finally, and Offer felt that it was a compliment, some testimony to his ability to walk with danger and not do any foolish or panicky thing.

Next day, Arab Ward – the name was beginning to stick to him now – was up and about an hour before dawn, and got Offer out of his blanket, too. They performed their morning ablutions, going sparingly with the water because still their greatest need for it was internally and they didn't have overmuch in spite of the nightly water party. Breakfast was hard-tack – rocklike biscuits which they soaked in their tea, and the last of some canned sausages. The magnificent food of their first days was rapidly coming to an end. From tomorrow, in fact, they'd be living entirely on army rations, desert style, which were sustaining but hardly exciting. There'd be trouble from some of the men over that, Offer thought, and wondered if he could get food from Siwa. Even fresh baked *koubes* would be welcome, but he couldn't see how it could be done without drawing attention to themselves in their isolated camp.

They walked while it was still cool, light coming but not yet the rim of the sun showing above the horizon. The air felt deliciously damp, a night dew which would skirl away in seconds when the sun appeared. Then they passed in amid the trees and got the scent of flowers and vegetation, and Offer was moved by it and thought, 'I want nothing more from life than this.' Just to be able to walk in coolness and peace in an oasis like Siwa.

Then he scoffed at himself. 'Don't be a damn' fool,' he jeered. 'It wouldn't last.' It would soon bore the tits off him. What he wanted was Shaftesbury Avenue and theatreland, all the lovely bitchiness that went with it and the sharp minds, the stimulation and challenge of each new role, the footlights and that glorious rolling response of laughter to greet wit well-timed. And afterwards the suppers, raffish friends making the night hours so short, and then bed with some little lovely who knew her timing, too.

Ah, that was the life for him, but then he was a rogue, he thought – didn't the law in some parts still equate strolling players with rogues and prostitutes? He liked being a rogue. He would leave the beauty of Siwa's morning to Max here. His flat in scruffy old Chelsea, not waking till noon, was good enough for him.

Long before they came into the town they heard the *muezzin* calling the faithful to prayer. From the minarets the cry came sounding through the palm trees, the great call for men to pay homage to their Moslem god, and at the appointed moment both went down on their knees and made ritualistic obeisance to the Deity. Ward had taught him the drill before leaving the camp. He only needed to show it to the former actor once, and Offer was perfect. That brought admiration to the lips of the Arab lover.

Finally they walked into the town, and Captain Offer, discreetly peering around, neckcloth drawn masklike over the bridge of his nose, was staggered by the size of it. All previous concepts of oases were fully shattered in that moment.

This was a town of size, which seemed to sprawl for a good mile in every direction. It was busy with seemingly thousands of people – everyone from black Nubians to fair-skinned Arabs from the north, but no Europeans – and it had its own market place with tented roofs to give shade, and bazaars and even quite rich-looking shops where jewellery was sold. Camels, and donkeys, and mysterious-looking Bedouins on fine Arab horses thronged the narrow streets. It was exciting, truly the colourful East and not the Europeanised version they found in Port Said, Cairo, Alex, or Ismaelia.

They had to pass right through the town to get out to the old L.R.D.G. HQ, and Offer enjoyed every moment of that walk. He had no fear now of his disguise being penetrated. When sherbert vendors or pedlars of fruit and violently coloured sweets tried to get him to buy, he just walked on as if not seeing them. When someone spoke to him – it happened twice, God knows why they picked on him to ask directions — Arab Ward was quickly there to say they did not know, they were in from the coast that day, from Mersa and were strangers, but Allah would surely be kind to the enquirer, and both agreed and said that Allah was great and reminded each other that Mohammed was his Prophet, as if that hadn't been dinned into every Moslem since birth.

On the outskirts of the town, where the cultivation began and men were already at work with their hoes, skilfully directing water from major irrigation channels into smaller ones that fed melons and giant pumpkins, banana groves, and citrus fruit, they began to see the outlines of familiar concrete buildings through the scattered trees.

Offer and Ward strolled along as if without any concern at all and finally they came to their destination. The buildings still showed signs of battering, Offer noticed, and there were changes. Now the vehicles parked in the shade under the trees bore the broad white stripe of the Axis armies, and the men who worked in the old maintenance sheds – fine men, with bare brown bodies that rippled with muscle in the shadowed light – sang German songs with a vigour and rhythm that British soldiery would never match.

Everywhere soldiers in German uniform marched smartly about. Again Offer experienced a thrill to see the enemy at such close quarters. Whose enemy? he thought cynically. Not his. He didn't want any trouble with these.

He and Ward strolled closer to the centre of activity. They were not alone – genuine Arabs were hovering about the place like flies around the proverbial jam-pot. The beggars, the pedlars, the suppliants after contracts and jobs were all to be seen congregating outside the buildings. Ward led him by them, though, to a place of lesser interest for Arabs on the make.

The tiny P.O.W. compound was behind the maintenance sheds, but detached from them on some hard-baked open ground about fifty yards away. Offer saw a barbed wire fence strung on stout wooden supports, perhaps eight feet high. It was well-made, the wire very taut, and though anyone could have crawled under the lower strand in time, it wouldn't have been easy and would have taken a minute or so to negotiate

The patrolling sentry would not have allowed them that minute of time. There was only one sentry on active patrol by day, though Ward said they put two on at night and had the compound quite well lit from some electric lamps strung across to a palm tree. The sentry carried a rifle, and looked an alert young German. Under a clump of palm trees that ran like a wall forty or fifty yards south of the compound was a guard tent. Offer could see figures inside it, the guard commander and the off-duty sentries.

A solitary E.P.I. tent had been erected within the compound. With the tent walls removed the thick Indian canvas would give good cooling shade to the occupants, and this would be helped by the tall palm trees over the guard tent. During the hottest time of day, there would be shade from them over part of the prisoner's big tent at least.

There was a rather forlorn pile of boxes and bits of ironmongery at one end of the compound, unusable equipment that the Germans didn't want, and at the opposite end a wooden hut of familiar shape which Offer knew to be the prisoners' privy.

Ward led him into the shade by some prickly bushes bearing little yellow flowers over which amber-coloured butterflies of large dimensions danced happily. Offer, remembering his schoolboy interest, thought they were the Monarch butterflies but wasn't sure and wished he had his book of identification with him, an absurd thought at such a time.

Ward said softly, 'Squat.'

Captain Offer was startled, but squatted. Behind his neckcloth his lips moved. 'But won't we look odd, just sitting here and staring at the prisoners?' Not that they could see any prisoners for the moment.

Where they were squatting was no great distance from the guard tent and in full view of the patrolling sentry. It seemed inviting trouble, just to sit there and so obviously take an interest in the prisoners, but Ward said, no, Arabs were curious people and did such things. It would look quite natural, he opined, and went on further to say he was pretty sure the prisoners had had similar audiences in their previous days of captivity.

The guard on the fence certainly took not the slightest notice of them, and Offer soon felt reassured. In time he began to feel that they were invisible to the Germans, no more to be specifically noticed than the prickly pears around them or the flowered bushes with their fluttering butterflies. So they squatted there and watched, each to his own thoughts. Ward's would be about Arabia and Arabs, and a possible future living the Arab way of life.

Offer's mind concentrated solely upon escape – the escape of these P.O.W.s.

Then they saw the first of their prisoners, and the instinct to help rose even more strongly in Offer. A man who is held against his will is a dejected being and shows it. The life seems to have gone out of him, and the will to live. Offer, jail-bird himself, recognised the symptoms of hopelessness and apathy that seem to attach themselves to any prisoner, like some uniform of identification.

A man had appeared in the tent doorway. Offer recognised him as one of his men who had been on the fourth Chev, a private named Salkirk, though known always as Sally. He was a man Offer didn't much care for, not an unfortunate who had been shoved into clink because of military stupidity but more of McTone's kind. Offer seemed to remember that he had a reputation for uncontrollable violence, excellent in one's army if it could be directed at an enemy, but a nuisance in base camp, as a few beaten-up N.C.O.s had testified. Ninety days in Sharafim.

But it didn't matter what sort of sod he was, Offer's instincts were unchanged. Someone was making a prisoner of him, and by Offer's code prisoners ought to be helped to escape.

Both he and Ward watched as the lean private stood in the doorway, clad only in shorts that looked in need of dobhi-ing, slowly scratching himself under a hairy armpit, his eyes dully surveying the scene before him. Then without haste, shoulders drooping, he padded a barefoot way to the little latrine, no hurry about him, as if he had all the time in the world – too much time, in fact.

Minutes later he came out of the latrine buckling the belt of his shorts. Again he stood and looked slowly round, like a man uncertain of his next movements, then he seemed to make up his mind and slowly approached the barbed wire where the young German guard patrolled. Two 'Arabs' watched every movement intently.

The two men came together at the fence, and Offer noticed how the German smiled a greeting at the prisoner. They could hear them talk – very broken English from the German – and it was all very amiable.

Offer murmured behind his neckcloth, 'Look at that. Just like Sharafim!'

His cynical mind thought, 'The enemy's a friendly chap; our own screws at Sharafim were bastards.' And here, prisoners of their mortal enemy, no one would work the P.O.W.s to death, no one would scream abuse at them and provoke them with intimate and closely detailed sexual activities of men's mothers, wives, and sisters, no one would get them alone in a cell and put the boot in. Better to be a prisoner of the German than of one's own people.

Another prisoner came to the tent door, but Offer didn't recognise him. He too made the little journey to the privy, to be followed by an approach to the young sentry. Then another prisoner showed up, again probably L.R.D.G., and went through the same routine.

Abruptly there was a low warning call from the guard commander, sitting almost invisibly in the shade alongside the guard tent. The sentry jerked round. An Afrika Korps captain, fully dressed in desert uniform of pouch-pocketed tunic, flared breeches, long lace-up desert boots, and peaked hat, was cutting across towards the M.T. shed. The little group along the fence hastily split up, the prisoners to wander towards their tent, the sentry to go through the motions of patrolling the wire perimeter. Offer saw the Afrika Korps captain turn his head to look towards the compound and caught the glint of sunlight on dark-lensed sunglasses. He thought the captain smiled a little. 'He knows. He's not being kidded.' But he was a good guy and didn't bawl out the lad on sentry-go. Again Offer was reminded of Sharafim – adversely.

Now the prisoners returned to their E.P.I. and began to take down the walling, revealing the usual sprawling disorder within. At this activity other figures stirred and sat up frowstily, scratching and rubbing themselves then finally crawling out of their blankets. 'Bet they stink,' Offer thought, having slept in E.P.I.s on long-unwashed blankets himself.

Now the others in turn made the trek to the privy, and a few of them, either more fastidious or remembering their army training, did something to tidy up the mess inside the E.P.I.

At exactly seven o'clock by Offer's watch, a new activity began. The guard commander now marched up to the compound accompanied by a second armed sentry. There was a wooden gate let into the barbed wire fence which was padlocked. The guard commander opened it with a key. As if this was a drill known to them, three prisoners detached themselves from the working party rolling up the braillings and walked over to the gate. They wandered off with the sentry, heading for the concrete blockhouse.

Quarter of an hour later they reappeared. The three men were in line, a tea dixie and a hot food container slung between them. On top of the boxy food container was a pile of flat *koubes*. Walking alongside them, and seemingly on terms of great amiability, was the sentry, rifle casually slung over his shoulder.

When they were near to the gate one of the flat cakes of native bread tumbled off the container and fell into the dust. Instantly the sentry was concerned. They saw him stoop and pick it up, then gently clean it with a dusting motion of his fingers. He replaced the *koubes* on the container, and said something which sounded apologetic.

'A bit of muck won't hurt us,' responded one of the prisoners good-temperedly. It was all very matey, Offer thought. He'd heard before how Rommel's men were always civilised towards their prisoners.

When the prisoners were at breakfast, and Offer and Ward had identified their own comrades in the group, Offer said, 'Let's go.' He wanted to get back to camp to do some thinking. On the edge of the town Arab Ward let him go on alone. 'No one will bother you,' Ward assured him a little glibly. All he was concerned about was going back into the *suqh* to chat up his new Arab friends.

'*Mamnun*,' said Offer at the parting, unable to resist about the only Arabic word he knew – 'thank you.'

And Ward responded as gravely as if they really were two Arab gentlemen, '*Hallat el baraka!*' which Offer guessed probably to mean, 'Don't mention it.' A graceful salute and Ward was away, and Offer was on his own to find a solitary way back to camp. He made it, and no one seemed to take a blind bit of notice of the rather portly

Arab slowly pacing his way under the slender palm trees. Even when he crossed the hot, open desert between the big oasis and their own small palm grove, Offer now had no feeling of anxiety.

In camp the men came round him to hear the news. He told them what he had seen, throwing off his robes because the walk had brought him on a sweat. Pom had char ready for him, which he drank gratefully.

The men were really interested in the information he had to give, especially in the names of their comrades who had survived. But the news seemed to make them restless, and they fidgeted about, and then Palfreyman, who had been a solicitor's clerk in Civvy Street, said with concern, 'What are you going to do about the boys, sir?'

Offer shoved the empty mug across to Pom for more tea. What was one pint in an arid climate like that? 'Do? Get the buggers out,' he said shortly.

The statement excited the men and brightened them. After nearly a week in the palm grove, lying around and doing nothing wasn't all that good, they were beginning to find. The prospect of action keyed them up, and they looked pleased.

'How?' came the awkward question.

'That,' said Offer, 'is something I've got to work out,' though he'd already got ideas simply from staring at the prison compound, and anyway escape plans would largely be dictated by this deadly desert that surrounded the oasis.

The rest of the day he spent detached physically and in his thoughts from his comrades, only breaking from his reverie when food came up. He was planning, and though the main structure of the rescue bid undoubtedly was dictated, the details of the plan took some thinking out.

Squatting by those prickly pears, Offer had stared at the barbed wire fence and thought, 'Well, that won't give much trouble.' A truck backed against it, a rope with an anchor at the end – a log of wood, for instance – the rope secured to the rear of the truck. A quick heave and the anchor would be over the fence and lodged under the barbed wire. A bang on the roof top and the Chev would start away and the whole damn' fence would come with it, and through the gap could race eight forewarned prisoners of war. Getting them out was no problem.

Of course he had to work out how to alert the prisoners so that they would know what to do when the time came, and there was also the problem of getting a truck backed up against a P.O.W. fence.

Curiously, the more he thought of it the less bothered Offer was by the problem of the truck. The rescue bid would be timed for early darkness – that was also dictated, if they hoped to have a full night in which to get away from pursuit – and no one, therefore, would notice the Allied markings on their Chev, driving through the oasis. Offer wasn't even sure if anyone would bother if they did see an Allied Chev wandering around Siwa. The Germans had already brought into use a 3-tonner Dodge, as he and Ward had seen that early morning, and were seemingly taking it on test runs through the oasis, trying it out for their own purposes.

No, they'd leave just after sunset, boldly, openly driving into Siwa, and no one, he decided, would look twice at yet another military truck bumping through the gathering darkness towards the German HQ.

Even when they reached the P.O.W. compound, Offer guessed their arrival would hardly be noticed. The M.T. sheds were there. All day long trucks were driving up to them or away from them, with much manoeuvring which sometimes brought them sweeping close to the wire fence. No, even reversing up to the fence wouldn't create alarm, not if it was smoothly, slickly done.

As for getting word through the wire to the P.O.W.s, that was Arab Ward's department, and should present no problem to him. He would go again to study the compound the following day, he decided, and Ward could do his stuff then about contacting the prisoners.

Breaching the fence was no problem, and with a bit of luck all eight P.O.W.s could leap into the back of the Chev without getting shot by the sentries. Offer began to wonder if they could also tear down that string of lights when they towed away the barbed wire fencing. Darkness would give better protection than anything against flying bullets. He also wanted to see if they could do their manoeuvring at such a point on the fence that their escape would be covered from the guard at their tent by the long, low maintenance sheds. He thought they could. Another thing he wanted to study was whether the German machine-gunners on the flat roof of the HQ could strafe them as they went down the trail in making their getaway.

But these were details. What concerned Offer all that day was what to do with the P.O.W.s when they were sprung from prison. Also, how would the rescue bid affect his men here in their camp in the palm grove?

It was no good getting men out of confinement if they couldn't be kept out of German hands thereafter. No, getting the men safely away was going to be a damned sight more difficult than holing the barbed wire fence.

By late afternoon Offer thought he was beginning to resolve his problems. For a start, his men were undoubtedly getting restive. Another desert journey might do them a lot of good; they were fit again, anyway. He himself did not relish the idea of making the long run round to Kufra, but if they were to escape completely from the Germans, where else could they head? That would mean getting the other three trucks on the move that night, quietly stealing south of the Siwa oasis, well out into the desert so as to be undetected, and making as much distance as they could during the dark hours before the morning German recce plane made its usual run. With a bit of luck, by daylight all four Chevs would have rendezvoused and driven beyond the orbit of the patrolling aircraft.

Offer was not at all enamoured of the idea of taking to the desert again. Personally he could quite happily stay on here in this palm grove; *he* would find much to occupy his mind even if they were here for a year or more. But most of his men weren't of the same mind. They were lost souls without the Naafis and canteen wallop, and drunken moments in native brothels. Offer knew they were restless, but he also wondered if McTone and his chums weren't exacerbating the mood with their growling and discontent with everything.

All day Offer made deep and devious plans. He wasted his time.

Arab Ward came walking into the camp in time to take out the evening water party. He had news. A camel train had come into Siwa from Kufra via Kharga. This meant it had to pass through the comparatively narrow gap between the Great Sand Sea and the Qattara Depression, the gap through which they would have to retire. The sheikh with the caravan had told Ward of a German patrol on guard across the gap. By his description Ward thought there were two patrol cars on regular beat in that wasteland.

Patrol cars? Offer knew at once that their Chevs, even with Lewis and Vickers mounted, were virtually defenceless against the superior fire-power that two such cars could concentrate.

So the Germans had put a plug in the gap, and all his planning to go out via Kargha was to no avail. Offer would have to sit back and think again. Yet in a curious way the news did not altogether displease him; it was as if he had wanted an excuse to remain near Siwa, as if he felt that the safest place for them was closest to an unsuspecting enemy. Anyway, the palm grove was more comfortable.

He got Art Weybright to send a signal to the L.R.D.G. at eight that evening, the time when all the desert irregulars listened in and talked to each other. 'Your patrol,' the signal ran, 'walked into an ambush. Two dead, three in hospital, four P.O.W.s. Am arranging to free P.O.W.s soon now.' He hoped he had established the right degree of nonchalance with that last sentence.

Having publicly committed himself to a rescue operation, Offer now had to get back to his planning. When he looked at the map he decided they hadn't much option but to work out a plan which would enable them to remain in hiding in their palm grove. The men would have to bear with their boredom a little longer.

The trouble was, if they did try to escape from Siwa, their way was cut off to the south, so which other way could they go? North? Little prospect of safety that way. There was an oasis, Jaghbub, over a hundred miles northwest, but if Siwa was in enemy hands, the betting was that Jaghbub had been simultaneously occupied. And if they went farther north still, eventually they would hit the Mediterranean coastline – Tobruk, Sollum, Bardia or Sidi Barrani – and the last news he'd heard was that the jackboot was firmly implanted on all those dusty little towns.

When he retired to his solitary blanket on the soft sand that night, Captain Offer's mind was toying with an idea about laying a diversionary trail away from the palm grove. Another part of his mind was building up that touch of worry about the absent O'Keefe. If they did continue to remain here near Siwa it was vital that the Great Sand Sea route to Kufra be found, just in case the balloon went up and their camp became unhealthy. What was keeping the R.S.M. in the desert? Had he fallen into trouble?

*

Arab Ward seemed in a curious, detached mood the following morning when they went off before dawn for a further recce of the P.O.W. compound. He seemed uninterested, bored with it all, and the only time he did speak was to say he was getting tired of the water-carrying fatigue.

Still, they went their deliberately unhurried way into the wakening town and then on to the compound, where they resumed their seat once more by the prickly pear hedge. The P.O.W. routine hardly varied this morning. The lazy awakening as the sun grew hotter on the big tent, the yawning figures, the walk to the ablutions, then the fetching of breakfast. Dullness, apathy, another day before them in which to do nothing.

Offer was watching every move, and measuring distances with his eye. He saw where the truck could sweep round up to the fence, and in the same moment, without stopping, the anchor on its rope could be tossed over the top strand, and all in seconds the fence would be down. Better have the tailboard down, too, he thought, so that the P.O.W.s wouldn't waste time climbing over it. It would flap and bang, but that didn't matter, and they might have time to stop and put it up again.

He visualised the men hauling themselves on to the metal floor of their Chev, then crouching there as it accelerated away. But they'd be exposed to any bullets from the rear ... All right, they'd build a nest of sandbags inside the truck and the men could take cover within it. Sandbags? They hadn't any. Well, empty cartons would do the trick.

And his memory had been right: making their getaway at this point meant that within fifty yards they'd put the maintenance sheds between them and the guard tent. The two sentries who would be on patrol were another problem, but if he knew sentries they would come together at times for a chat, and if they obligingly picked the north or west sides – likely because that would be farthest from a possibly disapproving guard commander – they would have little time in which to interfere.

John Offer now turned his attention to the posts that supported the naked light bulbs, switched off with daylight. One of the posts was also a support for the barbed wire fence, he noted with satisfaction, so if the fence came down, so would the lights. There'd be beautiful darkness to help their getaway. And the machine-gunners up in their nests on the blockhouse would see nothing of events, he was relieved to notice, because another building was between them and the compound.

'I know how it will be done,' Offer told himself. Though still not sure how they would get away after the rescue attempt. Now Arab Ward must get word through to the prisoners to be on the alert for an escape dash.

Offer wrote a brief message. 'Will attempt to rescue you shortly. Be ready every evening just after dark to escape through break in fence. A truck will be there. Destroy this note.'

For once Offer resisted dramatics in this note; he did not sign it or add 'G.G.C.U.' Instead, he thought it safer simply to put, 'L.R.D.G.' It would be more inspiring, anyway.

He gave the tiny, folded note to Ward. 'Now Max, old son, your job's to get that into the hands of the P.O.W.s without raising suspicion.'

Ward nodded, took the note and rose, carefully shaking the dust from his robe. He was away no more than ten minutes. Then Offer saw him in the distance. He had a small Arab boy with him, and in the boy's hands was a tray – probably a beaten-out butter can – and on the tray was a pile of luscious fruit. Ward was talking to the boy, and pointing, and then he gave him a little shove and the barefooted urchin came trotting up to the fence. Ward joined Offer at that moment. 'Boys come every day to sell things to the P.O.W.s,' he told the captain. 'The sentries don't mind. They're used to it.'

When the prisoner reached the fence, the boy said something and just shoved the tray into the soldier's hands, then ran away. They saw the surprise on the P.O.W.'s face at being given the fruit without having to barter, but he turned and walked to the tent, and then the other P.O.W.s came out and began to pick at the fruit.

One of them spotted the note. Holding their breath, Offer and Ward watched the careless way he handled it, almost as if he were going to throw it away. Then he began to unfold it, and all at once the P.O.W.s were close together in a group, heads down over the note.

'They've got the message,' Offer thought with satisfaction. He rose, 'Good man,' he said to Ward. Now he would go back to camp and get his thoughts on to final escape plans. As he rose he saw that all eight prisoners turned to watch them go, as if they suspected the 'Arabs' had something to do with the note. Fortunately the German sentry did not seem to notice their excitement or interest.

Again Ward did not accompany Offer back to camp. Offer made his own way back alone, leaving Ward to sit around and listen to gossip. Offer encountered no problems during his return journey. He had been taking a few lessons in Arabic from Ward, and was confident he could at least get by with customary greetings. But no one spoke to him.

Trudging back to camp, Offer's first reaction on reaching it was to glance round for O'Keefe. The R.S.M., though, had not come in during the cool of the morning. Offer's unease now became closer to alarm. O'Keefe was a damned long time finding that trail. Something must have happened to him.

Then the captain frowned. Could he go ahead with his escape plan before making sure of their back-door way out in emergency? Offer decided not. They mustn't try to spring the P.O.W.s, then, until O'Keefe was back and the escape route open to them if things did go against their plans. It was vexing and Offer was annoyed by the circumstance. But what else could they do? They couldn't take risks with a powerful force of Germans so close.

He said as much to the men when they gathered round. 'I don't suppose a few days makes any difference to the prisoners. They can wait. But we simply can't move till we know our way across the Sand Sea.'

'Suppose the R.S.M. can't find it? Do we drop the rescue bid?' Tulger asked the question. There was a growl at that, and Offer thought that some were opposed to the project while others were opposed to the idea of not trying to free their comrades.

He said, 'We'll make that decision when O'Keefe does come back and we know how we stand.'

Then he talked to them about his plans, so that they could come instantly into operation if events decided in their favour. There was a lot of loud arguing, of course, some of it coming from McTone, though he didn't seem clear himself what he was arguing about. The big ex-pro boxer had doffed his shirt this day, not a usual proceeding with him. Some men were like that, Offer thought, always keeping their shirts on, sweaty though they became, though most of the men revelled in going about bare-bodied.

McTone had been shadow-boxing for the admiration of his comrades when Offer returned to the camp, and the officer had stood and watched him for a few minutes. McTone had a hard body, tattooed on both forearms and with blue ears above each nipple, turning them into miniature pig's faces. The body was deathly white, unlike most other men's, with blue veins standing out markedly under the skin. Offer saw that formidable muscular body

194

and thought, 'And I've got to knock him out cold.' With one blow. Ah, well, he could but try.

Fortunately, though McTone did a lot of stupid talking he was not in a challenging mood this day, to Offer's relief. He didn't want a showdown too soon now, not with this worry about the missing O'Keefe, and the plans he had to hold on ice to spring the P.O.W.s, though ice was hardly an appropriate word, here in this great heat.

So he spent the rest of the day planning against the time when they could go into action. He had empty cartons taken out to the Chevs and filled and nested inside the wagon they would use. Then he walked to the edge of the palm grove, to the north side, and stood there, his back to the trunk of a tree, looking over the seemingly endless sand dunes that stretched as far as his vision could reach.

When the time came, another truck would go out heading directly north into those dunes, then, half a mile from their camp, would strike off north-east and keep going until they found some hard going where the tracks would be temporarily lost. The truck would make a wide circle, and then return on a parallel course, only this time it would drag camel thorn bushes behind it, sweeping away the patterns of their tyres. True, this sweeping action would leave a bit of a trail across the desert, but within hours, with this little wind constantly stirring over the hot sand, the marks would be obliterated. And according to his plan they had a whole night's darkness in which the wind could obligingly assist them.

Men from the camp would brush out the other tyre marks leading to where the truck turned north-east. So then Offer would have his diversionary track, leading nowhere yet keeping suspicion away from their camp in the palm grove. All that was needed was for their rescue truck, with the prisoners aboard, to drive on to those tyre treads making it look as if it had come that way direct from Siwa. After joining, abruptly the truck would swing off at right angles and head for the camp, dragging camel thorns, uprooted and left by the tracks for that purpose, behind them, again destroying the evidence of their tyre marks.

'It's a good plan,' Offer decided, at length pulling himself away from the palm tree. He couldn't think of anything better, anyway, so it would have to do. Now all they could do was wait for O'Keefe to come through, saying he could lead them to safety across the Great Sand Sea if something went awry with their plans and the Germans came into the grove after them.

O'Keefe did not return that evening. Neither did Arab Ward. Evidently he could not even stand those brief hours of return to the camp and had finally gone native. Offer shrugged when eventually he accepted the situation. He'd been a great help, old Ward, and they probably still could do with him, but now he wasn't altogether indispensable.

'Water party!' he finally called, later than usual. 'Tonight I'm afraid you'll have to rely on my Arabic,' he told them, and led the party out. The foray proved uneventful, and the party returned without having had any untoward encounter with the local population.

O'Keefe did not show up the following day, either, and now there was tension all round the camp at his non-return. Perhaps it was that which provoked McTone into unruly behaviour.

A desultory day passed, with the men increasingly restless and showing their frustration. Their hopes had been raised by the prospect of action, only to be dashed by this circumstance of the absent R.S.M. A further day of idleness began to get them down.

McTone, wise after the event, could be heard putting the verbal boot into Offer around the camp. 'We shouldn't have bloody stayed here,' he growled with a vehemence that grew louder and more uncouth as the long hours dragged through the heat of a particularly boring day. 'We should have gone on to Kufra with the other mob.'

Some more realistic souls argued against him, but not very strongly because McTone had his shirt off and looked far too nasty a customer to cross. 'Well, you never said anything about going on –'

'I soddin' did,' and the big McTone turned on his doubters and intimidated them with the ferocity of his being.

Offer sighed and thought, 'It won't be long now,' and was glad when evening came and there was a need to take out the water party and have something purposeful to do.

This night again McTone demanded to be allowed to go off with the water carriers. 'Why can't us lot go out an' have a look at the town?' Skipper, Sibrett, and Dodge were with him, looking little less unpleasant than their leader. 'Why are the same sods always picked to go out?'

Captain Offer spoke crisply. 'First, we don't go into the place. We also keep clear of all people and buildings, so our trip is scarcely a sightseeing excursion party. Second, the men I take with me know what to do now, and you don't.'

'We could bloody learn,' McTone argued, but Offer just cut him short.

'You're not going, so you can stop arguing.'

To his surprise McTone didn't pursue the matter. Abruptly he turned and looked at Sibrett, and Offer thought there was a bit of an unpleasant grin on the ex-pug's face. And then all four walked off and went and sat together beside the cooking area. Offer frowned, watching them, made uneasy by the way McTone had capitulated so easily. He had a nasty feeling that the big fellow was up to something, and if McTone was up to something it mightn't be very healthy for him, Offer.

Shortly before the water party went out, an incident occurred within the camp that brought everyone up and running. It was a flare-up in which McTone, again, was involved. It was all over in a few seconds, but at least it satisfied one aspect of mystery that had made Offer thoughtful for some time.

Tea had been dished out, the usual proceeding before the water party girded their robes around them and went off with their rusty jerricans. McTone and a few other men seemed to be having an argument, or it might have been just the usual noisy pointless conversation of his kind.

Abruptly big, loose Art Weybright was standing before McTone, talking with vigour and squaring up to the bigger man. Offer, who had been to the latrine area, was some distance off and saw it all through the palm trees. He could hear voices raised in sudden temper, though he couldn't catch what was being said. Buckling his belt he began to hurry to the scene of the commotion, wondering what had caused it.

Almost at once the altercation took on the appearance of a fight. McTone simply lashed out, but Weybright, surprising them all, rode the blow and it made little contact. His own fist, however, clumped hard on McTone's forehead, and Offer heard the pro roar with fury and annoyance. McTone had taken Weybright too carelessly, and now he came in to chop the wireless operator into a mood of bloody regret.

Somehow, though, Walker got between them, shouting to others to stop the brawl, and a few men with good sense crowded Weybright away to safety, and that was the end of that

Minutes later Weybright tramped over to where Offer was adjusting his robes, the time to fetch water now upon them. Weybright seemed a bit off, the captain thought, as if upset by the recent incident. He wanted to know if

Offer had any messages for the L.R.D.G. if he were able to raise them this night. The previous nights had been blank, radio conditions bad, and Weybright unable to contact the squadron.

Offer, perhaps to raise the spirits of his radio operator, said, 'Well, what can we do to cheer them up? What have we done today? Let's see . . .' He began to dictate a signal, and Weybright took it down on his pad. 'Have begun harassment of enemy preparatory to rescuing prisoners.'

Weybright's head lifted slowly from his writing. Offer saw blank astonishment on his face.

'Go on,' ordered Offer with great good-humour. 'Take it down. You would like to buck up the spirits of the old L.R.D.G., wouldn't you? I mean, they must feel pretty depressed at being kicked out of their glamorous Siwa home and having to submit to the rigours of the Kufra trail. So what'll cheer 'em most? Why, the knowledge that Jerry's getting hell, too.'

He resumed his dictation. 'Yesterday ambushed supply convoy from Mersa. Destroyed 8 trucks. Only 3 got through. Tonight intend to blow up enemy M.T. sheds. Now routine, we maintain sniper fire during night on German HQ to cause them loss of sleep.'

When Offer had run out of ideas Weybright replaced his pad and pencil and then looked levelly at his captain. 'Did you say you were a writer before the war?'

A shake of the head. 'No, an actor.' Offer was amused. He wondered what was coming.

'Sir, you've got the imagination, anyway. The one thing you missed out –'

'Oh, what was that?' Offer puzzled. Weybright's face was so serious.

Weybright dictated, 'At great personal risk to himself, Signalman Arthur Weybright put out of action German armoured car with soft transport, taking five prisoners. Recommended for decoration with the Naafi Star.'

Offer began to laugh, and the solemnity departed from Weybright's face and he began to laugh, too.

'Get me two dependable witnesses and I'll mention you in despatches,' Offer promised, and he meant it. Thus began the deception that was to fill with joy the hearts of military minds as far away as Cairo, right up to the mighty Commander-in-chief. It began as a joke, but thereafter was maintained because men of the G.G.C.U. insisted on new victories every day, and Offer solemnly radioed them because he could see they raised the morale of his unit. In G.H.Q. Cairo they'd be puzzled, of course, as well as pleased. Who the devil was this outfit doing such damned good work behind the enemy lines? The G.G.C.U.? Never heard of 'em. Must be a mistake. Tell Kufra to identify them. Probably turn out to be L.R.D.G. or Stirling's lot.

Weybright was turning away when Offer asked casually. 'You had a barney with McTone. What was it about?'

'Oh, a silly bloody argument.' The frown returned to Weybright's face, reminded of it. 'McTone was shooting off his stupid mouth, saying we ought never to take prisoners-of-war but just shoot the bastards out of hand.'

'Nice fellow. What would happen if the Germans or Eyeties did the same?'

'That's what some of us said. Then Mac got on his usual theme about how all Germans were Nazis and none of 'em was any good, though Christ knows what he's got to talk about. They were bastards, he kept saying, so I told him something.'

'What was that?'

Very simply Weybright said, 'My father was a German. He was a prisoner-of-war in England during the First World War. He met my mother, stayed on after demob, married and there was I. Our real name is Weibricht, but my father anglicised it because Germans weren't popular in the nineteen-twenties.'

So that explained Weybright's curious phraseology of some time back.

'I told that to McTone just now, because my father was a good man, as kind as you'll get anywhere. I told him there's good in every nation, and all Germans weren't Nazis.' Reluctantly Weybright now admitted – 'I also said there were bastards in every nation, and I let him see I put him among that lot.'

Offer laughed, delighted at the way he said it. 'So then he tried to knock the teeth out of you.'

Weybright grinned. 'But I knew it was coming and got out of the way and gave him a clout, too. Though he'd have killed me if the other chaps hadn't come between us.'

'He'd have killed you.' Offer nodded. Any day now, when the ugly mood took hold of McTone, he'd come swinging at the captain, too, their ersatz, phoney captain, as the bombardier kept saying with increasing insistency.

'Get the signal off. Send in code, of course.' No one in his right mind would transmit all that information in clear.

The talk with Weybright did much, at least temporarily, to smooth Offer's jarred nerves. O'Keefe simply had to come back within the next few hours, if he was to return at all, because his water if not his food must now almost have run out. Talking himself into a tranquil mood, Offer adjusted his Arab headdress, then led out his water party.

But things jarred that night. For the first time an elderly Arab came wading out to where they were filling their cans, and opened conversation. All that Offer could assure him, standing there In the moonlit water, was that God was Great and peace be to his kind, and *el hamdu lillah, mamnun* – I am well, thank you. It was probably puzzling to the old Arab to be told so repeatedly that this Arab, up to his calves in water, was well when he probably didn't want to know.

Finally the old man went away, but he kept looking back as if very doubtful about them, and they watched him stalk up the bank to the lighted part of the village and approach some coffee drinkers at one of the bare-looking open-air cafés.

When it was safe to lift the cans out of the water, Offer said, 'Come on, let's get cracking,' and they returned through the darkness to their camp at a pace rather less dignified than on previous occasions. Uneasily Offer wondered if the old man would look out for them on subsequent expeditions, and maybe bring his pals over to join in the elevating conversation. Perhaps it was tempting providence too much to take the pitcher to the same well too often, and maybe they should find another water-hole. A pity Arab Ward had deserted them.

Back in camp, Captain Offer made his customary enquiry. 'The R.S.M.?'

'Not back, sir.' Pom, with a mug of char for his captain. Offer's heart sank. He was sure now that O'Keefe had run into serious trouble – perhaps a breakdown, and they were stranded or even all dead by now in the desert. Offer's imagination built up depressing thoughts, moodily accepting his supper from Pom. Well, that seemed to have put paid to plans to free the P.O.W.s yet awhile, signal or no signal to the L.R.D.G.

It was quite a time later that Offer became aware of differences about the camp this night. For one thing, there was a feeling of restraint about the men, for they seemed unusually quiet, and he thought they kept looking at him oddly, though averting their gaze when he caught them staring his way.

The next thing was that subconsciously he noted that the camp didn't seem as crowded as it usually was. He made no count, yet in time the fact registered that there were fewer men around the fire-cans than usual.

Abruptly he rose, putting down his plate, and walked round among the men. Instinctively they seemed to know what was in his mind, and now they all sat and gave great concentration to their food, not a man lifting his eyes to meet Offer's until he had moved on.

By a process of elimination Captain Offer arrived at a conclusion: some men had left camp, and those men were McTone, Sibrett, Dodge, and Skipper. A few minutes later he realised that Busker and Cruiser were missing, too, and later he learned that a seventh man had also sheered off, Joe Bannister, quite a good bloke normally.

His new sergeant, Walker, did unhappily catch his eye. Offer jerked his head, walked back to his plate and resumed eating while standing. Walker came over, and Offer could feel the reluctance behind his approach.

'Well, sergeant, looks as if we've got some A.W.O.L.s.'

Walker said nothing.

Offer recited the names of the missing men. Then he asked. 'When did they go?'

'I don't know.' Walker was very emphatic. 'I think some of the others knew they were going, but they didn't let on to me. You must have passed 'em on the way back.'

'Well, they didn't advertise themselves if so,' Offer retorted. He was building up to a cold anger. Here it was, the challenge to his authority. 'They'll have gone into Siwa.' Not necessarily right into the native town, even they would have a bit of discretion in the enemy-occupied oasis. 'They're after women.' What else would they want on such an excursion?

Walker said, simply, 'They'll get them, too, even if they have to take 'em by force.' Walker was a hard case, but he had no liking for rape.

Offer smouldered. The stupid sods had really put the balloon up. They'd get their women, and he couldn't see how they could get them except by force. Some unfortunate walking in the dark, the randy sods picking her up, hand across the mouth, and carrying her off.

'The bastards!' Yet Offer wasn't thinking of a terrified native woman but of himself, their security now threatened here in this palm grove.

He said, 'She'll know they're not Arabs. With a bit of luck she might think they're Germans.' In which case the heat would not be upon them. But McTone and his kind wouldn't keep quiet while they took turns at rape, and she might recognise British accents from the recent long occupation by the L.R.D.G. and other Allied units. In that case, their goose was going to be well and truly cooked.

Offer said, 'If it gets back to the Germans – and it will – they'll give the place a thorough comb-out and it will only be a question of time before they come out here.'

'We'd better scarper before that happens, sir.'

Offer sighed. 'We'll see what McTone and Co have to tell us, first. But I think we'd better get organised for a move out tomorrow.' If only O'Keefe would show up!

John Offer did not go to sleep, turning in when the others did. Instead he draped himself with his blanket and squatted against a tree and waited while the hours passed silently. The moon was quite high and still waxing, and long shafts of cold light came streaming down between the heads of the palms, beautiful to the watcher, but eerie.

He listened to the grunts and snores of his comrades in sleep, and he thought of what he would do when McTone returned, though not tonight if he could help it. He wanted daylight, with every man there watching while he asserted his right to lead them.

What seemed a long time later, Offer heard a muted challenge from a sentry out on the edge of the grove. Coarse and less well-controlled voices responded, and they grew louder as the men came carelessly deeper among the trees. Finally they began to move out through the patches of moonlight, and Offer could recognise them.

And now he stood up and shed his blanket and walked across so that he was in their path. McTone, leading them, halted at sight of him, his face a white mask shadowed blue.

Captain Offer spoke with great clarity, and some of the men stirred, disturbed in their sleep. He noticed that Walker now made an appearance, as if he too had been keeping vigil, to be on hand if Offer required him.

'You've been out, strictly against orders. Where have you been, and what have you been up to?'

McTone, slow mind, was a second in replying, then replied predictably. He was coarse about what Captain Offer could do with his orders, and it was none of his bleedin' business where they'd been. Then, significantly, he threw in the question, 'What d'you think we went out for? Crumpet, of course!' A laugh from his pals, crowding truculently around him. 'And we got it!' and there was another laugh, and Offer knew there had been rape that night.

He said, 'I'll talk to you about this tomorrow morning.'

'I'll be waiting.' McTone jeered in Offer's face, but it wasn't Offer who moved. In the end all the men just went off and climbed into their blankets.

The showdown came right after breakfast. When it was done Offer, desert boots on this morning, no Arab robe to hamper his movements, just clad in bush-jacket and shorts, walked across to where McTone and his allies were still drinking their tea. He knew his new sergeant walked right behind him.

All in that palm grove that morning knew what was coming, and every eye was on Offer as he walked with unhurried pace to the sprawling group of men. And as he passed, slowly one by one they rose and put down their plates and mugs and came up behind his sergeant.

McTone looked up and saw them coming and at once said something to his pals, then laughed, loud and jeering. Offer halted before him, looking down at where he lay on his side in the sand, a picture of ugly, truculent insolence.

Captain Offer spoke very deliberately. 'You went out last night, all you men here. As I said, this was strictly against orders, and whatever you have to say about my orders, there was sound reason behind them – the safety of all of us, here in this camp. Do you realise what you've done in flouting those orders?'

McTone still lay on his side, his battered face contemptuous of Offer's logic. John Offer, hands in shorts' pockets, thought, 'I've got to get the big sod on his feet,' though he hadn't any doubts that McTone would soon get up when he'd done with this show of insolent behaviour.

McTone said he didn't know and he didn't fuckin' care, and all his pals, including Busker and Cruiser, joined him in laughter. McTone looked pleased at having made a laugh, and was emboldened by it.

'We had a good time, an' what's that got to do with you – *captain!*' A heap of contempt on the title. 'We caught two women and shared 'em and tonight we go out for another couple, an' it's none of your flamin' business what we do with ourselves.' The humour had gone from him with their laughter dying down. Now he was working himself into brutish anger.

John Offer deliberately toed McTone's foot. 'Stand up when you speak to me.'

McTone suddenly came rearing up from the sand. 'Who the fuckin' hell do you think you are, giving orders!' he mouthed, and all around men grew tense knowing they were within seconds of the showdown; and they thought,

'Poor bleedin' Offer, why doesn't he keep his big trap shut!' Big McTone would do worse things to their leader than any screw, because he was that much more powerful.

Offer told him, 'I'm your security. I'm the only one who can pass as an officer. I know the ropes, and while you have me in charge we can keep clear of trouble with M.P.s and screws.' And then he did throw down the challenge to McTone. Very briskly: 'Now, I know you, McTone. You're a bully with little sense. It's in your nature to want to be cock of the walk, and you've got ideas on taking over this mob from me.'

'I bloody will, too,' growled McTone, and he had worked his mood close to the moment when he would lash out and try to inflict as much damage on Offer as any man could do to another human.

McTone's body was weaving a little, the instinctive movements of a pro fighter coming into a fray, and he seemed to have risen on to the balls of his feet. He towered above Offer, again this morning without a shirt so that his body looked repulsively white but hard with muscle and intimidating with its projection of brute power.

And Offer – he looked nothing beside the big boxer. His bush jacket was slackly open, and in some way he managed to look slight, though comfortable living latterly had put some roundness on his limbs. The actor in him made him look physically totally unlike a fighting male, drooping his shoulders a little, slightly bending at the knees to reduce his smaller height even further. McTone must have only contempt for him, must be well off his guard when the moment came.

Offer shook his head. 'No, you won't because you can't do it. You haven't the intelligence to lead – we'd all be back in the Glasshouse or an Italian P.O.W. camp if we followed you – and you're too dumb even to beat me in a fight.'

It's an old trick, but Offer knew them all. Somehow it is expected of a man that he will finish what he is saying before he strikes out. So the ruse is to talk and in the middle of a sentence get a surprise blow in first. John Offer, who had few ethics and no scruples now, did exactly that.

The fury was almost boiling over in his opponent. Offer guessed that the moment he stopped talking McTone would be in to him. So Captain Offer stopped talking abruptly, unexpectedly, and before anyone knew it his right hand flashed in a swift vicious arc that connected with the unprepared McTone's jaw.

Offer was no pro and knew little about punching to the greatest effect. All the same, in the harsh world of the army John Offer had learned something of the art of hurting the other fellow. He might be a long way from being as effective as McTone, but still he could pack a good wallop.

Even so, that blow on McTone's chin shattered them all, watching its effect. No one had expected anything like this. And none, in fact, was more astounded than John Offer.

They saw the swift-travelling fist make contact. Some said they heard the sound of a bone breaking. Anyway, they saw McTone's head jerk round as if in frantic response to awful pain, then he began to turn on his feet and fall, and Offer – not looking so small now – was in to McTone's groin with his desert boots. Still turning on his heels, McTone crashed and rolled on to his back in the sand, his fall watched by comrades astounded by what they saw. One blow, just one blow from this little squirt, and that had done for the mighty McTone. Incredible!

They looked down on McTone's face. The jaw was curious-looking; no doubt it was smashed. The cheek was cut and there was blood trickling from inside McTone's mouth. McTone moaned and something eased between his painfully moving lips. It was a broken tooth. Another followed.'

Offer recovered his own wits, shoved his hands into his shorts' pockets and walked over to where the bombardier lay. Quite deliberately, hands still in pockets, he drove his boot hard into McTone's ribs. In Chelsea his friends would not have recognised him. John Offer had been an amusing, good-humoured man, a bit of a scamp in some ways, but never a man to suggest any sort of violence. An education in the army, but even more so in the Glasshouse – much of it brought upon himself – had changed the Offer character.

He poised, his foot held as if to drive a second time into those unprotected ribs, and his eyes looked coldly round at the startled men. 'Do I make myself clear? I'm the boss. Anyone else like to dispute it?'

Sibrett, a nasty customer, was first to stir. He began to come forward, fists bunched, face hard with the killer look. Skipper started after him – two of them could do for this little bastard ... though, Christ, where did he find that punch? And Busker's huge bulk heaved into the beginnings of motion.

Offer felt two men range by his side. One he knew would be Sergeant Walker, faithful old Walky. He didn't look to see who the other was. That brought Sibrett and the others to a halt. This wasn't going to be several on to one; the odds had changed. Then some of the men showed they were on Offer's side, probably secretly glad to see big McTone moaning in the dust. They called out, 'Lay off him! McTone asked for it, the big sod!' and their tones were rough and threatening, further quelling to the small group of McTone men. Offer knew he had won. But he had to take advantage of the moment.

He raised his right hand to get quietness. Christ, he could still feel that blow. He'd thought for a moment he'd broken all the knuckles in his hand ... hadn't expected it to be like that. But he couldn't show how sore it was.

He spoke, well in control of himself again, quite gently, allowing his habitual note of good-humour to lard his words.

'I should have warned Mister McTone that I am a champion in my own right.' Oh, you bloody liar, Offer, he told himself; but exhilarated by the moment he had to go on to worse excesses. 'Yes, a champion. I am a champion in a Japanese martial art known as –' He paused. Damn it, what did Japanese sound like? '– *hui tsui*.'

Again he paused, but this time it was in respectful admiration of himself and the fertility of his inventive mind.

'As you all know –' That was the usual audience flattery. How the heck could they know when he'd just made it up? '– *hui tsui* is Japanese and means, quite literally, jaw-breaking. Yes, jaw-breaking. Long ago the clever little Japanese developed this form of attack in a scientific manner. It is all merely a question of hitting the jaw at precisely the right angle, and with a fist conditioned to a degree of hardness not usual in most men.'

He was well away, intoxicated with his own words, an actor knowing he had his audience and wanting to spin out this moment as long as he could. But then he stopped because he was more than an actor now – he was a man imbued with a strong sense of danger, and there was danger in being carried away with his own words. He might talk too much and they might rumble him.

'But that's enough of that. Someone put a bandage round McTone's head and tell him to keep it still or it'll set badly.' Pity Ward wasn't with them.

McTone could probably hear and understand now, for he was sitting up, very dazed, but the moan was still issuing from his lips. One hand held his jaw. He must have been in too much agony even to think of having another go at Offer. Neither Sibrett nor Skipper offered to help him, and finally it was Dodge and some of the other men who took him away for first aid.

Captain Offer turned, restraining any show of jubilation. Sergeant Walker had indeed been one of the men who had ranged beside him. The other was R.S.M. O'Keefe.

Offer took one look at that lean, ravaged face and knew the worst. O'Keefe seemed to exude an air of defeat, as if he had lost ...

'You didn't find the way out?' O'Keefe, drawn and haggard from too long in the desert on a limited water ration, followed by a long night's drive back to camp, seemed to sigh and then his head shook slowly.

Offer sighed, too. The elation of victory was completely gone. 'You'll need a drink, R.S.M.' His glance took in three weary privates who had come in with O'Keefe. 'And your men. Any tea, Pom?'

There was no tea for the moment.

'All right, get a dixie on the boil. Meanwhile, R.S.M., some bottled warm beer will have to do.'

'Bottled warm beer sounds just great,' said O'Keefe and proved it by knocking back four pints with hardly a pause.

John Offer said, 'Come with me, R.S.M. We've got to talk –'

'I'd rather sleep,' said the R.S.M. tiredly.

'You can sleep,' his captain told him gently, 'but in a while. We're in an awful jam, my friend, and I need your experience and advice.' Put like that, O'Keefe had to defer the bed which his tiredness craved for.

'We've been planning to rescue some P.O.W.s.' Swiftly he outlined the situation. 'First idea was to grab 'em, then beetle off to Kufra. But Jerry's put a plug across the

Qattara-Sand Sea gap. Armoured car patrol,' he threw in by way of explanation. 'And if we can't go south, where else can we go? Jaghbub?'

O'Keefe shook his head. 'The Eyeties have that. We saw their flag.'

Offer was impressed. So the R.S.M. had been right up to Jaghbub looking for the lost trail. No wonder he was knocked up.

'And direct north just brings us into worse enemy territory. So we decided to wait for your return, and if you'd found the track we were going to spring the lads and trek off across the Sand Sea.'

'You'd better forget about rescue operations then.' O'Keefe's voice was harsh and bitter. 'I didn't find the bloody trail.' He was exasperated as well as tired. 'The trouble is, I don't know what we're looking for. There might be a cairn, and the sand might have covered that. More likely it begins with some permanent geographical feature, an outcrop or an escarpment or anything.'

He shook his head helplessly, mortified by his inability to find what he knew was there. He drank again, but the beer seemed to have lost its flavour, and when Pom came up with some strong sweet tea he went over to that instead.

'So you'll have to forget about the P.O.W.s and just go on lying up here until it's safe to go somewhere.' – O'Keefe, very tired.

'That's what I thought until a few hours back.' Pom brought tea for his captain. A man could always use a mug of tea in that dry heat. 'Unhappily, my friend, events now say it isn't safe for us to stay here, and where the hell can we go?' He looked at the R.S.M. still with the tiniest flicker of hope inside him. That was why he had asked the ex-L.R.D.G. man to talk with him before taking to his bed. If anyone could find a way out of this desert it was the R.S.M.

Offer told of McTone and his cronies' shocking stupidity the night before, and O'Keefe swore in many languages, including Urdu and Arabic. 'Good God, they're not in their right senses! To do a thing like that!' They couldn't have betrayed their presence here in Siwa better if they had advertised it, he said.

'You think the women will know the men were British?'

'Certain.' Offer's heart sank at the sureness of O'Keefe's tone. His last ray of hope in that direction was now finally doused. 'Until now there never have been Germans in Siwa, but we British have been here for years. I suppose most of the Arabs have heard the British accent by now and would recognise it.'

O'Keefe was right. 'So word will get to the Germans that there are still some British hiding in the neighbourhood.'

'Rape's a terrible crime, even more so to Arabs when it concerns their womenfolk. They'll put the Bosche on to hunting down the violators of their women, you see if they don't.'

'We can't stay here, then?'

'If we want to get shot, yes.'

And there was nowhere they could go, with the Great Sand Sea track still undiscovered. 'We're in a dicey do,' said Offer.

O'Keefe, swallowing his tea vigorously, choked a little, then was more frank. 'We're in a right proper mess, sir. A bleedin' bloody hole. Shan't wear this wrist strap much longer.' He gestured towards his R.S.M. badge of office.

They sat in silence for quite a time, and then Offer spoke again. 'I'm not sure — not sure we still can't diddle the Hun. Look, R.S.M., I had a plan. True, it was based on your finding the Sand Sea route, but we can still use it. It just means if it doesn't come off we've no back way through which to escape.'

John Offer began to tell him about his diversionary trail. 'If we can make Jerry think we've driven right out of the district he won't come rooting round this grove. So now, whether we like it or not, thanks to randy McTone and pals, we've got to rescue the P.O.W.s to make sure Jerry then thinks we've moved on out of the area.'

When O'Keefe was acquainted with all the details, he gave his opinion. 'It's a fair old plan,' he admitted. 'It could come off. We've just got to make that diversionary trail convincing. Anyway, I don't see any alternative.'

Offer agreed with him. He couldn't see what else they could do if they wished to keep their skins whole. 'It'll have to be tonight.' And all day they would be praying that any manhunt would not reach their isolated camp before dark.

'It'll have to be tonight.' O'Keefe rose stiffly on muscle-weary legs. 'And I want to lay that diversionary trail myself.'

'That's what I wanted to hear, R.S.M.' O'Keefe would do the job right.

'It'll have to be done in daylight, this afternoon. Not much risk, though – no one'll be out this way when the sun's up.' He sighed, at the end of his tether. 'God, I'm tired. A few hours' kip and I'll be all right, though.'

He walked away, and even now he carried that air of depression, as if dejected and ashamed because he, their desert expert, could not find the Sand Sea trail.

There was that weight in his right shorts' pocket. John Offer placed his hand upon it, a hand very bruised about the knuckles. He thought, 'I shan't need it again.' The men were solidly behind him now, and there'd never be any other challenge to his leadership. He'd better take the thing back to Pom.

Pom was sitting in all the disorder that was his part of the camp. A real little scruff, Pomegranate Face. Still, he had his uses. Good job he, Offer, had once spotted the shiny metal thing amid Pom's kit, though what on earth Pom was doing with it he didn't know. 'Wouldn't have the guts to use it himself,' was his opinion at the time. Just an ugly souvenir, perhaps.

'Here,' said Offer, 'take it.'

He dropped the thing on to Pom's blanket. Pom looked up at him through steel-rimmed glasses. *He* knew – knew how big McTone had been dropped by this much smaller man.

Offer said, 'Thank you for the loan of it, but if ever one squeak gets out about it, I'll break your bloody little neck, understand?'

Pom was convinced. He just nodded and shoved the steel knuckleduster to the bottom of his pack.

The day dragged slowly by. Perhaps there was less wind than usual, but that morning seemed unusually hot. Offer gathered all the men around him shortly after O'Keefe had gone to sleep and told them that the rescue bid, after all, was on, and it had to be that night. He held nothing back because there was no sense in being at all reticent. The men had a right to know the extent of their danger, and would react the better for knowing it.

Their parlous situation sobered them. It was all a desperate gamble, but, blast-McTone, they had no alternative. Everything depended on that ruse, on the success of their diversionary trail.

'R.S.M. O'Keefe will be in charge of that operation,' Offer told them. 'Thank heaven he came back when he did; he'll make a pukka job of it, if any man can.'

Someone said dolefully, 'I'd be happier if he'd found that back way out.'

Several times, more out of restlessness than need, Captain Offer made a tour of the camp. He also found some essential work for idle hands to do. One important job was servicing the Chev that had brought O'Keefe back to camp. Tiffy Jones went out with a party and gave the truck a thorough góing-over. Other men re-stocked it with petrol, food, and water, so that in emergency it could go instantly into operation.

Though where now could emergency send them in their trucks? There was nowhere for them to go.

On those tours of the camp Offer came across the stricken McTone. He was in a bad way, and as the day went on his condition grew steadily worse. His head was bandaged, so that his jaw was virtually in a sling, but it seemed to bring no comfort to the big fellow. Torn nerve ends and the great heat were driving the fellow mad.

Offer had no sentiment or compassion for the man. But for his own swift action, now *he* would be lying here with fractured bones, probably far more of them broken than McTone had. And the bombardier, he was sure, would have had less mercy upon him than he had shown. He'd have jeered and kept on kicking him when he was down – literally would have kicked the guts out of him, Offer thought. Well, the boot was on the other foot, but he didn't put it into McTone's ribs now.

When McTone saw the man who had done him so much hurt, his eyes did not show hatred or vengefulness. He was too far gone for that, the pain of his jaw obsessing him more than anything. He just moaned and looked ill, a powerful man reduced to comicalness by the bunny rabbit ears of the bandage round his head. Anyway, McTone was now the weakest man in the unit. Anyone could defeat him, if he got nasty, with one slug to that tormented chin.

What impressed Offer on those rounds was the way one man looked after McTone the whole day long. Offer hadn't expected such solicitude from such a man, yet he was constantly by McTone's side, pouring water or cooled tea between the parched lips that never seemed to get enough liquid through them. That man was Dodge, one of the raping party.

Dodge was a burly man, a coalman in Civvy Street, so he said, though by the sound of it he spent more of his time in jail than in coal-heaving. He wasn't gentle with his patient, and his bedside manner was somewhat distant from Harley Street.

'Come on, you stupid git, keep your fuckin' head still or you won't get any fuckin' water into your flamin' gullet,' Offer heard him say once as he came up.

All the same, Dodge was always there to tend to Mc-Tone, and John Offer marvelled at it. Skipper, Sibrett, Busker, and Cruiser never once went to the aid of their former leader. They'd just lost interest in him with his fall. They didn't want to know, in the words of more than one man around the camp.

The last time Offer saw McTone, before O'Keefe came reluctantly from his bed to organise his part of the operation, Dodge displayed real concern. 'The poor sod's goin' through it.'

Indeed McTone looked half the man he'd been, his eyes bright with pain, his face – what could be seen of it – thinned as if with agony. He was rapidly getting worse, and Offer suspected he would soon be in delirium. The chap ought to have skilled medical attention; even Ward would be better than nothing now. It was going to be awkward, hiding up in this camp with McTone off his nut with pain. Still, what else could be done about the matter?

Dodge told him, 'He ought to have a doctor.'

Offer said, abruptly, 'Well, there isn't one here.'

'No.' Dodge shook his head, agreeing with him. 'There'll be a German M.O. in Siwa, though, but that's no bloody good to Mac.'

'No; no good,' agreed Offer, and went the round of his outposts to make sure they were on the alert. They had doubled their sentries since that morning, just in case the enemy began to move across from the main oasis.

'Nothing to report?' asked Offer, and each sentry shook his head.

'Everything quiet, sir.'

Well, if the Germans were looking for some stray British rapists their search hadn't carried them this far yet, and if their luck could hold out until dark they might get away with their desperate plan.

O'Keefe came up from his blanket, eased the residual stiffness out of his limbs with a walk to the latrine area, consumed an enormous amount of tea, all ready for him, then got stuck into his part of the operation.

He seemed to work with ferocious determination. He kept saying, 'It's got to be done properly. By Christ, if we don't kid the bloody Hun, we get the chop – P.O.W. even if we don't stop a bullet.' But shrewd Captain Offer thought he was more driven by shame at his failure over the past week than by concern at what could happen to them.

O'Keefe was very thorough. He took four men with him, though Offer also joined him for the first part of the ride, hating though he did the prospect of the hot walk back afterwards. They boarded a Chev in the sandy rift, pulled out on to the sand dunes, and drove over the undulating surface due north of the oasis. Within minutes it was out of sight except when they topped a particularly high sand ridge.

The heat was searing, and Offer quailed as it came in at them where he sat in the cab. O'Keefe was driving. At some distance off – Offer was sure it was much more than the proposed half-a-mile away – the Chev took a turn that was almost at right angles, and then halted.

O'Keefe climbed down. So did Offer, reluctantly. He winced as the heat from the hot sand penetrated his desert boots, and the sun came scorching into his face from the desert. Still, the Germans wouldn't find it any more comfortable than they, and this would be in the Glasshouse Gang's favour, tending to make a search in the desert more perfunctory than it should be.

O'Keefe tramped round with a machete which he'd picked up somewhere and hacked off some camel thorn bushes. His men dragged them together, swearing vigorously as the sharp thorns too frequently found their mark on sensitive flesh, then tied them so that they were one great bundle. Ropes were left protruding so that without loss of time that night they could be tied to the rescue vehicle.

O'Keefe looked round critically. Two men would go on with him; the other two had taken palm leaves from the back of the truck and with no great show of enthusiasm began to sweep away the tyre marks that led back to camp.

'We'd better have a chap out here with a torch tonight, sir. Then your Chev can drive right on to these tracks.'

'Yes.' By torchlight, too, they could do a careful job of wiping out awkward tracks where they joined. And the torch would be useful when it came to tying on the camel thorns to his Chev. He thought, 'I don't envy the bloke with a torch; though, shining it when he hears a truck approaching.' Suppose the truck turned out to be a late wandering German?

O'Keefe drove off to make a long trail towards Jaghbub. He was a considerable time finding the hard ground where he could turn in safety and drag his tail-obliterating bushes behind him back to the oasis. In fact it was only about half-an-hour before Offer moved out that the Chev came in with its desiccated occupants. By that time Offer had supervised the careful wiping out of all tracks leading towards their camp. When it was done, standing there in the welcome green shade, Offer took one last look over the shimmering, dazzling sand dunes and it amused him to think there were now twin parallel tyre marks which mysteriously started then went a long way only to end just as mysteriously as they'd begun. His plan sounded crackpot, but it could work, he thought, and he turned away quite confident before going into action.

They went out to their Chev before dark. The last thing Offer heard from their camp was the moaning of McTone.

Offer took only four men with him. He couldn't use more than one Chev for the rescue bid, and another eight men aboard would be crowd enough in one vehicle. So four came, and two of them manned the Vickers machine-gun mounted in the rear, and one man – it was the reliable Sergeant Walker – stood by to hurl the anchor over the barbed wire fence. Offer's driver was Lashley, the Australian. The man from Sydney's Woolloomooloo did a lot of griping but he was a good and dependable chap in an emergency.

They drove by circuitous route into the big oasis, approaching from the south, and again they dragged camel thorn behind them so that no tracks could lead pursuit back to their hide-out. It was almost completely dark when finally they took the trail that led through the oasis.

Their nerves were keyed up, this night. All the men except Offer had seen some sort of front-line action, but this was different. Before, the men had been part of an army, moving forward or retreating in company with thousands of others. This night they were few in number operating within enemy-held territory. It made a difference.

There was nothing at first out of the ordinary. They ran past mud houses, occasionally through little clusters where some lights showed, then to the bigger villages where water came up from the sand and there was noise and people moving and quite a lot of light. Their Allied markings were clear for anyone to see, yet no Arab on the way seemed to notice them.

They had, too, to drive through Siwa itself, that crowded little town, knowing no other way of getting to the outlying German-held buildings. And still no one in the jostling throng took any notice of them. Their confidence rose. Lashley used his horn to get the camels and donkeys along with their owners to make way for them. It was going to be slow, coming through here on their way back, but it would be just as frustrating for German pursuit, Offer thought.

Coming clear of the town, they almost ran into another military vehicle. It was a big, open truck with parallel seats down the inside, and it was crowded with German infantry. Offer said, 'Oh, Christ!' and he heard Lashley start to swear under his breath. The two trucks drew level, passing within a yard of each other. Offer could see faces – incurious faces – within feet of him. Blurred faces, for the moon wasn't high and the light in the shadow of the palms hereabouts was fitful and seemed to distort objects.

Offer gripped his seat hard and waited for the shout, the challenge, the note of enquiry in a voice. The vehicles continued to pass each other. No sound from the German vehicle.

When they had completely passed, both men in the cab eased the tension out of their limbs with a long, long sigh of relief. Offer felt weak from shock. Right now, if their luck hadn't held, they could be in the middle of a bloody fight with bullets destroying them. There had been a lot of Germans on that truck, and all were armed. Yet it had gone on, uninterested in another military vehicle, not noticing any differences.

'Probably a new guard going on for the night,' Offer thought, and then Lashley said, 'Hope we don't run into the old guard coming off duty when we make our run for it,' as if he had had the same thought.

'No, I hope we don't.' For if there was shooting, warning everyone of trouble, they mightn't get past the enemy so easily next time.

And now they saw the buildings. There was no fence around them, no cordon of patrolling sentries. Ward had told him there was a guard posted within the main building, and the P.O.W. guard covered the maintenance area. Other German-held buildings could look after themselves. The occupying force was small in numbers and did not have the men to do things on a lavish scale.

They drove their Chev in boldly, headlights on, in no hurry, so as to rouse no suspicion. Ahead they saw the string of lights over the P.O.W. compound, the big tent in the middle, the P.O.W.s squatting outside it as if enjoying the cooler night air. So they were alert, ready if the rescue bid came this evening. Well, it would.

The Chev came up steadily alongside the dark M.T. shed, engine beating noisily, but in no way different from the dozens of other vehicles that had come to the area during that day. Offer's eyes were searching for the sentries. If they were in luck they'd be together at the far side of the compound, perhaps screened by the big tent from view of the approaching truck. But they weren't together. Offer saw only one. Perhaps the other was patrolling the rear of the tent. The sentry was ambling slowly along the wire to the left of the camp from Offer's point of view, not far from the guard tent. It could have been worse. Once they'd got back behind the M.T. shed with the P.O.W.s aboard the sentry would be out of sight, too, and unable to fire at them.

The barbed wire fence was looming up. Glancing back Offer saw Sergeant Walker standing balanced in the rear, the heavy anchor – just a log – in his powerful hands. Then Offer's eyes came round again as they cleared the

M.T. buildings and came into full view of the guard tent. A few figures were sprawled on the ground outside it, quite clearly seen under that string of electric lamps, off-duty guards taking it easy, Offer decided. Then their rifles would be inside the tent, he thought, a few vital seconds away from their hands. Events were running nicely in the commandos' favour.

'Here goes,' said Lashley, beginning to turn. Offer saw the P.O.W.s getting to their feet. They'd guessed this was it. The sentry walking up the side didn't even bother to look at the noisy truck.

Their turn brought them parallel with the high wire fence. Offer was craning round, watching. Walker mustn't miss. It had to be first time or never.

It was first time. The log left Walker's hands, soaring gently over the wire fence, then dropping. The Chev continued its turn. The anchor rope tightened. 'Now!' said Offer, and Lashley put his foot down to take the strain.

The fence disintegrated. It came tumbling down as the powerful Chev tore up the posts from their roots. Offer heard a shout of alarm. His head swung. The guards by their tent were on their feet, looking. One man did have a rifle and it was coming up.

Offer turned again, quickly. The sentry along the wire was unslinging his rifle hurriedly, nearly letting it fall in his agitation. Still no sign of the other sentry. The P.O.W.s were running towards the opening gap. The lights were coming crashing down.

Darkness all at once. 'Great!' thought Offer. A shot blasted off from the guard tent. 'Hold it!' They'd come for the prisoners and mustn't leave them behind. Walker would be frantically hauling them aboard. Their machine-gun behind him opened up with a tremendous din. 'Don't fire unless you have to,' had been Offer's instructions. The less noise the better. But a man with a rifle aiming at you was a case of emergency.

A lot of noise behind, men yelling. Then someone thumped the cab roof. All prisoners were aboard. Lashley gave it the gun. They took off, everyone lurching and clinging on under that fierce acceleration. Something hit the inside of the cab roof and Offer felt hot splinters of metal needle through his hair. Not a blow, and only a tiny scab when he had time to examine it later.

More bullets — that damn' guard had been quick at getting to their rifles — and a lot of noise from the banging tailboard. The long shadow of the M.T. hut. Then they were behind it, and safe from the guard.

Lashley belted down the dirt track that led a winding way out through the oasis via Siwa. Here there were only palms for half a mile, long densely black shadows thrown from them by a low, brilliantly bright moon. It was eerie, driving through shadow after shadow, the shafts of white moonlight hitting them in between with almost physical effect. They were tensed, still tremendously keyed up, and yet beginning to relax with joy. They'd done it, by God! So simply done, and they'd got away with it. If boldness could succeed like this, then who was to say the rest of their plan wouldn't come off, too . . .

Round a sharp bend they almost ran into an approaching vehicle. Offer found the glare of headlights in his eyes, partially blinding him. All he could make out was a dark bulk that must have been a big truck. His mind went instantly to the truck they'd passed only a few minutes earlier. Was it the same? Had something registered in one alert German mind — 'That isn't one of our trucks!' And had he caused the infantry lorry to halt and then turn round to make sure?

Both trucks had to clap on their brakes to avoid a head-on collision. Headlights glared at each other. Offer thought he heard someone bellow, 'Halt!' and then Lashley, with extraordinary presence of mind, was accelerating while they still had some movement and was dragging hard on the wheel, almost jerking them round the other vehicle.

Offer, helpless to do anything except sit and sweat and think, "We didn't get away with it!" saw figures standing in that other truck, black shapes against the light skyline, then flame – a lot of it suddenly – and he knew they were under fire from the German infantry carrier.

Behind them he heard their own Vickers go into action and saw red tracer zipping at incredible speed over the heads of the Germans. 'Too high, bring it down,' was Offer's frantic thought, and almost simultaneously – 'Too late!' Some of the Germans were on target. Offer dropped down on to the floorboards, and so did not see the finest bit of driving in the Aussie's young life.

Lashley did it deliberately. He was only a few yards from the infantry carrier's front bumper. He could have avoided it, though, pulling round. Instead, judging it superbly, Lashley drove into the front of the carrier, giving it a mere glancing blow. Not a hard bang that could have halted the Chev, too, and stalled their engine, just a bit of a bump that hardly reduced their acceleration, but it shook the German and had all the infantry tumbling one on top of the other. By the time they had sorted themselves out and could fire again they had a receding target, and their truck, anyway, had to turn in the track before they could take up pursuit. Of course the bump tumbled their own machine-gunners, who went down, but they were up in a minute with their gun belting off, and that brought Offer's face above the dashboard again.

He was in time to see more headlights. Behind the infantry carrier were two other vehicles. The suspicious German must have rustled up assistance en route.

The Aussie was shouting quaint Australian tribal obscenities. It was a paen of victory, a cry of joy. 'My bloody oath, I did the buggers that time! Stone the bloody crows, I thought we were goin' to cop it, my word I did!'

'You can tell me how you did it later,' shouted Offer above the noise of the engine, the rattle of straining body-work, and the intermittent firing from their Vickers. He opened the door, hanging on and looking back. There was a lot of movement of headlights behind, as vehicles frantically reversed in an effort to get round and take up pursuit. He saw their own tracer skipping away, vehicle high, but missing the moonlit shapes of those other vehicles, the bumpy track upsetting the aim of their machine-gunners.

In a lull in the firing Offer yelled, 'Everything okay behind? No one hurt?' There'd been a lot of lead poured at them, but if they'd all kept down behind the sand-boxes perhaps they could have escaped.

Sergeant Walker shoved his face round the corner of the cab, so unexpectedly close that Offer was startled and instinctively drew away. Walker bawled, 'Phil Bowen copped it, sir. Took a lot of lead back there.' He'd died instantly, Walker told him later. A pretty good bloke, Bowen, one of their two machine-gunners. Walker had taken his place immediately. And no one else, down inside that sand-walling, had suffered a scratch.

Offer shouted, 'We'd better get the tailboard up.' Headlights had swung round behind; the pursuit was on. What was more, Offer saw at once there was at least one swifter vehicle coming up fast behind. His men were vulnerable to any gunfire from the rear, with the tailboard dangling.

'It's up,' shouted Walker, and Offer realised he had subconsciously noted that there'd been no tailboard hanging for some time. Walker had seen an opportunity. Almost as soon as they went bouncing away from the darkened P.O.W. compound, Walker had seen the tailboard come lifting up within grasping distance. Walker had grasped. The tailboard swung into its catches and locked. Now they had some metal between them and flying bullets from the rear, and someone had shoved some sandboxes against the tail to give them further protection.

They ran into Siwa. The place seemed remarkably bright, and it was also remarkably crowded. Their speed dropped as Lashley drove, fist upon the horn button, scattering people and animals in their path. But how reluctant they were to get out of the way, and to men frantic to make all speed, how agonising to see the crowd's slow reaction.

A shout from Walker behind brought Offer out on to the footboard again, their pace so slow, there was no danger to him. Back along the narrow street he saw a German staff car. It was driving at reckless pace through the crowd and catching up fast. Offer thought, 'If we use the Vickers lots of Arabs will get hurt and the crowd'll lynch us.' All they could do was keep going.

They had the place in an uproar, horns blaring, headlights on, engines straining to gain every possible yard on the other. People went flying in their last-minute hurry to get out of the way. There were shouts, fists shaken, angry brown faces and furious brown eyes directed at them. Some animals went down, and a whole train of camels panicked and went loping off, shedding their loads and pursued by anguished camelmen.

And the staff car was gaining on them, and behind it another vehicle had appeared. Offer groaned inwardly when he saw it. It was some sort of German scout car, he guessed, lightly armoured and with a turret from which protruded two gun muzzles. He felt they could handle the staff car, away from the populated area, but that scout car would outrun them in the open, outgun them, and be protected against their bullets all at the same time.

His plan was rapidly falling to pieces. More than Offer on that Chev started to sweat badly with this realisation.

Gradually the roadway thinned of people and animals.

They were driving through the outskirts of the tiny Arab town now. The staff car was no more than a hundred yards behind them, still recklessly driving forward.

Offer shouted, 'You can nail that sod, Walky!' and Walker shouted back something unheard in the din.

They ran out of the town completely. Open track, very wide here, plenty of moonlight upon them. Walker let the staff car come well clear of any buildings, so close that someone in it began popping away with a pistol from the passenger seat, then he let them have it.

One short burst from the Vickers, the tracer flashing away behind them. Still a bouncy road, but this time it didn't spoil their target. The tracer smacked into metal. The staff car turned, as if perhaps the driver had also been hit, turned too fast for their speed and the turn became a roll and the car tumbled over and over behind them. Offer's machine-gunners set up a cheer, and Lashley responded to the news with a congratulatory hi-tiddly-hi-ti – pom-pom on his overworked horn.

The elation died swiftly. The scout car burst into view on the trail. It began to catch up. Probably not far behind it was the infantry carrier. All the scout car had to do was bring them to a halt and then the German infantry would soon winkle them out. It wasn't a happy prospect.

Walker kept ripping off with his Vickers, and the scout car gave occasional bursts back, but neither machine-guns got very close to their targets. The going was far too rough, bouncing over the cart ruts. The scout car was gaining, in spite of Lashley's reckless driving. It was inevitable, their being overtaken.

Offer's mind was in a turmoil; the situation had changed so quickly. Only a few minutes ago it had looked as though they'd pulled off a most daring *coup*, and now –? Now, within too short a time they'd be a target for enemy gunners at lethal range. Offer was no man for dying easily. If the going was too bad he'd have his hands up, he started to tell himself, walking in to surrender in no time. And then he recognised a place.

It was the broad rippling spring where nightly they drew their water. Offer found himself on familiar ground. At once his thoughts raced, the desperate efforts of a man seeking to maintain his life and liberty as long as possible. His mind pictured the village, the trail along which they had walked so often ...

'Lash! When I yell out, turn left, then stop immediately and be ready to go back hard in reverse!'

He'd conceived a desperate plan to put their formidable opponent out of action. It was no good trying to run away, he argued. With that thing hanging on to their tail all that business of a diversionary trail came to naught. They had to stop it, and keep it stopped while they got clear.

Offer saw what he was looking for. He'd seen it many a time, and always like this, after dark. The dusty trail took a rather quick bend here, diverted by a wandering irrigation ditch. On their left was a huddle of mud houses, an island of buildings in the open cultivated area.

John Offer timed the moment as they roared round the bend, shouted 'Now!' and Lashley had the brakes on and was hauling on the wheel and bringing them out of sight behind the last house in the Arab hamlet. That skidding halt must have sent everyone in the back for a Burton, Offer had just time to think, and he'd got a nasty jar up the elbow himself, though he had been prepared for the manoeuvre.

Instantly he had the door open and was looking back. Only seconds later he heard, above the ticking over of their own truck, the roar of an overtaxed engine approaching fast.

'Now!' he shouted again, just as headlight beams swung round the corner. Lashley had the Chev in gear. His foot stamped on the accelerator and the truck went lumbering in reverse from the shelter of the house.

It was nicely timed. A startled German driver saw a massive Allied truck moving backwards across his path. There was no time for delicate manouevring. The driver held his foot hard down on the accelerator and tried to squeeze through the narrowing gap between the irrigation ditch and the reversing vehicle. The scout car just failed to make it.

There was an almighty crash as the Chev caught the lighter car broadside on and rammed it into the narrow canal. Offer was thrown out of the cab and fell sprawling to the dust. From the Chev came cries of anguish and a lot of swearing. He got to his feet. The Chev had halted. The scout car was halted, too, nose into the ditch, its headlights still blazing along the irrigation channel.

Offer leapt for the Chev door, and started to haul himself inside the cab, shouting as he did so, 'Everyone all right, back there?' The swearing continued but someone was moaning, too. The last few seconds must have been undiluted hell for his men, he thought – probably all the sandboxes had tumbled on to them. Ah, well, this was war and people got hurt in wartime. He'd have his share of bruises to show next morning, if they got through till next morning, that was.

Lashley was doing things like lightning with gears and clutch. They were moving; no harm had come to them with that collision. A mighty haul on the wheel and their bonnet came round and once again they were bowling along the trail through Siwa Oasis.

'Keep going,' Offer advised his driver unnecessarily. 'I'm going to watch behind.'

He shoved the upper part of his body through the cab door window, hanging on hard in case the door swung open, but it didn't. Everything was working well on the Chev this night in spite of grievous punishment. He could see back to the scene of the collision, now rapidly receding into the distance. He could also see the headlights of the scout car and they were moving. Within a minute they had moved with such effect that they were beaming down the trail after them.

'Well,' thought Offer in dismay but also admiration, 'the buggers have got it out!' Tenacious and tough people, these Germans. But he hadn't thought they'd get out of that ditch so quickly – must have a four-wheel drive, he decided.

Walker's face came round the corner, very pale in the moonlight. He was an aggrieved sergeant. 'You might have told us,' he said indignantly.

'Didn't have time.' Offer's eyes were calculatingly on that distant scout car. At least the manoeuvre had given them over half a mile of lead. He saw other headlights far across the cultivated fields, a whole string of them. They'd turned the troops out at the German HQ and were in hot pursuit of them. It wouldn't be healthy if that pack caught up with them.

'Anyone hurt just then?'

Walker disappeared to find out. John Offer still hung out of the window, though it was playing hell with his guts. The scout car did not seem to be gaining on them; in fact the procession of lights seemed to be gaining on the scout car. 'Must have damaged it in that crash,' he thought, and his spirits rose. If they could maintain this lead over their pursuers they would still have a chance to link up with the diversionary trail and slip off undetected among the sand dunes.

Walker's face again. 'Just bumps and bruises, sir. Fellow called Addison – L.R.D.G. – thinks he might have a cracked rib. He got a tea chest of sand on top of him. But they're a bit peeved.'

Offer found himself laughing at the odd expression. Then the laughter went from him. All at once it seemed as if the scout car had started to spurt forward along the straight track across the fields. He groaned. Whatever had made it limp before had been righted or had righted itself and now it was surging after them with speed apparently undiminished by that crash. And the other lights, the lights from the following procession, were also undoubtedly catching up with their Chev. But then he remembered that the Chev was carrying a heavy load, with a dozen men and several tons of sandboxes ... more weight, in fact, than the truck was designed for.

They crashed over a succession of rough wooden bridges crossing irrigation channels, and the effect proved too painful for Offer who was obliged to withdraw and sit for a moment in his passenger seat.

'What's the score?' He'd forgotten that Lashley couldn't know what was happening in the rear.

'The scout car's picked itself out of the ditch and is catching up hand over fist.'

'Well, sod him. Can we do it again on the bastard?'

Captain Offer shook his head. He couldn't remember any more buildings before they cleared the oasis. Anyway, the scout car wouldn't fall for that trick twice.

Lashley took another crude bridge at speed and Offer rose into the air and cracked his skull on the metal cab roof. 'You'll tear the guts out of her,' he said, but it wasn't an order for Lashley to reduce speed. They had no alternative but to keep going until they cracked up or the scout car caught up with them or by some miracle they managed to give him the slip.

Offer shouted above the noise of straining engine, 'We'll be clear of the oasis in a couple of minutes. If we don't do something that chap'll run us down in no time on the open desert.'

And what was the good of keeping on running if the scout car had them in sight all the time? It was a waste of time rendezvousing with the poor bloke with the torch where the diversionary trail began. No, to go through with the original plan the scout car must be stopped now, so that they had a chance to link up with those red-herring tracks. In fact, Offer thought it was all too late now; nothing could shake the scout car from their trail.

If only they had more speed he was thinking, and associated the thought in his mind with that great load of sand behind, an encumbrance now outweighing its advantages. If only they could get rid of that –

Another damned bridge and up he went and another painful crack on the skull. And – 'Blast the bloody things!' he cried in anguish, and Lashley heard him and then was sure his commanding officer had gone mad.

To his astonishment he saw Offer disappear through a suddenly opened door. For one moment he thought the door had swung open and Offer had overbalanced. His foot automatically eased on the accelerator pedal, and then he realised that Offer had opened the door and was trying to climb round the cab to the men in the back, no easy feat at that speed.

One of the machine-gunners saw him coming and hauled him into the bouncing rear. In the moonlight Offer saw disorder. The boxes and cartons of sand were everywhere, no longer neatly lined against the walls of the truck. A dozen men were among them, squatting with backs to sandboxes, feet braced to keep other bursting cartons and boxes from converging upon them. Offer saw faces desperate with strain turn to look up at him. 'Christ, they must have had one hell of a time!' he thought again, but if they were to save themselves there was no time to commiserate.

'Quick!' shouted Captain Offer, making a frantic but uncertain way towards the tailboard. 'Build a wall!' He set an example by pulling a carton into neater line. Walker began to drag on a bigger sandbox. Offer shouted the swiftest of explanation, and enough men caught on to bring them working frantically. A wall of sandboxes, four feet high, began to go up against the tailboard. Then

Walker and one of the L.R.D.G. men got their hands on the tailboard catches but didn't let it drop yet.

Offer left them to it and somehow battled his way back over bodies and sliding sandboxes to the cab. He looked ahead. For one terrible moment he thought the idea had come to him too late. Then he saw ahead there was another log bridge over an irrigation ditch, probably the last one before they ran through a final belt of palm trees.

He got his head round, his lips close to Lashley's ear. 'Slow down, slow down. Take it easy, going over the next bridge . . .'

It was coming up fast. Seconds only left. The brakes going on, the speed reducing swiftly. A glance behind and Offer saw the scout car was a mere hundred yards away and catching up hand over fist. He realised it was firing at them, and perhaps only that sandbox wall they had built across the tailboard was saving his life, up front against the cab . . .

The rough log bridge. The front wheels were almost on it. Their speed slow now.

'Now!' yelled Offer, and this was the moment, they all knew, positively their last chance. If this didn't come off they were dead ducks.

Walker and the L.R.D.G. man let go with the catches. The tailboard began to fall. The other men heaved and sent the sandboxes toppling over. Offer thumped the top of the cab. Lashley got the message and picked up speed again, while everyone behind him, Offer included, fell flat on their faces because German machine-gun bullets were beginning to hose their truck.

But bullets or no bullets, Offer had to see what happened. His head came up. He looked back. The headlights blazed brightly at them, blinding. His own machine-gunners were scrambling for their Vickers, unusable these last seconds because of that sandbox wall behind. But if the trick were to succeed there'd be no need for Vickers' fire, Offer told himself.

The bridge receded. He saw a hump of broken sand-boxes right bang in the middle of the bridge. The German driver probably saw it too late. He hit it at speed, and that long-suffering scout car took off, turning in mid-air and landing for the second time that night in a ditch. This time it had the appearance of greater permanence.

Offer let go with a cheer, and that brought all the other men up. When they saw their pursuer was right out of it now, they too broke into noisy delight. They'd done it; they'd pulled it off! The men nearest Captain Offer grabbed his hand and shook it and thumped him with comradely enthusiasm on a back that could take anything suggestive of success at that moment.

Still, they weren't altogether out of the wood. Those German HQ vehicles were coming up too fast to give them any real sense of complacency. They would make it, Offer thought, but by God it was going to be a near thing.

They left the oasis and found themselves scudding over sand that hissed under their speeding tyres. Two minutes of switchback ride over dunes, taking a course north of their own isolated palm grove, a black mass sometimes seen against the reflecting white surface of the desert, and they saw a light waving. The bloke with the torch.

Lashley flicked his own battered headlights on and off, doubtless mightily reassuring to their comrade with his light. They came up to him with a rush, saw his white face in their headlights, then Lashley, slowing, was carefully running on to twin tyre tracks which started abruptly on the smooth desert surface. Only a few yards, then he pulled left and halted.

They all knew the drill. The bloke with the torch shone it where their tracks turned off, and someone with a palm leaf began to smooth out the tyre marks were they diverted. Within seconds there was no sign of any vehicle having turned off.

R.S.M. O'Keefe was there, hauling the big bundle of camel thorn up to the Chev and tossing ropes into the back for men to hold. Everyone worked at frantic speed. It was all done in less than two minutes, and all that time they watched with anxious eyes back towards the main oasis.

Headlights suddenly showed behind, lifting into the sky like twin searchlights as some vehicle breasted a rise. Their pursuers must have cleared the oasis. Quicker than he'd reckoned on, Offer thought. They hadn't two minutes left to them, and they couldn't make the security of their own palm groves in that short time.

'Get going!' roared Offer, and everyone scrambled aboard. Lashley got them moving in sand that was a bit soft hereabouts, going through the gears cautiously because he didn't want to start a wheelspin. Their slow start made everyone feel frantic.

'Lights out!' snapped Offer. They could progress by moonlight now. Lashley's hand flipped up the switch. Their lights died instantly. No light to betray them now ... except moonlight. No one could miss them on that brilliantly silvered bare desert.

More headlights behind, and the leading pair were creeping up a dune and once they came over it they'd catch the Chev in the full glare ...

Their truck began to run downhill at speed. The pursuing headlights were obscured suddenly by an intervening sandhill. They'd run into a hollow, Offer thought, and decided to take a risk.

'Halt! Switch off!' Lashley had the truck silent and still immediately. 'No talking – no noise now!'

They all sat in attitudes of frozen life, every eye looking across the moonlit rolling dunes, every man straining his ears for significant sound.

They heard engines. They were roaring furiously, driven

on by vengeful men, made wrathful by the impudence of that raid. They'd be following the tracks in their headlights, Offer thought – no difficult matter. In fact with that moon above even headlights weren't needed to see that deep rutted trail across an otherwise unflawed desert.

The noise grew to a crescendo. The leading German vehicle must be level with them, probably only two hundred yards away, a mere shoulder of sand separating British from German. They caught the white radiance moving beyond the rolling sandbank, and could watch the progress of the vehicle as it tore on past them.

Past them. It didn't stop, didn't hesitate. Nothing had aroused suspicion. Away it went, the noise dying away in the distance. Then another sound took up, the second pursuing German. This too came breasting the rise beyond, moving in its pool of reflected headlights so that they could track its progress beyond the ridge. And that too went on without halt, and so did the next, and the next. In all five vehicles went belting by along the false trail, and not one hesitated and turned and found them sitting quietly in their hollow.

'They'll have mucked up the track proper now,' thought Offer with relief, all his old good-humour back now he could relax. It would be instinctive for the drivers of those German vehicles to ride over their trail – no reason why they shouldn't, anyway – and by this time all those vehicles would have churned up the sand so that no one would notice where any other vehicle had turned aside. And now they were hurrying through the night, following the trail O'Keefe had left earlier.

Offer said to his driver, 'They're going to wonder, after a while, what sort of a truck we're driving, always to keep ahead of them.' It would astonish the Germans, but what else could they do but keep driving furiously along the false trail? Hour after hour racing along, then finally losing the trail on the hard ground, and probably waiting for daylight and then more hours of questing round like baffled hounds with never any more tracks to see. O'Keefe, he was sure, would have done a good job of obliterating his tyre marks back to the palm grove.

'I think,' remarked Captain Offer when the silence of the desert had completely returned, 'we could go back to camp now, Lash, my old Aussie. And there I think we could knock back the last of our beer in celebration, don't you?'

'Too bloody right,' agreed Lashley, and away they went, dragging the camel thorn behind them, until they saw the palm grove looming up ahead. They turned right then and drove up to the rift in the sand, where the Chev was quickly bedded down for the night under its camouflage netting. Back to the camp, men sweeping out their footmarks all the way. All the same, Offer decided he'd be up at first light with a party to make sure nothing had been missed in the darkness.

Camp. Men waiting for them in darkness. No fire-cans this night, not even in their hollow. The stink of burning petrol could carry a long way over the desert, and this wasn't the night to take any sort of risks.

Some moonlight in patches, though, and after a while their eyes got used to the uncertain light quite remarkably. Anyway, light or no light, the whole camp was jubilant, in an uproarious mood because of their night's success, and they'd have found where the celebration liquor was kept even if there'd been no moonlight or light at all.

The drinking began, but Offer kept it under control. No drunks were going to draw attention upon them this night, he told them flatly, and the men, rough customers though most of them were, agreed with him and behaved with commendable restraint.

The four L.R.D.G. men came in for a lot of hand-shaking and welcome, of course, and they certainly were the most delighted men in the camp. 'When we got your note we didn't know whether to believe it,' one of them told Offer, drinking together. He'd been introduced as Phil Maye, a sergeant who had known O'Keefe in the days of that man's glory when he too had held sergeant's stripes in the L.R.D.G. 'A first-class navigator,' O'Keefe told his captain some time later. Apparently one of the best.

They talked until midnight, a happy camp. Everyone was sure Offer's plan would succeed. The Germans would drive right on to Jaghbub, everyone was firmly convinced, and they'd be utterly baffled at the way a clumsy old Chev could outrun them and eventually give them the slip somewhere en route. It tickled the men to think of their enemies fruitlessly pounding all through the night on a false trail, and all were certain it would never occur to the Germans to return so close to Siwa to look for the daring raiders.

'It's the last place they'll think to look,' more than one man said exultantly, and Offer thought, drily, 'That's why I picked it.' He also wondered how long this honeymoon feeling would last, how long before even this safe hide-out began once more to pall upon the men and make them fret and want some activity. What diversion could he provide next time for them to dissipate any possible boredom? That gave him an idea. He called Weybright over to him.

'Better get a signal away to Kufra to tell them what we've accomplished tonight.'

Weybright drew out his pad and pencil. He had a good sense of humour as well as being an intelligent man. 'It will be in modest and restrained terms like the last one, sir?'

'Of course.' Offer looked his surprise, as if anything else was beyond his thoughts. 'Let's see. How do I begin?' Then he began to dictate.

' "Have rescued four L.R.D.G. P.O.W.s and four of my own men." ' He interrupted himself here. 'Better get the names of the L.R.D.G. blokes and send them off – Kufra will want them.'

He resumed the signal. ' "Heavy fighting occurred resulting in death of one of my men and some injuries. In running fight destroyed –" ' He paused. Scout car had an unimpressive sound. ' "– one armoured car and some soft transport." '

It didn't sound good enough for Offer, so after giving the matter full mental debate he changed his mind. 'Make that two armoured cars and a column of soft transport.' After all they had twice ditched the scout car, so why not make it two?

'Yes, sir.'

Offer continued, ' "Intend to remain in vicinity of Siwa to maintain harassment of German garrison." '

Weybright appeared to be taking a long time getting that short sentence down. Offer asked, 'What's all that you're writing?'

Weybright cleared his throat and read back the last of the signal. 'Intend to remain in vicinity of Siwa to maintain harassment of German garrison, now thoroughly demoralised by continuous night attacks." '

Offer gave approval with a nod of his head. 'Now, that's good. I was just going to dictate that information myself. But just add one thing more. "– continuous night attacks and mounting casualties." '

Between them they wrote a nice piece, mainly fiction, which went off to delight Kufra, Cairo, and several other places in the Middle East. Later Weybright came back with a congratulatory signal and a request from Kufra, relaying a message from GHQ Cairo, asking Offer to identify himself and his unit.

Offer looked at Weybright. Moonlight under trees did not allow a man's expression to be easily read. He wondered how Weybright had handled that situation.

'I kept replying, "Please repeat, reception getting worse." ' The radio operator supplied the answer to Offer's thought.

'Good man.' Offer knew now he could always rely upon the big signaller to handle delicate situations, and never again worried about Weybright.

Finally the party broke up. Contented men, only slightly drunk, took to their blankets and slept noisily, four happy L.R.D.G. men among them. R.S.M. O'Keefe went the rounds of the outposts, reporting back to Captain Offer before going off to his blanket. Offer was feeling some of his bruises now, but still retained a little of the euphoria that had held him from the moment they realised they had diddled the Germans.

O'Keefe found him, though the camp was now in greater darkness because the moon rode high and cast solid shadows from the tops of palm trees. 'That you, sir?'

'Yes, R.S.M.' Offer got to his feet, aching a bit. 'Everything all right?'

'Everything quiet, sir. We've nothing to worry about tonight, I think.'

'No, nothing to worry about.'

O'Keefe lingered. 'Just wish we had that back-door route known to us.'

'Across the Sand Sea?' (O'Keefe still felt as if he had let the side down.) But it wasn't likely to be a concrete highway through the treacherous sand. 'Still worries you, eh?'

'A bit,' O'Keefe admitted. 'I like to feel I can slip out of a tight corner if I'm pressed, and here – well, we wouldn't stand much chance if Jerry got wind of us here.'

'No. Let's hope he doesn't rumble us. Right now we certainly seem to have thrown him off the scent.'

They parted soon after that, O'Keefe to the patch of sand that was his bed, John Offer for a last minute visit to the latrine area.

He found his way in the shadowy darkness to the place. Someone else was standing there. A minute later, when

Offer turned to go he was attacked by a rabbit. He felt a stunning blow to his neck, a sick-making chop, a rabbit-punch, he managed to think, falling yet turning to see what had hit him.

The rabbit was standing there, silhouetted against a patch of night sky. It stood six foot two and had big white ears. It had a narrow face between white cheeks, and Offer saw the rabbit's eyes were filled with murderous fury.

The rabbit's paw caught his chin as he was going down, his head jerked almost off the spinal cord and consciousness slipped completely from him. His last thought before going out was that a hot pain was developing in his ribs...

The moon was shining on John Offer when he began to stir and come to consciousness. There was a scab of blood on his cheek where it had run from his mouth. He could see out of one eye only, the other puffed up and closed completely. His body cried against the torture of fresh bruises as he tried to stretch cramped muscles, and he relaxed and groaned and went off into unconsciousness again.

There was no moon the next time he came to, but it was still night and so dark that at first Offer thought both eyes were closed. Over a period of many minutes he gradually focused his confused thoughts and pulled himself together. Bloody rabbit, he thought.

He got on to his knees and rested a long while and the fire in his body told of a boot going in again and again. Probably cracked ribs. But he couldn't lie there. Somehow he got to his feet and began to walk slowly and painfully to where men slept. The luminous face of his watch told him it was nearly five o'clock, very close to dawn. He began to sweat with pain and knew he was going to be sick any moment. Never in his life had he known such pain, never did he want to experience it again.

In the dark he fell over one of his men who woke and grabbed him.

Offer said painfully, through puffed up lips, 'Okay, soldier. It's me, Captain Offer.'

'Anything wrong?'

'Find R.S.M. O'Keefe. Bring him to me.' Offer sat down and stayed down, the strength gone from him, his body one mighty pulsating bruise. The man went off. O'Keefe was suddenly shaking him, talking to him, a torchlight shining on his face.

'Christ, you're in a mess! What happened?'

Offer told him. 'A rabbit was waiting for me in the lats. It knocked me down and kicked me. Big ears, rabbit's.'

O'Keefe's voice behind the bright light, kindly: 'You're delirious. No rabbits here.' None powerful enough to do all this damage to Offer, anyway. Offer straightened a little. 'McTone,' he told them. 'He was the rabbit. Did me in ... put the boot in ... hard.' Oh, Lord, how hard he'd done it! Got his own back thoroughly. But he wouldn't be allowed to get away with it; Offer would see to that. 'Get McTone, R.S.M. Hold him till daylight. He's ... dangerous.' Offer's head slipped on to his chest, consciousness departing yet again.

The R.S.M. roused some men and got their officer on to a blanket. Then a very tight-lipped R.S.M. took several strong men and went looking for McTone. They searched by torchlight at first and failed to find him. Then O'Keefe wakened Dodge and asked him if he'd seen McTone. Dodge said not since last night, he'd been asleep, and was something up?

'Just given the Old Man the most thorough working over I've seen anywhere outside the Glasshouse. Come on, help find your pal.'

They were still searching when daylight came. Then O'Keefe roused the entire Glasshouse Gang and made a thorough search of the grove. Still no sign of the big bombardier. Growing more and more perplexed as time passed, the R.S.M. made one final effort. He had every man string out in line and walk the full width of the palm grove. When they had combed the whole place thoroughly, O'Keefe had to admit that McTone was no longer there.

He went back to Offer and got him cleaned up, and the process brought returned life to his captain. Some hot sweet tea did wonders for Offer and his one visible eye began to look bright again. O'Keefe gave his report. 'McTone's not here, sir. He's scarpered.'

'Scarpered?' The big man with the bunny rabbit ears? Offer's brain was working immediately. 'Have you questioned the sentries?'

'Yes, and no one saw him leave. But that's not surprising. When the moon went down anyone could walk between the sentries without being seen.'

'Help me up.' The situation was urgent. Offer wondered if O'Keefe fully appreciated the gravity of the situation. 'R.S.M., if McTone's left this camp, where can he have gone?'

'If we're lucky he's wandering across the desert, lost.' Offer had done the gap-toothed sergeant-major an injustice; O'Keefe was alive to their perils as much as he. 'If not, my bet is that McTone's somewhere inside Siwa Oasis looking for a doctor.'

'You think that's why he's gone off?'

'What else? Bloody terrible jaw you gave him. Probably doesn't give a damn what happens just so long as he can get medical attention. My bet is he's tramping on to the M.O. at the German HQ.'

Offer nodded. O'Keefe had expressed the situation exactly. He thought, 'The Arabs will wonder what the devil's happening, seeing Mac walking by with his bunny ears.'

Offer gratefully accepted more tea from Pom who couldn't keep his fascinated eyes off his commanding officer's battered features. 'I've lost my boyish good looks, haven't I, Pom?' Offer said through cracked and swollen lips, humour not entirely quenched by pain.

Pom agreed with him. 'Cor, not 'arf,' and withdrew with obvious reluctance.

'You know what this means, R.S.M.?' O'Keefe thought he did. Offer spoke their thoughts aloud. 'He'll give himself up to the Germans. They'll be astonished, one Britisher turning up like that. They might suspect other British troops are hanging around, too, which means we're not as safe here as we thought we'd be.'

'Sod McTone!' Very fervently from the R.S.M.

'Even worse, Mac will talk or be persuaded to talk.' A man in such need of medical attention would tell them anything they wanted to know to get relief from pain. The Germans would know how to exploit such a situation.

'So he'll tell them we are here and they'll come out in force.' A ring of mortars round the grove; perhaps some field guns ranging on them, and they'd be driven out in no time. It was hardly the place for a successful stand.

O'Keefe asked, simply, 'What do we do? We've got the trucks.'

'All right, we've got the trucks, but where can we go in them?' Just nowhere. The alternatives seemed to be to fight it out here in the shade of the palm trees or fight it out in the desert where there was no shade. But Offer knew in the end they'd make a run for it over the desert. It wasn't in man's nature not to run, even at the price of great discomfort, if only to buy a few more hours of time.

Captain Offer spoke as briskly as his bruised face would permit. 'Put more men on watch. The moment they see anyone coming, out we go in the trucks.'

'That might be too late.'

'Any time's going to be too late, I think. Let's hang on, though, just in case we've got it wrong and McTone isn't in German hands right now. He might be lost in his delirium out there.' His head nodded towards the open desert. Mac wouldn't last long if he was. 'So don't let's panic and bolt for it unnecessarily.'

O'Keefe said, 'I suppose you're right,' but he was dubious. It was no good disguising the fact that they had never been in a tighter or more unenviable situation.

Offer began to walk round the camp, trying to work off his stiffness. The men knew all about McTone, but for the moment their captain did not tell them the full implications of the bombardier's desertion. No need to get them worked up unnecessarily. There was just that ray of hope still to cling to, that McTone hadn't given himself up to the enemy.

The L.R.D.G. men were stirring and yawning and getting up now. They hadn't been wakened for the search, enough Glasshouse men being available without them. They looked with curiosity at the battered captain limping slowly by, but didn't know him well enough to ask what had hit him.

O'Keefe came back from the perimeter guard. 'All quiet,' he said, but of course it would be quiet, right up to the last minute. Armoured cars and infantry carriers would only take two or three minutes to sweep out of Siwa Oasis and cross the half-mile stretch of sand to their palm grove. If Offer's men had to leave they would have to withdraw in a mighty hurry. But the Chevs were ready; the camouflage nets could be cast off without holding up their departure. They'd have time to steal away while the enemy was cautiously recce-ing the palm grove.

The hours passed. The sun climbed and beamed down upon them, and though they had shade it grew very hot where they sat or lay quietly under the palms. By midday, with no move from an enemy, the ray of hope began to widen. Could it really be, after all their fears, that Mac hadn't gone in to Siwa? Had they nothing to worry about?

Tiffin came up and everyone ate heartily, all except Offer who found masticating a trying business. Shortly afterwards there was an alarm.

A sentry came doubling up to O'Keefe. 'Someone's heading towards us from Siwa.'

'One man?' O'Keefe was startled.

'An Arab – coming this way.'

'One man.' O'Keefe looked at his captain and repeated the word thoughtfully. 'One man shouldn't give us much trouble.' He went off with the sentry and a dozen men to lie in wait for the intruder.

Offer thought, 'It's probably the owner of this grove, coming to check on his date harvest.' Why had he to pick this day to visit them?

But it wasn't the palm tree owner. They heard sounds of men coming through the grove towards them, and waited, hands on guns. But it was only the R.S.M. and party returning. With them was an Arab. Offer recognised him immediately.

'Ward!' Their errant medical orderly had returned. He was also walking very briskly in spite of all he had said about Arab gents being leisurely people.

'You gave us a scare, Ward, my lad.'

'Did I, sir?' Ward's face looked vaguely into his captain's. Then he recollected why he had returned. 'Sir, the Germans have picked up McTone.'

Crash went Offer's hopes at that. Until that moment he hadn't realised how much he had built on McTone's not being in German hands. But hope had been misplaced. The big fellow was a captive, after all. How soon before Jerry came?

'Where is he?' As if that was important now.

'He's in their field hospital.' Ward must have done some good scouting or have established a neat intelligence service within the hospital area, for he continued, 'He's unconscious, sir. He collapsed and some Arabs told the

Germans and they came out with a truck and took him in. Now they're waiting for him to come to so that they can question him.'

Offer nodded, then regretted it, a stab of pain hitting his injured neck. So McTone's unconsciousness had given them a brief reprieve. But he wouldn't stay unconscious for ever, and when he came to they wouldn't be long in getting the truth out of him.

Before Offer gave the order for them all to abandon camp – what else was there to do now? – he had to satisfy one little piece of curiosity. 'Why have you returned?' Just to warn them? Big of Ward if that was so.

Ward was very frank. Not bulsh about devotion to his comrades and coming out to save them. 'You don't think I can stop in Siwa if McTone starts to talk? He's bound to remember I'm here, living Arab, and how long before they pick me up if they started to search for me?'

'Well, we could do with a medical orderly again,' Offer told him and looking at that face Ward nodded emphatic agreement. 'Gather the men round, R.S.M.'

So the men gathered round, the L.R.D.G. types among them, and Offer made his last speech before pulling out of the grove.

'Looks as if our nice little plan's gone for a Burton, chaps. McTone's upset everything – no holing up here in comfort while Jerry wastes his time searching for us as far away as Jaghbub.' He explained about Mac being in the German hospital tent. 'So, though we've nowhere to go, I think the best thing is for us to take our trucks and get a lead on the Germans before they turn up.'

Everyone agreed with him. Run for it, keep alive a bit longer. One never knew. O'Keefe began to rattle off orders. Every man on the trucks within three minutes. Take what they absolutely needed, and leave behind everything else.

There was confusion, men beginning to turn, to talk, to shout things to each other, what they needed to take, what mustn't be forgotten, and who was going to recall the sentries. Everyone seemed to start running and all in different directions, so that Captain Offer hardly heard the voice, 'But what about the Great Sand Sea route?'

At that moment something whined through the trees. For a lot of the men it was a familiar sound and instantly they dropped flat on their faces. It was followed by the crack of a rifle going off, then the sound of many rifles but also machine-guns rattling away and bullets whizzed dangerously overhead and dug flakes out of inoffensive palm trees.

Offer said to someone next to him – he didn't know who: 'Looks as if Jerry's arrived.' Everything too late now? He heard their own machine-guns, Brens firing from the perimeter, and then R.S.M. O'Keefe came crashing up from somewhere and threw himself alongside Offer.

'They came out of the main oasis – Jerry – a minute ago. They've got armoured cars, mortars, and hundreds of infantry. They're moving round to outflank us.'

Captain Offer showed energy at that. He clambered to his feet, though the effort nearly killed him, and oblivious to the flying lead marched most resolutely out towards where their trucks lay hidden. It cost him a lot, that effort, but it had to be made if he were to escape death or imprisonment.

As he walked he shouted, 'Come on, everyone. On your feet! Let's make a break for it. R.S.M., give us two minutes then pull back the sentries.'

He took control quite briskly, and had everyone going at the double instantly. Offer did not try to keep up with them; in fact his pace slowed as the pain hit his bruised ribs. One man only kept pace with him, the fellow he'd spoken to a few seconds ago, he thought. Now he had a look at him. It was one of the L.R.D.G., their sergeant. Offer ought to have remembered his name; O'Keefe had said he was an absolutely first-class desert navigator. Maye, that was it, Sergeant Phil Maye. Back of Offer's mind was the thought that Maye had said something interesting, earlier, something he ought to have paid more attention to ...

A deafening crash near to them, and a tree reeled as a mortar bomb lobbed into the grove and went off. Smoke, and then fire as the dry palm leaves on the ground ignited.

Captain Offer staggered as the blast hit him, then the smoke rolled over him and he choked and coughed and it was hell to his ribs. He had to halt, smoke or no smoke and Sergeant Maye halted too.

More bombs, deafening them, fountains of sandy soil erupting, trees crashing and palm tops falling towards them.

'Here, let me give you a hand.' Phil Maye began to drag him along and it was very painful. The place was blazing all round them now – well, not all round; Maye was finding a way through the flames.

Some men seemed to skip through the fire carrying a couple of Bren guns. The outposts, recalled by R.S.M. O'Keefe. The Germans wouldn't be long, following up. Maybe they were already in a position to shoot at the trucks as they accelerated away; then Offer, still keeping his senses, decided they hadn't had time to get into position.

Bullets positively screaming around them now; a wonder they weren't hit. And the mortar-pounding increasing in intensity. Just erupting earth and choking smoke, fire and deafening noise.

Offer, right on the edge of the burning grove, had to halt. His bruises were too much for him. 'You go on,' he told the sergeant. Good chap for staying with him; none of his own bastards had done that. Ahead he could see a Chev pulling up on to a sand ridge. What if they all went off without him? He sighed. It didn't seem all that important now, keeping alive or out of German hands. He wanted to drop, too aching, too drained of strength to hurry.

Sergeant Maye, concern in his young voice, said, 'You've got to keep going. I don't trust them to stay with the Germans coming through.'

A tree seemed to be uprooted and began to fall towards them. The shock wave hit them both, then Maye grabbed him by the arm and began to drag him, though Offer cried out in agony.

Another halt, this time only thirty yards from the last remaining Chev. The other trucks were noisily climbing the sand ridge. Offer saw faces, his own men, looking back at him. Then he saw Weybright peering round from the driving seat. He didn't think Weybright would go without him. Or would he?

The noise inside the grove grew to greater fury. And the Germans would be racing round the perimeter for certain, intent on cutting off their retreat. Any moment now. And still the strength was gone from him and he couldn't move.

Maye shouted above the din, 'Make one last effort.' Oh, God, the Chev was beginning to move.

'Why?' Desperately, wearily, suddenly giving in because of pain more than he could stand. 'There's no place of escape for us . . .'

Phil Maye shoved his face, just as desperate as Offer's, close to the captain's. 'Didn't you hear me, back there? What's wrong with everyone? Why don't we take the Sand Sea route to Kufra?'

Drugged with pain though he was, Offer had the answer to that one. 'Because we don't know where it is. O'Keefe can't find it.' And if O'Keefe couldn't find it, who could?

Sergeant Maye said something. It took seconds for the words to register with Offer. Then he peered through eyes nearly closed behind their ugly swellings and said, 'Did you say you know the way?'

'I ought to. No bloody picnic, but I've crossed it twice, the back way, as we call it.'

Offer found strength because those words brought hope. He began to run, an awkward, stumbling run, but faster than a walking pace. 'Take us,' he shouted. 'Get us out of this hell-hole.'

Hands reached down and dragged their captain over the tailboard. He passed out, so they laid him on a blanket. Sergeant Maye ran round to the driving seat. 'Shove off,' he told Weybright. 'I'll take over. I've got to pilot you through the Sand Sea.' He took the wheel and began to sound the horn, a signal to the other Chevs to hang on and wait for him, and then he got their Chev into the lead.

When Offer came to painful consciousness they were already inside the worst desert in the world, but around him the lads were beaming and saying, 'We're safe! We made it! We gave Jerry the slip after all!'

'Roll on Kufra,' whispered Captain Offer through puffed up lips, and almost content, fell asleep.

ANTHONY DESTEFANO WRITES WITH A FEROCITY OF PURPOSE AND A CLEAR IDEA OF THE NETHER WORLD

THE SORCERESS
☐ 15285 ★ $1.50

MONDO: MAN OF VIOLENCE
☐ 12333 ★ $1.25

COCAINE KILL
☐ 12487 ★ $1.25

A MINUTE TO PRAY, A SECOND TO DIE
☐ 15272 ★ $1.50

★ ★

Manor Books Inc.
432 Park Avenue South
New York, New York 10016

Please send me the MB books I have checked above.
I am enclosing $ _____ Check or money order, (no
currency or C.O.D.'s). Enclose price listed for
each title plus 35¢ per copy ordered to cover cost
of postage and handling.

☐ Send me a free list of all your books in print.

Name _____

Address _____

City _____ State _____ Zip _____

THE UNTOLD STORY OF

DOUGLAS MacARTHUR

BY FRAZIER HUNT

The definitive story of one of the most controversial military men of all times, told by a reporter with a background of information and experience that better fitted him than any other to tell the intimate MacArthur story.

$2.50 ★ #25101